TO WIN HIM BACK

"Is there something I need to know about you and Dom?"

Ava held her breath, wondering if Mac was aware that he had stopped treating her injuries and was now stroking a fingertip along the sensitive skin of her arm, causing an involuntary shiver. If he noticed, he gave no indication. He continued to touch her while waiting for her answer.

"Would it bother you?" she asked quietly. She knew it was juvenile to insinuate that there was something romantic between her and Dominic, but she wanted— no, she needed—Mac to care.

Mac expelled a breath before his hand moved from her arm and glided up to her neck, lingering on the pulse beating wildly there. "You have no idea, Avie. He's my brother, and I'd give him everything I have . . . but not you, baby. Never you. You. Belong. To. Me."

Also by Sydney Landon

The Danvers Series
Weekends Required
Not Planning on You
Fall for Me
Fighting for You
No Denying You
Betting on You (Penguin digital special)

ALWAYS LOVING YOU

A DANVERS NOVEL

SYDNEY LANDON

A SIGNET ECLIPSE BOOK

SIGNET ECLIPSE
Published by the Penguin Group
Penguin Group (USA) LLC, 375 Hudson Street,
New York, New York 10014

USA I Canada I UK I Ireland I Australia I New Zealand I India I South Africa I China
penguin.com
A Penguin Random House Company

First published by Signet Eclipse, an imprint of New American Library,
a division of Penguin Group (USA) LLC

First Printing, February 2015

Copyright © Sydney Landon, 2015
Penguin supports copyright. Copyright fuels creativity, encourages diverse voices, pro-
motes free speech, and creates a vibrant culture. Thank you for buying an authorized
edition of this book and for complying with copyright laws by not reproducing, scanning, or distributing any part of it in any form without permission. You are supporting
writers and allowing Penguin to continue to publish books for every reader.

SIGNET ECLIPSE and logo are trademarks of Penguin Group (USA) LLC.

ISBN 978-0-451-47280-9

Printed in the United States of America
10 9 8 7 6 5 4 3 2 1

As always, to my love—my husband: He is the inspiration behind every word that I write. He is my forever person.

To my amazing aunt Nancy Ida Cash.

To my friend Larry Browning and his best friend, Max: Thank you so much for being a blessed part of my life.

Chapter One

Ava Stone stood concealed in the parking garage of the Danvers International Office Building staring as her longtime friend Mac—McKinley Powers—greeted his new girlfriend. Mac was nothing if not polite, so if he had noticed her, he would have insisted on introducing her to Gwen. But Ava already knew all about the other woman. When she found out that Mac was dating someone who also worked for Danvers, she'd made it her business to find out everything she could about Gwen for two reasons. First, Mac was a friend and in her mind, no one was good enough for him, including—and perhaps most especially—herself. Second, Ava had been in love with Mac for years and if she couldn't have him, then she didn't want to see him end up with just anyone.

The relationship between Ava and Mac had been complicated for many years. Mac had grown up next door to their grandfather. Ava and her brothers, Brant and Declan, had come to live with their grandfather when their parents were killed in a plane crash. At the time Ava was thirteen and her brothers a few years older. Their grandfather had been an indifferent bastard who accepted responsibility for them but mainly just wanted them out of his hair.

Ava and her siblings had known Mac and his family for most of their lives, since their parents had insisted that they visit their grandfather on a regular basis, even though they weren't particularly close to him. Their grandmother and grandfather had divorced when Ava's father was still young. She had packed her bags and walked away. As far as Ava knew, her father had never seen or spoken to her again. Actually, no one mentioned her—ever.

Ava thought the visits with their grandfather were more about her parents having a couple of weeks away without having to drag their kids along than any real family bonding time. One of those solo trips to Florida had taken a tragic turn when they didn't come back. Their plane had crashed, and they were simply gone in the blink of an eye.

Ava had been crushed at the death of her parents, seemingly more so than Declan or Brant. Later she came to realize that they all just handled the grief in different ways. Brant, as the oldest, had grown up almost overnight and tried to watch over her and Declan. He had also attempted to keep the peace with their grandfather, feigning an interest in his company that she wasn't sure he'd had back then. Hell, she wasn't sure if he had ever really developed a genuine interest for the business, but he felt it was expected of him as the eldest. And Declan, well, he turned into a hellraiser. The old man chewed his ass out almost as an afterthought every time he got into trouble, but Declan didn't care. She was pretty sure that their grandfather had secretly loved it. She suspected he felt as though he was reliving his youth through his younger grandson.

She, on the other hand, had struggled to find her place in the world with the loss of the two people she had depended on to watch over her. They might not have been Ward and June Cleaver, but they were her parents and a life without them seemed unimaginable. So, on the days that she just couldn't cope, she turned to Declan's friend Mac. Even when she was a teenager, he had been a caring presence in her life and he always made time for her. She felt special when she was with him. He always acted as if he wanted to hear her thoughts and dreams. She also had a huge crush on him, which she was sure was no secret.

As the years passed and she got older, she started to resent Mac for not returning her feelings. Her resentment had come to a head around the time she was seventeen and had been dating at that point. No matter how alluring she dressed, he still ruffled her hair and slung his arm around her shoulders in an affectionate gesture whenever they were together. He asked about her dates and told her about his. Unlike with most boys from school, she never caught him looking at her in any way other than as just another brother.

Her emotions had been all over the place as she dressed for the senior prom. She was looking forward to wearing the pretty dress that her grandfather had given her the money to buy, but she was less than thrilled with her date. She had gone out with him several times, mainly to take her mind off Mac, but she wasn't really interested in him. He was handsy and determined, and those hands were always trying to get under her clothes. Sometimes it seemed as if he had way more than two hands. As soon as this evening was over, she planned to tell him they were through. He was simply a means to a social end tonight.

Later, she would come to know him as the animal who stripped away her innocence and left her lying in a bed of dried leaves in the woods, a mile from her house. It would take her what would seem like hours to walk, stumble, and finally crawl toward the lights of a house in the distance. Mac's house. She had lain bruised, cut, and bleeding on his doorstep, unable to summon the strength to reach the doorbell. The beautiful iridescent gown that she had twirled in earlier on the dance floor was tattered. The delicate material had been ravaged by first her date, then by the weeds and briars as she crawled through the dark forest.

She had no idea how long she had lain there, staring into the starry night as if in a trance, when the door suddenly opened. The bright light in the room beyond made her blink in surprise. She was no longer even certain where she was.

A foot connected with her bruised leg, causing her to cry out in pain. "What the hell?" she heard as she tried to struggle into a sitting position. Suddenly, strong hands were on her shoulders. She was breathing hard, terrified that he'd come back. She twisted away frantically, terrified of what would happen next. "Ava? Honey, is that you?"

She stopped suddenly, causing the hands holding her to slide. She knew that voice. He'd never hurt her. Even as her body screamed in protest, she climbed onto the man's lap squatting next to her and held on with everything she had. She was shaking so hard she could barely keep her arms looped around his neck. "Mac . . . please help me," she remembered whispering frantically.

He stood in one swift movement and swung her up higher in his arms. Without saying a word, he walked back into the house with her, kicking the door shut behind them. When they reached what she thought was the living room, he sat down with her still in his lap. Soft light flooded the room as he used one arm to flip on the lamp on the table beside them. "Honey, what happened?" He tried to move her, but she continued to hold him tight, afraid of what would happen if he let go. He stroked her hair, murmuring words of reassurance against her head, until the shudders subsided. When he moved her back again, she let him put just enough distance between them to see his face. She heard his quick intake of breath, then a barrage of profanity. She started crying then, not able to handle him being angry on top of everything else that had happened.

"I'm sorry. Please don't be mad at me, Mac."

A harsh laugh tore from his throat. "Honey, I'm not mad at you. But I need you to tell me what happened. Were you in an accident?"

She wanted to say yes and just forget the rest, but she had never lied to Mac. He was the one person in her life whom she trusted without reservation, even more so than her brothers. She didn't know what to do or where to turn . . . and she hurt so bad . . . everywhere. "No . . . he . . . hurt me."

His eyes never wavered from hers as he asked, "He hurt you how?"

Tears rolled down her cheeks as she revealed the truth to him. "He forced himself on me, Mac. He held me down, and he . . . raped me." She saw the exact moment that her words sank in. His face blanched an alarming shade of white before turning a dark red.

That was the night that they both had shattered. Mac would spend years trying to put her back together again, and she would spend years trying to convince everyone, including herself, that she was okay. And the bastard who raped her . . . his only punishment ended up being to leave South Carolina and agree never to contact her again. That sentence would be decided by her grandfather, who had never liked having the family's dirty laundry aired in public. Always better to handle things privately.

Ava was brought back to the present by the sound of a slamming door. Apparently, Mac had finished his conversation with his new girlfriend and had helped her into her car. No doubt, they had made plans to meet later. Just a few months ago, that would have been her walking out with Mac. They would jump in one of their cars after work and go for dinner somewhere. Now, though, she had been shoved firmly into the casual-friend zone. Granted, they had been only friends for years—but she had always had the hope of something more between them. Now Gwen was the woman in Mac's life, and Ava was just the screwed-up friend of the family.

As if sensing someone's eyes on him, Mac turned suddenly in her direction and there was nowhere to hide. He'd seen her standing in the shadows. Hell, she'd spent most of her life in them. For just a moment, he looked at her as he used to. His mouth pulled into a smile and his eyes softened in the way she had always loved. God, he was so handsome. He kept his dark hair in the short buzz cut favored by the military. His tall body was lean, without an ounce of visible fat. The cargo pants and T-shirt that he was wearing did little to disguise the muscles rippling in his shoulders and thighs. Mac was, without a doubt, drool-worthy. He was the kind of man that women turned to stare after as he walked by. And . . . now he belonged to Gwen.

As he started to walk toward Ava, she had the urge to tuck tail and run. She was still too raw from seeing him with Gwen. But . . . she couldn't deny herself this moment with him. There had been too few of them lately. She needed to see him, to talk to him one-on-one, just for a moment. "Hey, Avie." He grinned as he drew close to her. She had long ago given up on trying to get him to stop calling her that silly nickname. She'd never admit it to him, but it made her feel special.

"Hey, McKinley." She used his full name when she wanted to tease him. He winced slightly but let it go without comment.

"It's good to see you, even if it's in the parking lot. I've missed your face."

She was in danger of breaking out into ugly school-girl sobs right on the spot. Maybe talking to him right now wasn't the best idea. Instead she admitted, "Yeah, me too. I . . . um, do you want to go get a drink or something?" He looked surprised, even though this would have been a normal question between them not long ago . . . before Gwen had entered the picture.

He ran his hand through his hair, something he did when he was uncomfortable. "I wish I could, but I've kind of got plans. But we'll do it soon, okay? Maybe Declan and Brant can meet up with us too."

And here we go. Now all of our meetings have to take place with other people present. The new girlfriend probably doesn't like him hanging out with me by myself. Just smile and act as if it doesn't bother you. You've had plenty of practice at that.

"Oh, sure," she said, starting to back away. Ava made a point of looking at her watch. "Wow, it's getting late. I've got . . . er . . . to get going. Good to see you." He stood there, looking sad while she continued backing toward her car and smiling like a freaking loon. What right did he have to look like that? He had turned her down, yet again. Fuck it; she didn't need him, or anyone else. Even as Ava tried to convince herself, she knew it was a lie. She was dying without him. She couldn't sleep, and she was barely eating. If her existence was pathetic before, it now transcended what she'd even thought was possible. She didn't know how to live in a world without McKinley Powers as her constant and she had no idea what to do now.

Chapter Two

Mac walked to his Tahoe in the parking garage of Danvers International. He slammed the door behind him as he settled on the leather seat. Seeing Ava was still like a punch to the gut. Yeah, this whole thing of dating and moving on with his life had been his idea, but fuck, it was hard. At least before, he was spending a lot of time with the woman he loved, even if she couldn't admit to feeling the same way about him. Hell, maybe she didn't love him. Maybe he'd spent years of his life loving her and needing to believe that she felt the same way. For years he told himself she just needed time to come to terms with what had happened to her. Only, nothing ever changed. His twenties were behind him now. He'd served two tours in the military, and he was ready to settle down and get on with his life.

He'd loved Ava for most of her adult life. In fact, when he looked back on it now, it seemed he had spent his teenage years waiting for her to grow up. She had started out more like a little sister to him. She had always been the girl next door. At some point, his feelings for her had started to change. He had been determined to wait until she was older, but damn, she hadn't made it easy. When she started to date, he had nearly lost it. No one was good enough for his Avie, but still he'd waited. Then that night had happened, and nothing was ever the same again. For either of them.

When he found her on his doorstep, he had almost lost his mind. She was so broken. Clearly in shock, with her ripped dress and blood on her face. He had taken her to the hospital and was ready to go after the guy and kill him with his bare hands. But he knew he had to inform her family before he did anything else, and Ava's grandfather had insisted he would take care of it. He forbade him to go to her date's house. Then the whole thing had just gone away. No police involvement, no reports filed . . . nothing. It was as if it had never happened. Money could make things disappear, and that had never been more apparent to him. It made him furious. Ava had deserved justice, but instead she only received indifference. At the hospital when Declan had told him that Ava refused to report the rape to the police, he had longed to persuade her otherwise, but her grandfather said that she was refusing to see visitors.

In the days and weeks that followed the attack, the Ava he knew and loved disappeared. He tried to talk to her, to be there for her while she recovered, but she distanced herself from him. He had attempted to talk to her brothers about what she was going through, but they both insisted she just needed time. His frustration and the pain he felt at what she was clearly going through, alone, just grew. When Declan had asked him to join the military with him, at first he'd said no. However, in the end, he just needed to get away. Ava still wouldn't see him and it was eating him alive. He figured maybe they both needed some time apart. He came back home to see her on every leave, but his Avie never returned. The little hellcat he had once known was now a reserved shell of her former self. When his tour ended, he was in complete limbo, so he re-upped with Declan, needing time to figure out what happened next for him.

After he left the military, he'd decided to take advantage of the training he had received in the marines and opened his own security company. A couple of guys he'd served with wanted to come in as partners, and East Coast Security was born. Now, several years later, they had been successful beyond any of their expectations. He, Dominic Brady, and Gage Hyatt mainly ran the day-to-day operations while their employees handled the work on-site. Jason Danvers, the CEO of Danvers International and a client, had offered them space for their corporate offices, which was convenient since they were located in a high-rise in downtown Myrtle Beach, South Carolina. East Coast also handled personal security for Jason's family. His wife and child were rarely without a security tail.

Mac had also made sure that Ava was covered. Since the bastard who raped her all those years ago was never arrested, Mac made it his business to make sure nothing ever happened to her again. After he'd been home from the marines for a while, they managed to resume some part of the friendship that they'd once had. A lot of their free time was spent together, but for Mac it hadn't been nearly enough. Sometimes he thought he saw something that looked like romantic feelings when she was looking at him on the rare, unguarded occasion, but they were gone so fast he wasn't sure if they were ever there. He had loved Ava for years . . . and he had no idea how she felt about him.

Watching over Ava so closely also had a downside. He knew entirely too much about her personal life. Every couple of months, someone new would spend the evening at her house and walk out the door looking rumpled but satisfied. It was never the same man twice, though. It tore him up to read those reports from her security tail. To know that someone else was touching the woman he loved while he was standing around on the sidelines. In those moments he would worry about invading her privacy and consider whether to continue monitoring her safety from afar, but he couldn't take the chance that any harm would befall her ever again.

Of course, he couldn't say that he'd been a saint either. He was a man and he had needs. He had slept with the occasional woman when the need was there. He wasn't vain, but he knew that women found him attractive, and it was never a hardship to find a willing woman to spend a night with. He and Declan had found many of them during their tours of duty. It had just never meant any more to him than filling a physical need. Had Ava said the word, he would have stopped seeing other women and been faithful to only her without a single qualm about stepping into a serious relationship.

When Declan had surprised them all by falling in love with Ella Webber, the receptionist at Danvers, Mac suddenly took notice of the hollowness that he had felt for years. Suddenly, it had become almost unbearable. Then when Declan married and started a family almost overnight, it had forced Mac to make a difficult decision. He had to move on with his life. He wanted a wife and a family in the near future, and he had to accept that Ava might never be at the same point in her life.

There was no choice left but for him to start pulling away, inch by painful inch. He had asked Gwen Day, who worked at Danvers as well, out on a date. She was an attractive woman with long red hair and an outgoing personality. Although she didn't make him weak in the knees, he was attracted to her, and she seemed to feel the same.

They had been dating for a couple of months now and his frequent dinners with Ava had all but stopped. He knew he couldn't have both. There was no way he could move past her with someone else and still spend so much time alone with her. It was one of the hardest things he'd ever done. He missed her so much he physically ached. But he couldn't keep going on as he had been. He wasn't doing either of them any favors. Maybe without him as a crutch, Ava would be able to move forward. Sometimes you had to take the training wheels off and see if you fell on your face or made it on your own. This was as much for her as for him. He just had to remember that.

Chapter Three

"Oh my God, what's he done now?"

Ava scowled at her assistant and future sister-in-law, Emma Davis, as she settled into a seat in front of her desk. Ava had been a vice president at Danvers International since she and Brant sold their family business to Jason Danvers. Truthfully, she enjoyed the work as well as the challenge of something new.

Ava gave an unladylike snort at Emma's question and resigned herself to playing twenty questions. There was no way her nosy assistant was going to let her off without explaining her shittier-than-usual mood. She gave her best innocent look and said, "I have no idea what you're talking about. Don't you have some work to do in your own office?"

Emma smirked back at her disgruntled expression, knowing by now that her bark was worse than her bite. Ava didn't have many close friends, and with Mac now mostly avoiding her, Emma was pretty much it. Oh, Ava would never let the other woman know it, but she had grown to love her dearly since her engagement to her brother Brant. Between Emma and her other brother

Declan's wife, Ella, family occasions were no longer akin to a gathering at the morgue. Emma and Ella had breathed some much-needed life into the Stone family. "Nah, I'm on a break, so I have time."

Rolling her eyes, Ava said, "A break, huh? You seem to have a lot of those." Secretly, Ava knew why Brant had enjoyed arguing with Emma when she worked as his assistant before their engagement. It was just freaking fun. Emma was actually fabulous at her job and took a lot of the load from Ava's shoulders.

"All right, enough of this stalling crap. What's happening with Mac? I take it you've spoken to him again, since you're acting like someone with a monthlong case of PMS."

Putting all pretenses aside, Ava said, "Yeah, I ran into him and—her—in the parking garage yesterday."

"Oh, shit! Did you, like . . . speak to the tramp?"

Ava smiled even though she felt the need to defend the woman who'd stolen her sorta man. "I don't think she's a tramp, Em. Mac wouldn't be interested in anyone like that."

Emma shook her head in disgust. "You're totally missing the point here. This woman is messing with your guy. We don't take that lightly. Until we get rid of her, she is the 'tramp' to us. So . . . how did it go?"

Ava tried to hide her pain as she relayed her run-in with Mac. "Well, he was walking *her* to the car when I saw them. He helped her inside and kissed her, and then she drove off. He saw me and we talked for a minute, that's it."

"Why do you put yourself through all this? If you

leveled with Mac about how you really feel, he'd probably kick the *tramp* to the curb faster than you could
say bye-bye. He loves you. According to your family,
he's never made a secret of that fact. And . . . you love
him. Are you really going to let *her* have him?"

It all sounded so simple when Emma put it like that,
but the reality seemed anything but simple. After years
of being terrified of intimacy and feeling as if she
wasn't good enough for Mac, Ava had finally decided
to do everything she could to overcome her fears. She
had purchased every self-help book that she could find
and was seriously considering going to a therapist. She
was so very tired of being afraid all the time. Just when
she was on the brink of confessing to Mac how screwed
up she really was, and how she felt about him, he had
pulled the rug out from under her. Apparently, they
had both arrived at the same conclusion—that they
needed to move forward. Only she had wanted to
move toward him, but unfortunately, his moves had
taken him away from her.

Since then, she had been reeling in shock. What
now? He had been her reason for finally getting her shit
together. He had waited for her all these years, and just
when she thought they might be on the same page, he
was gone. He'd freaking left her behind. And damn it,
she couldn't even blame him. "Em, it's not that simple.
What am I supposed to say? 'Oh, Mac, please toss your
new girlfriend aside. I've decided that although I'm too
fucked-up to have a relationship with you myself, I
can't let anyone else have you. I'm going to need you
to masturbate for life and remain true only to me'?"

Emma cocked an eyebrow, saying, "Well, that wasn't quite what I had in mind, other than the tossing of the new girlfriend. Seriously, though, grow a pair or whatever the female equivalent of that is and take Mac back."

Ava reluctantly smiled. "So you're going the tough love route today, huh? Given up coddling the poor, messed-up girl?" She saw the look of sympathy that Emma tried to hide as she stood, turning toward the door.

"You're one of the strongest people I know, Ava. I have no idea what it's been like for you all these years. But I know if you lose Mac, you'll never move forward. He's your white knight, but this time you're going to have to charge to his rescue. You need to save both of you from living a life without 'the one.'"

When the door closed behind Emma, Ava turned to stare out the window of her office. The beach town was bustling with the last of the summer crowd before cooler weather took over. She hardly noticed, though, as her friend's words echoed through her head. Was she strong enough to finally show Mac how she felt? God, where did she even start? He wouldn't agree to have a drink with her last night, so it was unlikely he was up for an impromptu date. Emma would probably laugh her ass off if she knew that at this moment, Ava was sitting at her desk searching "how to show a man that you love him." Great, the most popular search result was just telling him. Fucking Google. Always making everything sound so simple.

*   *   *

When Ava walked into her apartment, she was hit with a wave of loneliness as she realized she was no closer to a solution than she had been earlier. Embarrassingly enough, she'd even resorted to stopping at the store on the way home and buying almost a hundred dollars' worth of women's magazines. If there was anything on the cover pertaining to men or love, she bought it. Walking into her kitchen, she pulled out the bottle of wine she had also purchased. You had to love today's conveniences. You could now buy everything short of a car at Walgreens. While she was shopping, she'd even paused by the condom aisle as if trying to think positively that she might need them soon. Yeah . . . that really looked likely.

Uncorking the bottle, she filled a glass nearly to the brim and walked back to the couch with her overflowing bag. The first cover promised twenty sexual moves that would drive her man crazy. She laughed under her breath. She'd have to actually have a man for that to work. She had bought it, though, just in case she ever moved on to the next level. As she set it aside, the headline on the next one immediately caught her eyes. WANT TO CATCH HIS ATTENTION? UNLEASH YOUR INNER DAREDEVIL! Okay, maybe she could work with that. Flipping it open, she found the page number in the table of contents and went to the article. The picture showed a woman about her age holding a motorcycle helmet in one hand and a pair of skates in the other hand. She grabbed a notepad and a pen off the coffee table. Her brother Brant was an organizational freak and she was more like him than she cared to admit.

How many women would buy a magazine for help with landing their man and take notes along the way? She was even tempted to highlight relevant paragraphs but suppressed the urge.

Hours and almost one bottle of wine later, she had filled her notepad with suggestions from the ten magazines she had spent the evening scouring. The overall advice was the same in all of them except for the one encouraging her to be a daredevil. Shit, it was either that or start dressing like a slut and making sexual advances toward Mac. One even suggested in a roundabout way that she invite her man to her house for dinner, wear a dress, and sit in front of him. Then after a few moments of small talk, she was to open her legs and start touching herself. According to the author of the article, it would have him eating out of the palm of her hand . . . or eating *something* for sure. She could feel herself blush furiously just thinking about doing that. Mac would probably have her committed. "Poor Ava's finally snapped."

She wanted Mac in every way, but damn it, she was essentially a twenty-eight-year-old virgin. She had never had a real sexual relationship with a man. Like most single women her age, she had needs and desires. Her vibrator took the place of a real man in her bed and she had learned to live with that. It was the safe way out. When she needed to take the edge off, she used it. Sometimes . . . most of the time it was Mac's name that she called as she reached orgasm.

She didn't know how to function outside of that, though. She could probably talk to her sister-in-law, Ella.

She had confided that she had been a virgin when she met Declan. That was where their similarities stopped, though. Ella might have lived a sheltered life before she met Ava's brother, but she hadn't spent her life running from past trauma. She wasn't scared of intimacy or afraid she'd freak out during sex and humiliate herself.

Part of her knew that Mac would take care of her and help her overcome her fears, but the other part didn't want him to know how messed up she was. His opinion of her mattered. She wanted him to see her as strong and confident, not scared and insecure. God, what would he think if he found out that she had picked men up in bars for years, paying them to come home with her for a few hours, just to keep up the pretense that she was normal? She knew it sounded bad when she thought about it, but it seemed to make people look at her with less pity when they believed that she was dating. Normal, unattached women her age had sex, right? She wasn't normal, and she wasn't having sex, but it was all about perception. Throw people a few tidbits here and there and they drew their own conclusions. In this case, the assumptions were wrong.

Ava had spent years believing that one day she would cross some invisible line and she would be worthy of Mac. It was kind of like holding on to an outfit in a smaller size thinking you'll lose weight and fit into it in the future. Well, fast-forward ten years and the damn outfit still didn't fit and she was no closer to making it happen. That was where she was: still dreaming of the day that it all came together and she woke up normal, in love, and with Mac.

Looking down at the magazines spread over her couch and coffee table, she felt a wave of despair. This was it? All that was standing between her and losing Mac to another woman was a bunch of magazine articles? Self-help and advice for the romantically hopeless. Shit, short of the boob job, she planned to try some of the other suggestions. What did she have to lose? Mac was probably with Gwen tonight, maybe having sex. While she was sitting home alone, just like always. When had she given up? At what point had she stopped trying to get better and instead accepted that she was broken beyond repair? Had her friendship with Mac unwittingly become a replacement for a real relationship with him? While he was in the military, there hadn't been any real pressure. Actually, it had made it easier for her to communicate with him knowing he was too far away to drop by unexpectedly. She saw him when he was home on leave, they wrote and talked on the phone, but she didn't see him every day. When he finally came home for good, they just fell into the routine of spending most of their spare time together. They went for drinks, had dinner, hung out at each other's apartments, and attended family events together. They were more of a couple then than many married people she knew. Things had been going so well that they were almost back to where they were before her attack, only now they were both very much adults.

Mac had never been one to verbalize his feelings, but he showed her in a million different ways that he cared for her. In the last year, though, it was as if his patience was wearing thin. His touches had gone from fleeting to lingering. A few months ago, before he had started dating Gwen, he'd kissed her. Not the usual brief peck either. There had been lips and tongue involved and . . . she'd freaked out on him. They'd been watching a movie at her place and she'd been curled up next to him, half-asleep. When she felt hands sliding through her hair, stroking her neck, she had nestled closer, instinctively seeking the comfort of his touch. When he had lowered his mouth to hers, she had allowed it, more curious than anything. But things had quickly escalated. She had found herself returning his kiss, tangling her tongue with his. Desire raced through her until he pulled her closer, embracing her solidly against his hard chest. Then she'd panicked. She couldn't breathe; she had to get away. So she had jumped from his arms and crossed to the other side of the room to put some distance between them.

Things had gotten awkward after that. He had apologized that night and she had thought things were okay until he started pulling away. Day by day, she lost him gradually. Until finally he was formally dating someone else right in front of her for the first time since they were teenagers. Oh, she knew that Mac had sex; she wasn't that naive. But he didn't have relationships, and she never saw him out on a regular date. Ava always came first with him, but no longer. Now Gwen was the priority and she felt a very distant second, if even that. He gave up on her that night just as plainly as if he had said it aloud. He was no longer content to wait around; he wanted more out of life. He wanted the fairy tale. He wasn't going to be satisfied with half measures; it was going to take more to get him back. And scariest of all, he wasn't coming back to a friends-with-no-benefits relationship. In order to get Mac, she would have to become part of his fairy tale. She would have to put the ugliness of her past behind her and become his freaking Cinderella.

She put the notes that she had made from the magazines in her purse. "Okay, *Cosmo*, let's give it our best shot."

Chapter Four

Ava looked at herself in the full-length mirror and cringed. She wasn't used to going to work and showing this much skin. The one thing all the magazines had agreed on was dressing more provocative and sexy. She usually just wore pantsuits, and as she hadn't been shopping since putting her plan in place, she was wearing the same today, with one change. She had unbuttoned her blouse far enough to take her from all-business to a mix of business and pleasure. She had also dug through her vanity drawers until she'd found the tube of red lipstick that she had received free with her last makeup purchase. Instead of wearing her hair up, she left it hanging in loose waves around her shoulders— another suggestion from *Cosmo*. She planned to have Emma go to the mall with her at lunch to buy some less conservative clothing. She needed a new look for the next item on her agenda, "unleashing her inner daredevil." She couldn't very well do that in plain black slacks. Her last addition to today's outfit was a pair of high-heeled black sandals. She preferred her lower-heeled flats, but apparently that wasn't sexy enough.

Shit, she looked like a stranger . . . but an attractive one, she admitted grudgingly. Before she could talk herself into changing back into her usual conservative ensembles, she hurried out of her apartment to her reliable white BMW sedan. It didn't match her sexier new persona, but she had to draw the line at buying a sports car, right? Wouldn't that be taking things too far? Besides, she had purchased this car because of the safety rating. Everything in her life it seemed was based on how safe it was. She consoled herself with the fact that she had opted for the sunroof, which was strictly for fun.

The drive into downtown Myrtle Beach was one she always enjoyed. It was still early morning, so the crowds were relatively quiet, as it was nearing the end of the official summer season. In the afternoon, these same streets would be filled with people walking, biking, or skating along Ocean Boulevard. On the weekends she spent a lot of her spare time on the beach, since she had very little social life outside work. She didn't partake in any of the other tourist hobbies, though. Maybe it was time to make a change there as well. If you lived somewhere like Myrtle Beach, shouldn't you enjoy more of what it had to offer? They had just installed a new zip line near her home. Did she dare do something that far out of her comfort zone?

She was pondering her first choice of activities on her daredevil agenda when an idea literally roared into the parking lot at Danvers. What she had always thought of as a death trap on two wheels was pulling into a space beside her. In reality, it was a sleek black

Harley-Davidson motorcycle driven by one of Mac's partners, Dominic Brady. Ava sat in her car, trying not to gawk out her window at the man dismounting next to her. She might be emotionally stunted, but it didn't mean she couldn't appreciate the sexy picture that Dominic, or Dom, as his friends called him, presented. He was wearing the typical uniform of East Coast Security—cargo pants and a shirt with their logo on it. The poor shirt looked as if it were doing everything it could to cover the broad shoulders it was stretched across. And the pants . . . Oh, sweet God, her breath hitched in her throat as he bent over to do something with his bike, putting his ass directly in her line of sight. When he stood and looked toward her car as if sensing her there, she jerked her gaze away, fumbling with her keys. She knew if she looked into the mirror, her face would probably be bright red.

Finishing with his bike, he walked over to her car and opened the driver's-side door for her. She blinked up at him in a daze before finally pulling it together enough to step out and let him shut the door behind her. "Ava." His deep voice rumbled her name in greeting.

"Er . . . hi, Dominic. Riding your bike today?" *Oh my God, of course he's riding his bike. Way to state the obvious, dummy. Next, I'll just point out that he's wearing pants too. Maybe mention his damn shoes. What happened to all the information from the magazines I studied last night?*

He gave her an amused look before saying simply, "Yep." She saw his eyes rest briefly on the expanse of flesh left on display by her blouse before moving up to her face. Okay, that was a good sign. She'd never noticed Dominic checking her out before, so maybe her wardrobe changes were getting her somewhere. Of course, it wasn't as if his tongue was hanging out or his breaths were coming in jerky grasps, but he'd totally looked at her boobs, so that was something.

"So, how fast does your bike go? Do you know the safety rating right off the top of your head?" By this time, he had started edging slowly through the parking lot, no doubt trying to get away from her. He stopped, surprised by her questions.

"It'll go over a hundred." Then, grinning, he added, "I don't think anyone buys a Harley for the safety rating, honey." Pointing to her car, he said, "If you're into stuff like that, then you stick with a car like the one you're driving." He turned back, continuing toward the door to Danvers International where East Coast Security had an office. Ava trailed behind him to the elevator. When he got off on his floor, she stepped off as well. He gave her a curious look over his shoulder, since they both knew this wasn't her floor. "Mac's not in yet. He had to make some stops on his way. Want me to have him call you?"

When Dominic opened the door to their office, she followed him inside. "Um, no. Actually, I wanted to ask you something."

He flipped on the lights in the reception area before leaning back against the desk behind him. His look of curiosity was gone, and he was now studying her as you would a science experiment. This man probably knew as much about her life as she did. After all, he had no doubt spent a lot of time watching out for her at Mac's request. She felt the urge to tell him that she hadn't really been having sex with any of the guys she had brought home over the years, but it might actually drop her down a couple of levels in his opinion. It was better to seem like a woman with normal sexual urges to a man like him. "What can I do for you, darling?"

Her thoughts scattered to the wind for a moment when his sexy voice uttered the endearment. Dominic was ex-military along with Mac and Declan, and even though she tried not to think of her brother that way, they all just oozed masculinity.

She wanted to run, to tuck her tail between her legs and forget all these crazy ideas, but then she thought of Mac and where he might actually be this morning. Probably either giving the new girlfriend a ride to work or, worse, getting a late start because he'd spent the night with her. Gwen was no doubt fun and carefree. Ava would try something new. Hell, she was trying something new, Mac! Taking a deep breath, she took the plunge. "I want to learn to ride a motorcycle. Could you teach me, you know . . . with yours?"

If she hadn't been so embarrassed by the whole thing, she would have found his expression comical. His mouth opened and closed several times and his eyes blinked rapidly. She had a feeling that very few people surprised the man in front of her, but she sure had. "You want to, like, ride on the back of my bike? Yeah, I guess I could take you for a ride."

He looked relieved just for a moment until she shook her head. "No, that's not it." Then his relief turned to shock when she said, "I want to drive the bike. You could ride with me, I guess, on the back, but I want to steer the thing. You know, do it all myself."

She wanted to die on the spot when he looked around the room suspiciously. "Is this a joke or something?" Oh crap, was the idea so absurd to him that he thought someone was having fun at his expense? She was pretty sure he was looking around for the culprit now.

Unbidden, tears started to well as embarrassment raced over her. What was she thinking asking a man like Dominic to teach her to ride a bike? He probably thought this was a pathetic attempt to hit on him. Unable to take any more humiliation, she turned toward the door, whispering an apology. She was surprised when hands landed on her shoulders, halting her progress. When she turned back to face him, he looked plainly terrified at the moisture gathering in the corners of her eyes. It was true, you could take the strongest man alive, and he would crumble under the weight of a woman's tears. "Never mind. Just forget it," she said as she tried to pull away.

"Ava, stop. Look, I'm sorry. I didn't think you were serious. You're just not . . . I mean, shit, you really want to drive a bike?"

She nodded, thinking it didn't really matter anyway. There was no way he was going to teach her.

He expelled a loud sigh, before dropping his hands. "You know Mac's going to fucking kill me, right?"

Surprised, she looked up at him, trying not to react to the mention of Mac. Was he saying . . . ? He narrowed his eyes as he studied her until she started shifting uncomfortably. Finally, a smile curved the corners of his mouth as he shook his head. "Well, well . . . sure. It looks like I'm your guy. How about we take a ride after work this evening so you can get a feel for things?"

She gave him a hesitant smile in return. She had the feeling that he knew exactly what she was up to. Either that or he was trying to pick her up. Whatever the reason, he was suddenly friendlier than she had ever imagined. She half expected him to pat her on the ass on the way out the door. Sadly, it would have been one of the bigger thrills in her life recently.

Mac walked in the door of East Coast Security after dropping off a coffee to Gwen. As always, he noticed Ava's white BMW in its usual space in the parking garage. She usually arrived early and left late. In truth, he would rather have taken a coffee to her and chatted for a few moments, but that wasn't his routine anymore. Now he had a girl he dated. He couldn't bring himself to label Gwen as his girlfriend yet. He was too old for that anyway. He smiled at their receptionist, Melissa, and stopped to chat before heading back to the security monitors where Dominic was sitting. Their other partner, Gage, was out on a new job this morning and wouldn't be in the office until that afternoon. They were all three ex-military and coexisted within their company in a way that only brothers could do. They might not be related by blood, but their bonds were just as strong if not stronger. "Hey, man," Dominic muttered as he settled in a chair next to him.

"Everything tight?" Mac asked, knowing that Dominic would have called already had there been any problems.

"Yeah, it's all good. Just zipping through the feeds from last night before filing them away." It was their daily routine to do a quick check of the security feeds for the previous twenty-four hours each morning even if no problems were reported just to ensure that nothing was missed and that their employees were doing their jobs. In this business, your reputation was all you had, and they depended on it to acquire new clients.

Mac was half watching the monitor while flipping through his e-mail when the sight of a familiar blond head caught his attention. He looked at the monitor before Dominic could run it forward. The time stamp showed just an hour ago. "Did Ava come by here this morning?" It was a stupid question because the camera clearly showed her standing in the reception area with Dominic. Was it his imagination or was Dominic smirking at him?

When the other man simply said, "She did," without saying anything further, he gritted his teeth.

"Was she looking for me?"

"Nope." Dominic continued running through the security feeds without saying a word. Most of the time Mac loved that he, Dominic, and Gage were able to communicate with only a few words or a look. He was a firm believer in the motto "less is more," but today he was finding it as annoying as hell.

"Why. Did. She. Come. By?" Surely to God, he could get an answer now. How much clearer could he be?

Dominic rocked back in his chair, before throwing his feet up on the desk in front of him. Was the fucker actually laughing at him? "Well, Mac, she followed me in from the parking garage to talk. She didn't really mention you."

Mac felt a wave of jealousy that he had no right feeling. He was dating Gwen, so he didn't have a say in who Ava chose to talk to. It was probably just a perfectly innocent, friendly conversation between them anyway. Still, it was unlike Ava to seek out someone she barely knew, especially a man. But he'd be damned if he would ask Dominic any more questions, because the smug look the other man was giving him let him know that he was enjoying watching Mac squirm. Bastard. Instead he tried to act as if he didn't care as he made an excuse to walk toward his office. It galled him more than he cared to admit that Ava had been to his office space earlier with no intention of seeing him.

Chapter Five

Ava handed Emma some folders and said, "I need to go to the mall during lunch for some jeans and leather stuff. Can you go with me?" When there was no reply, she looked up from the e-mail she was composing to see Emma staring at her with a bewildered expression on her face. "What?"

"You can't just drop stuff like that on me and not expect that I'm going to have questions. The jeans, yeah, I get why you need those, but what kind of leather stuff are we talking here?"

Ava knew it was hopeless to think that she could get Emma on board without telling her everything. The girl was like a bulldog with a bone when she wanted to be. Rather than going into a long explanation, she picked her purse up and pulled out the notes she had made last night from various magazines. She handed them over to Emma, who gave her a questioning look before she started reading. After a few minutes, the other woman looked up at her with a huge grin. "I have no idea where you got all this, but does this mean what I think it does?"

"And what do you think?" Ava hedged.

"You're going after Mac, aren't you? You're taking your man back. Finally! I can totally help you with this. Well, everything except the second page where it says 'have a threesome with your best friend.' I don't think Brant would be into me getting it on with you and Mac."

Ava handed her a pen. "Mark that one out. I shouldn't have included it. The thought of a twosome sends me into a panic, so an orgy is definitely out."

Seeming genuinely happy, Emma said, "This is great, Ava. I know how you feel about Mac, but I was afraid that you were just going to let him go, and I know you'd never get over that. Okay, enough of the serious stuff! I need to ask, though, why the leather? Are we talking some bondage stuff here? Don't you think that's a bit ambitious for a beginner?"

"No! That's not what I want." She couldn't contain her giggle at the other woman's serious expression. Good grief, did she think she had suddenly turned into a closet dominatrix? "I need some clothing to wear on a motorcycle. Don't you usually wear some kind of leather for that? Maybe a jacket?"

Emma looked confused as she asked, "Motorcycle?"

Settling back into her chair, Ava gave a proud smile. "Yep, I'm working on the daredevil part of my plan. Well, actually, it kind of fell into my lap. You know Dominic, who works with Mac?"

Emma gave an appreciative smile, and Ava was sure she licked her lips. "Oh yeah, I sure do. I love your brother, but I'm not going to lie, Dominic starred in a few of my preengagement vibrator sessions. That man just breathes sex."

"He does look good." Ava found herself agreeing. She wasn't used to having this kind of girl talk, because before Emma came along, she really didn't have any close friends, especially women. She had spent most of her time with Mac. Maybe what they were talking about was silly, but it was nice to do something so normal for a change. "Anyway, he's going to teach me how to ride his motorcycle. He was a little hesitant at first, but he said yes. I'm meeting him after work tonight."

Emma jumped up out of her chair, pumping her fist in the air. "Yes, yes! You are my new hero!" Brant picked that exact moment to stick his head in the office, looking at his fiancée in amusement.

"I believe you said the same thing to me this morning, baby."

Emma whirled to see him behind her, and Ava was surprised to see her assistant blush as she gave Brant a soft smile.

"Cool it, Mr. Stone. Your sister and I are trying to get some work done here."

He smiled at them both, looking curious. "I can see that. Just wanted to know if you ladies had lunch plans."

Before Ava could make an excuse, Emma jumped to it first. She took Brant's arm, steering him toward the door. "I'm sorry, babe. The girls invited us to lunch earlier. Ella's having some of those Braxton Hicks contractions and she wanted to discuss them with the girls. You know, get a second opinion."

Ava had to choke back her laughter as her brother started to shift uncomfortably. Obviously, the man thought this was some kind of code for "female problems." "Oh yes, you need to do that, then. We can have lunch another day. I mean, no big deal at all." The whole time he was talking, he was edging backward. Emma blew him a kiss, saying that she loved him as he turned to flee.

"You're really bad, you know? Brant was sweating bullets when he left. The poor man is too uptight for his own good."

Emma grinned in return. "He is cute, though, right? And I was serious. Not about the Braxton Hicks thing, but about meeting the girls. They asked me this morning to have lunch. We'll eat at the mall and get them on board as well. Mac will never know what hit him with all of us working together."

Ava started shaking her head, beginning to feel apprehensive. "Em, I can't go to lunch with your friends. I hardly know them. I just . . . I'm not good with crowds. I don't know what to do with other women."

Emma sat back down in the chair in front of her, giving her a look of sympathy. "Ava, you'll be fine. You already know Ella—and Suzy, Claire, and Beth are awesome. You'll have a great time, I promise. If you get uncomfortable, just give me a sign or something, and I'll make an excuse for us to leave. You can consider this part of your daredevil challenge. Having girlfriends is a wonderful part of life, one I think you need."

Ava felt as if she were agreeing to a voluntary root canal as she said, "All right, I'll try it. Don't blame me, though, if your friends don't want anything to do with you after this. I'm not only sexually stunted; I'm socially stunted as well."

"You'll be just fine," Emma assured her. "Now, I'll let the girls know that we'll just meet them in the front of the mall. I'll cut you some slack and won't make you ride with them . . . this time."

"Gee, thanks." Ava smiled. She was secretly relieved, though. She hadn't thought of how uncomfortable being in the confines of a car with a bunch of women she barely knew would be. It sounded like hell. Yeah, she was completely and totally socially inept.

"So, Ava, I'm really digging this look you've got going on today. Your boobs look much bigger than I first had them pegged for."

Ava almost spat her drink across the table as the cool redhead openly assessed her breasts. "Er . . . thank you, Suzy. That's . . . good to hear." They were having lunch at a Mexican restaurant inside the mall. Emma had arranged it so Ava was sitting between her and Ella, and that had helped lessen the discomfort a bit. Unfortunately, that left Suzy, Claire, and Beth across the table. So here she sat, fiddling with her glass and trying to follow the flow of conversation around her. She felt as if she had entered some Lifetime movie where each woman talked about her husband. She knew who these women were married to and she suspected they must be thrilled to go home at the end of each day.

When she and Brant had originally met Jason Danvers, she had been so tongue-tied she couldn't speak.

She hadn't been expecting someone so young and gorgeous. But the real crush had developed once he started talking. The man was brilliant. She had fallen in love with his mind that day. Ava had always had a thirst for knowledge, and Jason was a master teacher. To watch him in action closing a big deal was a thing of beauty. One of his most attractive qualities, though, was how much he loved his wife and the fact that he didn't bother to hide it. Ava had had dinner with them a few times through the course of various business functions, and Jason seemed to think that the world revolved around the woman he had chosen to be by his side. Ava knew that Claire had once been his assistant at Danvers but was now his wife and the mother of his child.

Suzy was married to Grayson "Gray" Merimon, who had also come on board at Danvers when Jason acquired his company. Gray's brother, Nick, worked for Danvers as well and was married to Suzy's sister, Beth. Just trying to keep up with all the connections seemed mind-boggling. And of course, there was Ella, who was married to Ava's brother Declan. Ella was adorable and currently only a month away from giving birth to their first child. Lately Ava felt a pang of emptiness when she saw how happy other people were as part of a couple. She could have had that if only she hadn't been such a coward. Mac had wanted a real relationship with her, but now it might be too late.

"Yoo-hoo, hellooo!"

Ava jumped as Emma's shout jostled her back to the present. She felt herself flush as all eyes at the table were on her.

"Good grief, woman, you were completely zoned out there. So, anyway, I want to talk to the girls about your mission and see if we can get some insight. Is that okay with you?"

Ava smiled politely, thinking, *I am so going to kill this big mouth when we get back to the office.* "Um . . . I guess so."

Emma gave her a wink in return as if trying to reassure her before diving in. "Ladies, you know that Mac and Ava are close, right? Or they were before he started dating someone else. Now, to be fair to Mac, he did want Ava first, but she wasn't ready. Anyway, now he's moved on and we just can't let that happen. We need to help Ava get his attention back and help him to see that she's ready to take the next step."

Suzy rubbed her temple, saying, "I think you've left out a lot of details there, but we can still work with what we've got. So, who is the woman that Mac's dating?"

"It's Gwen, you know, the redhead who works in accounting?" Ella offered.

"G-lo?" Claire blurted out before slapping a hand over her mouth.

"No shit, really?" Suzy smirked. "Wow, I guess Mac likes big butts and he cannot lie."

"Oh my God," Beth groaned, looking at her sister. "I can't believe you went there. Her butt isn't that big."

"It's not that it's big," Suzy corrected, "it's just quite round and juicy, like Jennifer Lopez, aka J-lo. Hey, I'm not insulting her; I'd like to have an ass like that myself."

"Me too," Claire admitted. "If I lose a pound, my butt takes a leave of absence. I've always wanted a big one."

"Yeah, hell, me too," Emma added. "Sorry, Ava, but men do love the big butts."

"She's not shy about showing that sucker off either," Ella chimed in. "She was walking in front of me last week and her dress was glued to it like a second skin. I almost ran into a ficus tree watching her walk."

Ava dropped her head onto the table, ready to admit defeat. "If you're all in love with her or at least her ass, what hope does that leave for me? The magazines didn't mention butt implants."

Suzy leaned forward in her chair, patting her on the top of the hand. "Honey, you've got more going for you than a good set of buns. Mac was into you first and men don't get over stuff like that as easily as they want to believe. Also, you've got us. I'm sure G-lo is a nice person and all, but she's gotta go. There are plenty of other ass-gawking men out there for her, so she'll be fine. Now, Emma said something about you needing clothes for a date with Dominic?"

It seemed that all jaws dropped when that name was mentioned. He appeared to have quite a few admirers at the table. When Ava told them about her plan to start trying new hobbies to catch Mac's attention with her adventurous streak, everyone applauded. "I think you're onto something." Claire laughed. "Mac has been to our house on several occasions going over security things, and Jason just loves how OCD he is over safety. Truthfully, it drives me crazy sometimes, but I go along with it because otherwise Jason would be a nervous wreck when my daughter, Chrissy, and I are alone. I bet you suddenly doing things so out of character will drive Mac out of his mind! Riding a Harley with Dominic, though, is really hitting the big leagues. I'm impressed."

The other girls nodded in agreement as Ava admitted, "I want him to see that I can be fun and exciting. For years, he's known only the quiet and repressed Ava. I need to show not only him, but more important, myself, that I can be like other women my age. I don't have to be so serious about everything anymore. I'm scared to death, but go big or go home, right?" Of course, most of the women at the table didn't know about her past and the baggage that she was trying to overcome. They just assumed that she had dragged her feet and let Mac slip away. It was as much as she was willing to share at this point. Heck, she couldn't be sure whether her past was a secret, because most things at Danvers seemed to be public knowledge. Maybe they all knew more than they were letting on, but she wasn't about to discuss it openly with them . . . not yet and maybe not ever.

Looking her over, Suzy said, "So we need some clothes to make Mac sit up and take notice, right?"

Claire, the sweet one as Ava had come to think of her, added, "Not that there is anything wrong with the way you dress. I think you always look so nice."

"You do," Beth agreed, giving her a friendly smile. "Maybe just some casual clothes for the new hobbies you plan to take on."

"What she needs," Emma interjected, "are some tit-displaying shirts to put those babies out there. Mac has to be behind G-lo to appreciate her big ass, but hello, your girls are right there on eye level for him. There is no way he can miss those suckers if you open those buttons up."

It felt so strange to have female friends rooting for her that Ava wasn't sure if she wanted to jump up and high-five everyone, yelling something about girl power, or run for the nearest door. Instead she followed the others out of the restaurant as they made their way into the mall, clearly women on a mission.

The next hour was something akin to a horror movie as the women she barely knew threw an alarmingly large stack of clothing before her and demanded that she model it, save for the underwear, thank God. When the whirlwind shopping spree was over, it took all of them to carry the bags. She had spent enough money that she could have put an impressive down payment on a new car. What did it matter, though? All these years of having no social life meant that she rarely spent money on anything other than living expenses.

She promised Suzy that she would continue wearing her hair loose and was grateful that no one had suggested a new haircut. Her hair was her one vanity, and even though she mostly wore it up, she still loved her long blond tresses. She groaned in exhaustion as she climbed into the passenger side of Emma's car. How could anyone love shopping? It was total hell.

"So." Emma wiggled her eyebrows. "This is it, then. No backing out now."

"Nope, I'm all in. There is no way I'm taking back these clothes, and I'd never be able to sleep again if I wasted this much money for nothing."

"Yay, that's the spirit. Now let's get ready to unleash hell on poor, unsuspecting Mac. He's going to find out that hell hath no fury like a woman kicked to the curb for one with a bigger butt."

Ava snickered, unable to control herself. Emma was a total nut, but boy, did she have a way with words!

Chapter Six

Oh crap, oh crap, oh crap. What am I doing? Ava looked down at herself, cringing at the unfamiliar clothes she was wearing. She had arranged to meet Dominic at his bike around six, and she had made it with five minutes to spare. She had on some of her new clothes, picked by Suzy for her first motorcycle ride. The outfit consisted of formfitting jeans, a black belt, a white tank top, and a lightweight black leather jacket. A pair of black boots completed the look. Ava felt as if every curve of her body was screaming, *Hey, look at me!* She did have to admit that even though she wasn't comfortable with the way the clothes molded to her curves, she did feel just a little sexy in them. Maybe too sexy. Dominic would probably think she was coming on to him. Before she could have a panic attack at that thought, the man himself sauntered up to her with a sexy grin on his face. Yeah, he definitely sauntered; there was nothing normal about his walk. He moved like a man who knew who he was and didn't care to pretend otherwise. Of course, Mac and Declan both had a similar gait. Maybe it was more like a military swagger. She gave him her brightest smile, trying not to look terrified. "Hey, Dominic."

"Hey, Blondie. Wasn't sure if I'd see you here or not."

Suddenly, she felt awkward and embarrassed. Had he been hoping she wouldn't show up? She had kind of put him on the spot this morning. He was no doubt just trying to be nice by agreeing to the ride, since she was friends with Mac.

Looking down at the toes of her new boots, she said, "If you don't want to bother, that's fine. Really, it was probably a silly idea anyway." At that moment, Ava saw movement out of the corner of her eye and looked over to see Mac and Gwen exiting the elevator into the garage. "Oh, damn, perfect," she muttered under her breath. That was all she needed, Mac and his new girlfriend with the big butt witnessing her humiliation as Dominic sent her on her way.

"Blondie, if you want to do this, let's make it good. Here's your big chance to get Mac's attention. Just play along and I guarantee he'll be fucking flipping out."

She snapped her head around to look at Dominic, gaping at him in surprise. "What?"

He grinned in response, before settling on his bike and telling her to climb on behind him. "Baby, I wasn't born yesterday. Sometimes it takes a hard right to the heart to realize how bad you've fucked up. I'm thinking you've taken the hit and now you're ready for some return fire. And lucky for you, that's my specialty."

Ava quickly but awkwardly climbed on the big bike behind Dominic, not realizing until she was settled that her crotch was going to be sitting right in the curve of his ass. It was official; this was her most intimate moment with something that didn't require batteries. She tried to ignore the throbbing between her thighs at the foreign feeling of a masculine body nestled there. She might love Mac, but she couldn't ignore the little flicker of desire that she felt at being this close to a man. She saw Mac and Gwen gawking at them before Mac started forward, almost dragging poor Gwen across the pavement. "Oh, shit, here they come. Why are you helping me? Mac's your friend."

Dominic rocked the bike backward, releasing the stand before he turned sideways to say, "Because he has something I want . . . and I have something he wants."

"What are you talking about?" Before he could answer, Mac and an out-of-breath Gwen reached them and sparks were flying.

"Dom, what in the fuck do you think you're doing?" Mac's hot gaze flew over her, and she saw him visibly swallow. In a gentler tone he added, "Avie, get off the bike."

Dominic ignored his friend, simply smirking in response. "Ava and I are going to dinner and then I'm giving her a riding lesson."

Ava watched Mac, fascinated, as a nerve ticked away in his jaw. She couldn't remember the last time she had seen him so angry. He usually showed her only his gentle side, even though she was aware that he, like most people, had a harder side. "What kind of lesson?" Oh, yikes, he thought that was a code for sex, didn't he?

"He's teaching me to drive his bike. I've been wanting to try it for a while." Uh-oh, he had his hands in his hair now, looking for all the world as if he was going to yank some of it out in frustration. Wow, if Ava had wanted to get a reaction out of him, this was it. He looked as if he was going to detonate. Beside him, Gwen's eyes jumped from Mac to Dominic to Ava and then back again. She looked as if she was on the verge of solving a big puzzle and just needed a few more pieces. Ava didn't miss the quick, appraising look that Dominic shot Gwen before looking away. Apparently, he also liked big butts and was ready to help Ava get Mac so that he would be free to have G-lo. Wow—weren't there reality shows about stuff like this? Ava had never thought she'd actually be a part of some type of love triangle.

Mac's eyes drilled into hers as he continued to speak to her in the same soft voice. "Ava, bikes are dangerous. There is no way you can drive a Harley. You're going to get seriously hurt. Now please get off and I'll walk you back to your car." Something about his tone was really starting to piss her off. She was tired of being treated like an invalid. Maybe she had done nothing to prove to him that she was capable of living a normal life, but that was about to change. This was no longer just about getting Mac back from Gwen; this was about showing him that she had a backbone. She wasn't the same scared teenager anymore. Well, maybe she was still scared, but damn it, she needed to prove that she could do something other than cower in a corner. She could be fearless and fun.

She gave him a bright smile before tightening her arms around Dominic's waist. "I'm ready if you are," she said against his ear. Beneath her, the big bike roared to life and Dominic threw a wave at Mac and Gwen before taking off. Ava heard Mac yelling at their retreating backs, but she had no time to try to decipher his words; she was too busy holding on for dear life.

Oh God, Mac was right, this bike was way out of her league. Ava buried her face in Dominic's back and started reciting every prayer she had ever heard. She even threw in Now I Lay Me Down to Sleep for good measure. A prayer was a prayer, right? She finally turned her head sideways when she was close to asphyxiating in Dominic's shirt. The Atlantic Ocean glimmered on her right, and she realized that they were on Ocean Boulevard. Even through her death grip she noticed how vivid the view from the back of the bike was compared to the countless times she had traveled this same route by car. There was something about the warmth of the sun on her face and the feel of the wind in her hair that made her feel alive. She hesitantly loosened her grip enough to ease back slightly and gasped in surprise. It was still scary as hell when she looked down at the road flying by, but there was also an unfamiliar rush racing through her veins. She was actually doing it. She was trying something new, something kind of dangerous, and she wasn't having a panic attack or a nervous breakdown.

She heard Dominic yell at her over his shoulder, "Not bad, is it, Blondie?" She laughed in reply, feeling her body relax further. She felt like Kate Winslet in *Titanic* when she stood on the bow of the ship with her arms in the air. She laughed again and figured that

Dominic must think she was losing her mind. She didn't care, though; she wanted to revel in the moment. All too soon, the bike slowed and pulled into a parking space next to the boardwalk. Dominic set the bike back on the stand and cut the engine. She held on to his shoulder as he helped her climb from the bike before getting off himself. "I thought we'd grab a sandwich and eat outside since it's such a nice evening." Normally, she would have listed all the reasons that she would rather eat indoors in the cool air-conditioning, but what the hell? She was turning over a new leaf, and after riding a motorcycle, surely eating a hot dog outside would be tame in comparison.

"Sounds good," she agreed, and followed him to the small café on the corner. They walked in the door and she fought the urge to suggest an indoor table. Dominic was more comfortable outside and she was just along for the ride, literally. As her eyes scrolled over the menu on the wall behind the counter, she suddenly clapped her hands in excitement before grabbing Dominic's arm. "Funnel cake! Oh, please, can I have that instead of real food?" Dominic started chuckling and Ava's cheeks colored when she realized that the few people in the café were smiling at her childlike enthusiasm for the sugary treat.

"Blondie, you get whatever you want. You're a bike-riding badass now. Break a few more rules and have dessert first." Dominic ordered two foot-long hot dogs for himself and the funnel cake for her. He also ordered them both Coke, which made her cringe slightly. She usually stuck to diet drinks, but that seemed silly when she was eating a fried treat with no doubt thousands of calories in it. She wondered idly how many calories riding a motorcycle burned off. *Surely anxiety raises your heart rate.*

Dominic balanced their food on a tray while she ran ahead and opened the door for them. Soon, they were settled at a table on the boardwalk. She had to admit that the sound of the waves breaking against the shore beside them was better than listening to the chatter indoors. Maybe Dominic was onto something. After taking her first bite of the fluffy, fried cake loaded with powdered sugar, she wiped her lips and looked at the man across the table from her. It seemed strange to be sharing a meal with him, since they had never really done it before. She had eaten with him, Mac, and Gage, but that was hardly the one-on-one they were having now. "So, you like Gwen, huh?" she blurted out before thinking better of it.

He lifted an eyebrow, looking surprised at the personal question for a moment before shrugging. She thought he was going to let the subject drop, but after a long sip of his drink, he finally answered, "Gwen and I are neighbors. I saw her first, I guess you could say. I didn't even know she worked for Danvers until Mac started dating her."

She gave him a sympathetic look, recognizing a kindred soul. "So you waited around too long and someone else moved in on your girl? Yeah, I can relate to that. I mean . . . not the moving-in-on-the-girl part, since obviously no one moved in on my girl . . . um, not that I have a girl, but . . ."

Dominic laughed, holding his hand up to stop her fumbling explanation. "I get it, Blondie. Yeah, we do have some things in common, although you kind of dropped the ball in a much bigger way than I did. Hell, I had just seen Gwen around our apartment complex and thought about asking her out. Honey, Mac has worshipped the ground you walk on for years. He was so messed up over you when we were in Afghanistan, I'm surprised he didn't get his ass blown off." In a gentler voice, he continued. "I get that you had some bad shit that happened to you and you've been hurting over it, but time waits for no man or woman, Blondie, and it looks like you're starting to see that. Hell, I am as well."

He saw her look of surprise when he mentioned her past, and he covered her hand briefly with his. "Declan, Mac, Gage, and I are brothers in every way that counts. There are few secrets between us. We lived in too-close quarters for many years for that. Secrets get you killed over there. I don't know all the details, but I know someone hurt you, and I'm sorry as hell about that. I really am. I know that the kind of emotional baggage that normal people never experience even in their worst dreams does something to you. It changes everything you are. Believe me, I know that. We all do. It makes me hesitate to do something seemingly easy and normal like ask a woman out who I'm really attracted to. It makes you afraid to show the man who loves you that you feel the same way and it makes Mac afraid of ending up alone. We all have the pieces we need to make something good happen in our lives. We're just fucking up with putting the puzzle together correctly."

Ava sat staring at Dominic, shocked by the almost poetic way that he spoke. He seemed to give new meaning to the saying "still waters run deep." She found herself responding to his speech by wanting to do one of two things: cry her eyes out until she was a blubbering mess or blurt out some deep, dark secret just to see what his take on it was. "All your reports were wrong; I haven't dated anyone or been with a man since that night."

She studied Dominic's almost comical reaction as the hot dog he was holding froze on the way to his mouth. "Come again." He blinked as if he had misunderstood her statement. *Shit, maybe this confession isn't such a good idea.*

"I picked men up in bars periodically and paid them to come home with me for a while. I knew that Mac kept a tail on me to . . . watch over me, and I didn't want him to know that I'm not normal."

Dominic set his hot dog back down without taking a bite and leaned forward on the table, looking stunned. "What did these men do who came home with you, then? Some of them were there all night."

Ava looked down, rubbing her finger in circles on the tabletop. God, this had gotten embarrassing. Admitting how messed up she was to a macho man like Dominic was almost impossible, but there was no way he would let it go now. He looked determined to get some answers. "Well . . . I told them all I was trying to make my boyfriend jealous and offered them a couple hundred bucks to come home with me for a while. We, um . . . played video games, Monopoly, or sometimes they fell asleep and I just let them stay on the couch until morning. I also locked my bedroom door, though," she rushed to assure him.

Rubbing his head, Dominic slumped back in his seat. "Blondie, do you have any idea how fucked-up that is? Aside from the fact that you almost killed Mac every time I had to report in that you had some guy at your house for the evening, do you have any idea how dangerous that was? Shit, you of all people should know that you can't trust a complete stranger. How could you possibly let someone you didn't know into your house with you? Damn, you even let some stay while you slept. Ava! Shit, that's completely whacked." When a tear slid down her cheek, his expression softened in apology. "I didn't mean to yell at you, Blondie, but it looks like you've been living on the edge for years without evening acknowledging it. Riding a motorcycle is nothing compared to what you've been doing. I just . . . I'm blown away here. I'm the last one to judge, but Mac needs to seriously spank your ass for pulling a dangerous stunt like that repeatedly. I mean, what were you thinking?"

More tears fell now as she realized the truth of what he was saying. She had risked her life repeatedly and for what? To prove to Mac that she had a normal life with normal desires? When she really thought it through, it sounded absurd. She had been raped by her prom date, someone she actually knew after several dates together. Yet she had trusted complete strangers to spend hours alone with her in her home. God, she had seriously lost her mind. Even though she now realized how bad it sounded, she felt the need to defend herself. "After the first few, I had a referral system of sorts. Most of the men in graduate school here are really broke. So they started telling their friends about me." She didn't add that one of them had accidentally let it slip that the other guys had said that the crazy cat lady from the bar would pay you two hundred bucks for a few hours to pretend to be her fake boyfriend. "They were actually nice guys. One of them fixed the drip under my kitchen sink and a few of the others repainted my kitchen. They even took the trash out when they left."

Suddenly, Dominic's body started convulsing in laughter. Ava watched him warily, wondering if she had pushed him completely off the deep end. It seemed unusual for a man whom she had rarely seen smile before today to actually fall against the table as full belly laughs erupted from him. "You're . . . too . . . much!" he gasped out as his big frame continued to shake. She sat waiting patiently for him to catch his breath, wondering what the joke was. Finally, when she was getting ready to upend her Coke over his head, he managed to reel it back in. Taking a couple of deep breaths, he settled for grinning at her while shaking his head. "Mac should pack his shit and move to another state, because he's never going to survive you. You know he's going to blow his top when he finds out about this, don't you?"

"So maybe I don't tell him that part?" She had meant it as more of a statement, but it came out as more of a question.

He still looked vastly amused as he shook his head again. "Blondie, if you want to have a real relationship with Mac, then you have to tell him the truth. Trust me, as a man, I can tell you that he will be constantly dwelling on the fact that your bedroom seemed like the local Do-Drop-In for years. He's got to be wondering why, if you're screwed up by your past, you're more than willing to sleep with a lot of other men, but not him. That's actually pretty cold. Couldn't you have found a less painful way to convince the man that you were functioning normally? Hell, even a pretend lesbian relationship or two would have been fine."

Groaning, Ava rolled her head, trying to release the tension there. "Okay, it wasn't my best idea. I just . . . wasn't ready to be involved with anyone, and I didn't know if I ever would be. It seemed like the only way to keep him at a distance, romantically, but still have him in my life. He didn't push me for anything else as long as he thought I was . . . seeing someone else. Plus, it made it appear that I was capable of . . . you know, of sex." Suddenly, it hit her that she was telling a virtual stranger all her secrets. Was this it, then? Was she so desperate for a friend that she had moved Dominic into the role of her own personal Dear Abby? Of course, she had talked to Emma and her friends at lunch, but that was different. Dominic probably thought a lot like Mac, which gave her some much-needed male insight.

Dominic started clearing off the remains of his food from the table, signaling the end of their meal. When he had cleared Ava's place as well, she stood to follow him back out to the bike. "All right, Blondie, for tonight, I think it's enough that you just rode on the back of a bike. You need to get used to the sensation before you try to actually drive one." Ava wanted to drop to her knees and thank him. She hadn't been looking forward to her first lesson and was grateful to have a reprieve. When a couple of girls rolled past them on skates, Dominic pointed after their retreating backs. "Want another way to drive Mac crazy? Take up that hobby. Do your skating on the sidewalk in Garden City, though. Mac goes right through there on the way home every night."

Her eyes brightened as she looked around at the other people skating down the boardwalk. Wow, it looked a lot safer than riding a bike, and if she could manage to make sure Mac saw her at least part of the time, it would be perfect. She gave Dominic an impulsive hug, saying, "Great idea! That's exactly what I need to try next. Do you think you could text me when he leaves the office every evening? If I try to wait on him at work, I'll never make it to the sidewalk in time."

"Ava . . . babe, I was kidding. That looks kinda dangerous actually."

"No, no, it's brilliant. I could just stand around with the skates on. Like not really moving, but acting like I have been." She jumped on the bike, pointing to the seat in front of her. "Hurry up. I'll have time to stop at Walmart on the way home. They have everything there."

Dominic gave her a hesitant look for a moment before shrugging. "There is no way this is gonna go well, but what the hell?" With those words, he climbed on the bike, and soon they were heading back toward Danvers and her car. She was able to enjoy the ride back without fearing too heavily for her life. When Dominic dropped her off, she thanked him before hurrying to her car. She was determined to buy everything she needed for her next mission: Ava Stone, skating queen.

Mac threw his keys on the entryway table upon entering his home. He heard them slip off the table and onto the floor, but he continued without stopping. He was too pissed right now to pick up after himself. He had barely been able to contain his anger as he walked Gwen to her car. They were supposed to go somewhere for dinner, but she had made a last-minute excuse about needing to pack for her planned weekend away with her sister. No doubt, the thought of spending another hour with him in his present mood was more than she could take. He'd been so damn grateful for the cancellation that he had just barely caught himself before he thanked her. As it was, he was pathetically relieved that she was going to be gone for a few days. What did that say about the state of their relationship?

He wanted to strangle Dominic, who was supposed to be his best friend. What in the hell was he thinking having Ava on his bike? And he planned to teach her how to ride it? Un-fucking-believable. Mac wanted to call and chew his ass out, but he didn't want to risk distracting him. Damn it, his friends knew how much Ava meant to him. He'd never thought he had to worry about any of them putting the woman he loved in danger. Was that the worst of it, though? Was Dom interested in Ava? Things had sure looked friendly enough with their bodies plastered together on that damn Harley. Seeing her slender arms gripping Dom tightly was enough to make Mac lose his shit. He would probably have done something completely stupid and careless like taking off after them if not for Gwen standing there looking as though she was putting two and two together and coming up with a solid four.

He stalked into his bedroom, jerking a pair of basketball shorts out of the laundry basket sitting on the floor. He might not be the best housekeeper, but he figured he got points for the clothes at least being clean. He made quick work of jerking off his usual work attire and pulling the shorts on. After a quick stop at the door to put on his running shoes, he made his way across the sand and to the nearly empty beach beyond. As his feet hit the wet sand, he quickly found his rhythm. He desperately needed an outlet for the anger coursing through his body, and it was either run until he dropped or go kill his best friend. Not much of a choice there at all.

Chapter Seven

Ava hadn't thought about it being the weekend when she concocted her master skating plan. Mac wouldn't be on his regular schedule today, which would make it a little trickier to get him to notice her on the streets of Garden City. She had also had a moment of panic when she thought that maybe he might not be alone. What if Gwen was with him? She'd already had the other woman staring at her on the back of Dominic's bike last night. After she calmed down, she realized that she had one ace in the hole; she knew that Mac took his mother to breakfast almost every Saturday morning without fail. She had gone along with them a few times, and Mac always met his mother at nine. Therefore, at eight thirty she was on the practically deserted streets of Garden City in a bright pink tank top and black running shorts. She had her new speed skates, which the gum-popping teenager in the sporting goods section of Walmart had recommended. She had looked at the safety gear, but realized that Mac wouldn't recognize her in a helmet. It didn't really matter; she just intended to stand around, not actually do much skating.

The only thing she hadn't taken into account was the fact that skates tended to roll even without you trying, and coupled with the incline on the sidewalk, things happened . . . fast. She was sitting on a bench when she saw Mac's black Tahoe turn the corner. She jumped up quickly, hoping he saw her before he passed. As it turned out, she didn't have to worry about catching Mac's attention, because she caught the attention of everyone within a two-mile vicinity as she flew wildly down the sidewalk before wrapping briefly around a No Parking sign, then ultimately running into the bumper of a Dodge Neon and finally falling backward spectacularly onto her ass.

Birds were tweeting above her head like something out of a *Tom and Jerry* cartoon as she lay there stunned. "Honey, are you okay?" someone asked helpfully before yelling down the line of onlookers, "She's conscious but has some road rash." *What does that even mean?* she idly thought as she lay there wondering if anything was broken. Seemed she would have been better off on the damn Harley after all. She now hoped fervently that Mac hadn't seen her. This was way too humiliating.

"Ava?" She blinked like an owl when she heard her name uttered in a familiar voice. She moaned as she turned her head to the right, blinking against the glare of the sun. Mac stood in the middle of the crowd looking as if he'd seen a ghost. His mouth was moving, but nothing appeared to be coming out of it. Maybe some silent swearwords. She was sure she'd seen him mouth something that started with an *F*. He seemed to shrug off whatever trance he had fallen in and jumped into typical Mac damage control. Kneeling beside her, he took inventory of the scratches on her body. "Where does it hurt, baby?"

She choked back a hysterical laugh before trying to pull herself up. "Where doesn't it hurt would be a better question," she muttered before her feet flew out from under her and again she landed backward on her sore ass. "Shit, that hurt."

He put a hand on her stomach, holding her down. "Avie, let me take these damn skates off before you kill yourself. What in the world were you thinking?"

She looked at the crowd still standing around them. "Can we please save the lecture for when we're alone? Just get me out of here."

At that, Mac looked around, seeming to finally realize that they were creating quite a spectacle. He quickly removed her skates before leaning down to scoop her up effortlessly into his arms. "Wha . . . what are you doing?"

She sputtered as he ignored her protests. He carried her to his Tahoe as if she weighed nothing. "Mac, my car is right over there. Just let me down."

He continued to ignore her, shifting her weight on his hip to free his hand for opening the door. He settled her on the seat, slamming the door on her complaints. He stalked back through the crowd, picking up the skates and throwing them in the backseat before getting in the driver's side. He turned the big SUV back toward his house before punching a button on his hands-free phone mounted on the dash. When Ava heard his mother's voice come through the speaker, she slunk down farther in her seat, hoping Mac wouldn't tell her what had happened. Luckily, he just said that something had come up and he'd call her later.

They parked in front of his two-story beach house. "Stay where you are," Mac ordered as he left his seat before coming around to her side of the car. One look at his tight face was enough for her to keep her mouth shut and let him carry her again. Normally, she would have taken a moment to appreciate the beauty of the rustic house with cedar siding that Mac had so pains-takingly restored, but today it passed by in a blur. He refused to put her down while he struggled to get the key in the front door and disable the security alarm.

Finally, they made it into the spacious living room, where he sat her down gently on the couch. He left the room, coming back a few moments later with a first aid kit and the same scowl sitting heavily on his handsome face. Wow, he looked seriously pissed. He lowered his large form to the coffee table in front of the couch and barked out, "Take your shirt off."

Now, that got her attention. "Um . . . do what?" Surely, she had heard him wrong.

"Take your shirt off. I need to see if you have any damage to your back or your stomach. It looked like you damn near fell on every single inch of your body."

Ava sat silently for a moment, feeling the old famil-iar panic set in. Damn it, if she couldn't even take her shirt off in front of the man she was supposed to love, then how would she ever convince him that she was ready for a real relationship with him? She was so tired of being scared all the time. Taking a deep breath, she silently cursed the fact that she had worn a plain white cotton bra this morning. She dearly hoped he didn't notice the slight tremble of her hands as she gripped the edge of her top and slowly pulled it over her head. He removed the shirt from her nerveless fingers, dropping it to the floor. His gaze seemed to zero in on the creamy swells of her breasts exposed by her no-frills bra, and she was horrified to feel her nipples hardening under his attention.

After a moment, he put his hands on her shoulders, and she groaned inwardly as she did a full-body shiver. Something about the feel of his warm hands on her bare skin was causing her pulse to rocket. The moment was broken, though, when he started mumbling under his breath before touching an area of her upper back that felt as if it were on fire. "Ouch!" Was he . . . ? Alarmed, she asked, "What are you doing with my bra?"

With obvious strain in his voice, Mac said, "Relax, Avie; I need your bra strap out of the way. You've got a nasty laceration back here. The asphalt ripped a hole in your shirt. You must have hit the ground even harder than I thought. You're damn lucky you didn't break anything." Suddenly, his face was back in front of hers, looking her face over anxiously. "I didn't see you hit your head." His hands started roaming over her scalp, looking for signs of injury. "Shit, tell me you didn't. I can't feel anything. If there is any possibility of a head injury, we need to go to a hospital and have it checked out. I should have checked for that before I moved you. I just . . . panicked."

Ava grabbed his forearm, pulling his hand back down. "Mac, my head is fine. I think most of the damage was to my butt and my pride." When he looked down at her shorts, she knew what was coming next, and her cheeks were already coloring in response.

"Er . . . take your shorts off, then. I need to see what we're dealing with."

"No! I'm not taking my shorts off. I'm perfectly capable of looking at my own . . . butt later." She might have caved to pressure to remove her top because truthfully the feel of the fabric against the scrapes on her back was painful. But there was no way she was removing her bottoms. She had worn her granny panties, and it'd be over her dead body that he would get a look at them. When she finally worked up the nerve to disrobe completely for Mac, she would be wearing something sexier than one hundred percent cotton. He looked ready to argue with her, so she shifted his attention back to her upper body by wincing and moving her shoulder. "Could you put a Band-Aid or something there? It hurts like the devil." Now that she'd mentioned the pain, it seemed to be all around her. As her adrenaline dropped, her body started throbbing. Running into a parked car was damn painful. "Ouch!"

"Hang on, baby; let me get you some Advil before we clean all your cuts."

Ava wanted to swoon when Mac called her baby. He had used the endearment a few times over the years, but that was twice already today. He mostly called her Avie, which had always made her feel special, but baby . . . yeah, she liked that a lot. Unless . . . did he call

Gwen that? She looked down at the couch she was sitting on. Had Gwen been here with Mac? Had they held hands, touched each other, had sex together . . . right where she was sitting? The thought made her physically sick, and she wanted to do nothing but run. She didn't want to be anywhere that another woman had staked a claim to the man Ava loved.

Ava winced as she tried to move off the couch. Agony raced through her body as she leaned down to pick up her discarded shirt. She needed to get out of here . . . now. She was balancing unsteadily on her feet when Mac walked back in carrying a bottle and a glass of water. He looked surprised to see her standing there, with her shirt gripped tightly in one hand. "Mac . . . I'm just going to . . . I mean, I need to get back to my car."

He shook a couple of tablets from the bottle that he was carrying out before setting it down. He handed them to her along with the glass, waiting until she had taken them before commenting on her sudden need to leave. "Avie . . . sit down, please. I need to patch you up before I take you back."

She stood there uncertainly before asking, "Could we use a kitchen chair? I, um . . . just don't want to sit back down on the couch." No doubt, he thought she was cracking up, but after a moment's hesitation, he walked toward his kitchen and returned seconds later with a wooden chair. She was so glad that he hadn't questioned her aversion to his leather couch. What could she possibly say? "Oh, sorry. I'm afraid that you had sex with your girlfriend on it and the thought of sitting there makes me want to puke"? Nothing strange about that statement at all. Especially when she had handed him to Gwen on a shiny platter with a damn red bow attached to it.

Mac picked up his first aid kit and started cleaning her abrasions with an antiseptic wipe that stung bad enough to bring tears to her eyes. Having his hands gently touching almost every exposed inch of her skin was torture for a different reason. She only hoped that he thought the few times that she hadn't been able to stop herself from flinching was from the pain and not the foreign feeling of his warm hands touching her body. She both feared and craved his touch. How many nights had she lain awake wishing he were there, lying next to her? Wishing she were a normal person who could wake up in the arms of the man she loved— without remembering another man's hands on her body, holding her immobile and stripping away her innocence? The one thing she had wanted to give Mac from the moment she had started to see him as something more than her brother's friend. It was always supposed to be him and only him, and that had been brutally stolen from them both. They could never get that back, but if she continued on the path of avoidance that she had taken for so many years, then the bastard who had raped her was still ruining her life, and she didn't want that. She wanted to be free. She wanted to know what it felt like to be touched by someone who cared about her. It had to be Mac, as it was always meant to be.

"Avie . . . what's going on with you? First, you go

roaring off on the back of Dom's bike, and next you're flying down the streets of Garden City wrapping yourself around a car. This isn't you; this isn't the woman I know. I mean . . . is there something I need to know about you and Dom?"

Ava held her breath, wondering if Mac was aware that he had stopped treating her injuries and was now stroking a fingertip along the sensitive skin of her arm, causing an involuntary shiver. If he noticed, he gave no indication. He continued to touch her while waiting for her answer.

"Would it bother you?" she asked quietly. She knew it was juvenile to insinuate that there was something romantic between her and Dominic, but she wanted— no, she needed—Mac to care.

Mac expelled a breath before his hand moved from her arm and glided up to her neck, lingering on the pulse beating wildly there. "You have no idea, Avie. He's my brother, and I'd give him everything I have . . . but not you, baby. Never you. You. Belong. To. Me."

His hand rested against her neck, and their eyes locked. His expression was wild and fierce and for the first time she wasn't scared. She wanted to taste his lips more than she wanted her next breath. Without allowing herself time to think, she raised her other hand, reaching up to pull his head lower. A hint of uncertainty flickered across his face just before their mouths connected and then her body sizzled with awareness of him. Unlike with their other kiss, Mac seemed to wait for her to take control, to deepen the contact. She tentatively touched her tongue along the seam of his lips, wanting to taste him. He groaned deep in his throat before opening his mouth and tangling his tongue with hers. In that moment, she understood for the first time where the inspiration for every romance novel and romantic movie came from. It was this . . . feeling as if you were on the verge of unlocking all the infinite secrets of the universe with just one kiss.

Time seemed to stand still as she experienced her first real kiss as a grown woman. Mac had kissed her one other time, but her fear had kept her from truly getting lost in the moment. This time, she was more than a willing participant. She took the lead in kissing him. She explored every corner of his mouth, tasting coffee and the minty flavor of his toothpaste. As his hands threaded through her hair, pulling her closer, she felt a small trickle of unease. She reminded herself that this was Mac. He'd never hurt her, never force her. She murmured a protest when his lips left her mouth only to kiss down her jaw, then her neck. "Mac . . . oh, Mac . . . please . . ." Something was buzzing on the table beside them, cutting through the haze of desire she was in. Mac cursed under his breath before pulling back. Almost in sync, they both looked over to see his phone lighting up and on the screen in bold letters it said CALL FROM GWEN.

"Fuck," Mac rasped out, reaching over to hit the IGNORE button on his phone. Ava guessed she should be grateful for that at least. After all, she was the other woman here, not Gwen. Even knowing that, she didn't think she could handle hearing Mac talk to Gwen as if he hadn't just had his lips all over Ava. By now, they were both breathing hard, trying to come down from the high they had just experienced. Ava's face colored in embarrassment when Mac looked at her. Had she really just been sucking on his tongue? Part of her felt the need to yell, "You go, girl," and part of her wanted to crawl under the chair she was sitting in. She had kissed Mac, and it had felt better than she could ever have imagined. She squeezed her legs together as her core ached for her to finish what she had started. Being reminded that Mac had another woman in his life, though, had ended her moment of boldness. "Avie . . ."

Ava jumped to her feet, not wanting to answer all the questions that she saw on Mac's face. She needed time to gather her thoughts and her courage before anything else happened between them, including a conversation. "Mac, I really need to get back to my car now. I, um . . . have plans soon, so I need to get home and change."

Mac put his hands on his hips, looking suspicious. "What kind of plans? They had better not involve a damn motorcycle or skates."

"Ur . . . no. I'm meeting Emma for lunch today."

"I thought Brant and Emma were visiting her parents this weekend."

God, was there nothing the man didn't know? "I meant Ella. I'm meeting Ella. You know, last-minute baby things."

Looking skeptical, Mac asked, "What kind of baby things?"

Suddenly, she remembered the conversation between Beth and Ella at lunch yesterday and blurted out, "Breast pumps." Mac's cheeks flushed, and if she hadn't embarrassed herself as well, she'd probably have laughed. Apparently, mentioning anything to do with breast-feeding was the equivalent of discussing your period with men. They simply folded right in front of your eyes.

"I . . . yeah . . . okay . . . sure, that's good," Mac stuttered as he dropped his gaze, shifting his feet on the floor restlessly. He gathered himself and walked over to help her when she struggled to pull the shirt back over her head. Ava limped back out to his Tahoe, and all too soon, he was pulling in next to her car.

Turning to him, she said, "Thanks for taking care of me today."

He grabbed her wrist before she could open the door, halting her exit. "No more crazy stuff, right? You're not the type of person to risk your neck like that."

Ava put her hand over his, saying simply, "Maybe I've changed, Mac. I need to take more risks now—I have to."

Clearly irritated and even more confused, Mac asked, "What could you possibly hope to gain from all this?"

Pulling her arm from his hold, she opened the door of his vehicle. Before slipping out, she turned back to him, finally answering his question with one simple word—"You."

With that, she slammed the door behind her and hobbled back to her car. Mac was still sitting there staring at her when she drove away. She didn't think he understood fully what she was trying to say, but between the kiss that she had initiated and her answer to his question, he was surely starting to realize that something had changed. She only hoped that she didn't break a bone before she gained his full attention. She would be a good girl and not do anything crazy today as he had asked, but she wasn't finished yet by a long shot. She had gotten under Mac's skin more in the last twenty-four hours than she had in months . . . since Gwen came along, and she intended to keep going. Just maybe with a helmet and pads the next time.

Mac scowled as he watched Ava limp to her car and drive away. She had him reeling and he didn't know whether to kiss her or spank some sense into her. Both options held strong appeal. He and Ava seemed to be on the same page with the kiss today . . . oh, fuck, the kiss. Ava finally laying her lips on his, taking the initiative. His cock had already been straining the zipper of his jeans ever since she had removed her shirt. The plain white bra she wore had somehow seemed sexier than every piece of lingerie that Victoria's Secret had in their whole damn store. It was Ava to a tee. Innocent white cotton, but add in her full breasts straining against the cups, and it was enough to bring him to his knees. Truthfully, he had been grateful that she refused to remove her shorts. He wasn't sure he could have held out with Ava in front of him in nothing but her panties. As it was, he'd taken a few deep breaths when he went to the kitchen for some Advil for her. He'd also adjusted his throbbing cock, trying to make his state of arousal a little less noticeable.

Now he felt something he didn't often feel—complete and utter confusion. If asked, he would have said that he knew Ava better than anyone else, including her family. He knew her favorite color, how she liked her coffee, how she loved watching reruns of the *Golden Girls* and, when she was feeling particularly daring, *Sons of Anarchy*. She always cried at every remotely emotional scene in a movie, even an action film. She was addicted to green apple Chap Stick, had a serious hang-up on buying shoes that she rarely ever wore, and sometimes she snored, even if she'd never admit it. He knew that from the many nights he had fallen asleep on her couch after watching a movie.

"Oh, fuck," he muttered, thinking back to her interest in *Sons of Anarchy*. Maybe she really was attracted to Dominic. Hell, he was probably the closest thing to a biker that she'd ever come across. However, if that was true, why had she kissed him as if she was starving for his taste? How far would things have gone if Gwen hadn't called when she did?

Oh, great, Gwen . . . truthfully, he'd been so caught up in Ava and Dom being together the night before that he had given little thought to the woman he was supposed to be dating. Moving on had seemed like a good idea at the time, but now he had to wonder if he hadn't just complicated an already impossible situation. Ava had been showing no signs of ever letting him out of the friend zone, and it had become more and more painful to pretend that he was content with that place in her life.

If he was honest, maybe he thought it might shake

her up to see him moving on, but that hadn't appeared to happen. Sure, she seemed sad when he stopped spending so much time with her, but she didn't show up at his house naked and professing her undying love. Instead she had given him looks around the office that had made him want to slink off while apologizing for being such a fucking prick to her. The fact of the matter was that time waits for no man, and he was getting older. Sure, he was only in his early thirties, but he was tired of spending his life alone. He fucked when he felt the need, but that was it. There was no one waiting for him at the end of the day, and it had gotten old. He could admit that he wanted a wife and a family sometime in the near future. He didn't still want to be sitting around ten years from now hoping that Ava would let him love her.

Yeah, it all sounded perfectly reasonable and rational. However, if that was true, why was he so conflicted about his master plan suddenly? Maybe the same reason he had yet to return Gwen's call. As he pulled into the near-empty parking garage for Danvers and saw Dom pull up beside him, he gnashed his teeth. This wasn't a good time to see his best friend. If Dom had any sense of self-preservation, he would crawl right back on his Harley and hit the road.

Instead the bastard walked over to his door as he opened it, giving a lazy grin at Mac's closed-off expression. "Morning, bro. Beautiful day, isn't it?"

Mac looked into the other man's eyes and tried to talk himself out of the unfamiliar feelings of jealousy coursing through his veins. This was Dominic, his brother. He'd never hit on Ava. He knew how Mac felt about her. "Morning," he answered, trying his best to keep his tone light.

"You're here early," Dominic said, looking down at his watch. "I thought you were having breakfast with your mom first."

"Yeah, so did I. I ran into a little problem on the way and had to cancel."

"What kind of problem?" Dominic asked, looking curious. No doubt, he thought it was something to do with their business.

Walking toward the doors of Danvers, Mac said, "Well, Ava decided to try some sidewalk skating and wrapped herself around the bumper of a parked car not far from my house. I saw the whole damn thing happen on my way."

Dominic looked surprised before bursting into laughter. "Holy crap, that girl's just not right, is she?" Before Mac could chew Dominic's ass out for insulting Ava, even if what he said did appear to have some truth at the moment, Gage came swaggering across the lobby as they walked inside.

"Good morning, ladies. You two need some extra beauty sleep this morning or something?"

Mac grinned as Dominic flipped off their annoying coworker before he could work up the effort. Out of the three of them, Gage was probably the most laid-back. Their employees and every woman within a hundred-mile radius seemed to love his infectious personality. If there was ever any bad news to impart, Gage was nominated to do it. He could tell a woman her hair was flat, her shoes were ugly, and her butt was big and the woman would probably hug his neck and thank him. He was just that good.

Dominic was more of an "it is what it is and fuck you if you don't like it" kind of guy. And Mac was more of a details man. He liked making things work, making them better. His life mostly revolved around making the rules and seeing that they were enforced. After being in the military, he enjoyed structure and didn't like it when things didn't adhere to the norm. That was one reason that Ava's sudden need to endanger herself doing something crazy was freaking him out. It was out of the normal for her, and he sure as hell didn't understand it.

Yeah, he, Gage, and Dominic were as different in personality as night and day, but the differences worked well. Between them all, they had every aspect of their business covered. Mac had grown up as an only child, but along with Declan, these were the brothers of his heart. He couldn't imagine loving a blood relative any more than he loved the men he had served alongside in the marines. They all had a tattoo that said "brotherhood," and it wasn't just an inked word to him.

Dominic jabbed Gage in the side as they walked through the door of East Coast Security. "Why are you so damn cheerful this morning? Get laid last night?"

Without missing a beat, Gage dropped into a chair in front of their bank of monitors. "Of course." Then smirking at them, he added, "Didn't you?" When they both just frowned in answer, he laughed. "Oh, come on. What's so difficult about it? You see woman, pick up woman, fuck woman, then repeat. If you two would stop sitting around talking about your feelings and buying tampons, you might actually get lucky. Tell you what, I'll go out with you both tonight and be your wingman."

Mac shook his head, then flicked his hand to Dominic. "Go ahead and do it before I kill him." Gage looked around in confusion, but it was too late. Dominic jerked the chair he was sitting in backward and suddenly his feet were up in the air as he hit the floor.

Dominic smirked, saying, "Thank fuck, I couldn't listen to another word from this cocky little bastard."

Always the good sport, Gage started laughing as he rolled out on the floor and to his feet. "All right, have it your way. Don't say I didn't try to help a brother out, though."

They all spent the next few hours running through the security feeds and finalizing assignments for the next week. When a text message buzzed through on his phone, Mac looked down at it distractedly.

DECLAN: Evan's birthday party at McDonald's @ 2:00. Be there, asshole.

Mac chuckled, wondering not for the first time if everyone called their friends such flattering names or if it was just them. Maybe something left over from their days in boot camp.

MAC: I hear ya, dickhead. What does the little guy want?

DECLAN: Who the hell knows? The list changes every
day. Ask Ava. Ellie gave her the latest list last night.
Appreciate you coming. His mom is out of town on her
honeymoon and I'm trying to provide a distraction to
her being gone, ya know?

MAC: Yeah, man, I hear ya. I'll make sure Dominic
knows. Gage is heading to a customer site this
afternoon, so I don't think he'll be there. Later, brother.

Mac immediately sent a text to Ava concerning Evan's toy list.

MAC: Avie, what does Evan want for his birthday . . . ?
You feeling okay?

He was starting to worry when it took her almost
twenty minutes to answer his text.

AVA: Skylanders. Are you coming to the party? I could
pick up something from you and me if you like . . . I'm
fine.

Shit, Mac thought, Gage was right. He was turning
into a pussy. Why else would he get a big thrill out of
giving a joint gift with Ava? His cock was twitching in his
pants as if she had said something dirty. Truly pathetic.
Before long, he'd start setting his DVR to record *Ellen*.

MAC: Yeah, thanks, Avie. I'd like that. Need me to pick
you up on the way there?

And just like that, Gwen was out of town and he had fallen back into the habit of looking for ways to spend time with Ava. He tapped his fingers on his desk impatiently before her response finally came through.

AVA: That's okay. Dominic is picking me up on his bike. You know, if you fall off, you should get right back on. Didn't want my skating accident to scare me off. Thnx, though. See u there.

Mac stalked out to the lobby just in time to see the asshole in question walk out the door, giving him a shit-eating grin as he waved good-bye. "I'm going to kill that fucker," he snapped to the empty room. It seemed that life was not only shitting on him, but taking a colossal dump. What. The. Fuck?

Chapter Eight

Ava grimaced when she threw her leg over Dominic's bike. The last thing she felt like doing today was riding a motorcycle after damn near breaking her neck on a busy street that morning, but it was too good an opportunity to pass up. Luckily, Dominic had been on board when she texted him while talking to Mac. She had enlisted Emma to stop by and pick up the presents she had bought for Evan from her and Mac, since she wasn't sure if Dominic had anywhere to store them on his bike. Luckily, Emma had left Brant in the car and God willing, he was in the dark about her mode of transportation to the party.

"I hear you've been a busy girl this morning," Dominic yelled over the roar of the bike.

She tried to shake off the embarrassment she felt knowing that someone else knew what a fool she had made out of herself that morning. It couldn't be helped, though. Dominic was likely to witness even more humiliating moments in her quest to get Mac's attention if he planned to help her. "Yeah, you could say that. I was going to see if you would help me out, but I didn't have your number. I had to get it from Declan this morning. By the way, he's a little suspicious as to why I suddenly wanted to contact you."

"I'll bet." Dominic chuckled, obviously vastly amused by the thought of Declan's discomfort. What was it with these guys and their need to get under each other's skin? Of course, when she thought about it, that was exactly what one brother would do to another. "I was hoping that you'd just let the whole skating idea go. I didn't think you'd be out on the damn sidewalk twelve hours later putting on some roller derby. I'll give you credit, though, Mac's nerves were totally frayed over the whole incident."

Dominic's words distracted her from the ache in her injured shoulder long enough to ask, "Really? What did he say?"

"It wasn't so much what he said as how he stomped around the office with a stick up his ass. I mean, more than usual. You've got his attention, Blondie. Not that I think you ever really lost it. Maybe you should just leave it at that for a few days before you break a bone."

Ava smacked his back, shaking her head emphatically. "No, I can't stop now. I just need some ideas on what to try next."

Dominic sat quietly for a moment, appearing to ponder her statement before snapping his fingers. "Hey, I got it. How about the new zip line place right in the middle of town? That would be pretty easy to bring Mac by. We're riding over to North Myrtle Beach tomorrow to talk to a new customer, so we'll be going right by there."

Every ache and pain in her body seemed to pick that moment to remind her how stiff and sore she was after the debacle this morning. She didn't know if she was ready to get back on the horse quite that soon. "Er . . . I don't know. I was thinking of something later on in the week."

Dominic rolled the kickstand up on the bike, preparing to set off. "I hate to say this, Blondie, but you might get more results with Gwen gone this weekend. If you wait, she'll be back in town, and even though I'm already sort of plotting against her, I wouldn't feel great about her having her face rubbed in it."

Ava instantly felt guilty about what she was doing. It was obvious from the tone of Dominic's voice that he genuinely cared for the other woman. It had been far too easy to forget that there was someone else involved in the whole scenario, someone who would be hurt if Ava got what she wanted. "Crap, I'm a horrible person, aren't I?"

Dominic planted his feet squarely on the ground, turning his head slightly to look at her. "All's fair in love and war, Blondie. Unfortunately, there has to be a loser. If I thought for a minute that Mac loved Gwen or vice versa, I wouldn't be helping you regardless of how I feel about her. He may not be able to admit it to himself, but Gwen is just a temporary replacement for you. Mac wants someone in his life and he made it happen. If I know him like I think I do, though, he's feeling right about now like he's made a mistake."

"And Gwen?" Ava asked, wondering why he was so sure she wasn't in love with Mac.

"If Gwen had serious feelings for Mac, she wouldn't be watching me around our apartment complex like she does."

Ava snorted, unable to hold it in. God, was this man vain! "Have a high enough opinion of yourself?"

Rolling his eyes at her tone, he said, "Men just know these things. I've busted her for looking at my ass several times, and she got all flustered over it."

"Okay, so obvious question here. Why don't you just talk to Mac about the whole thing? I can't imagine he would ever go out with someone if he knew that you were already interested in her. That's just not how he is."

"But I didn't make the first move, Blondie. He did. I fucked up. He just needs to remember that it's always been you for him and you need to show him that you finally understand and return those feelings. Hell, why don't you just talk to him?" At the look of panic on her face at his suggestion, he grinned. "That's right, isn't it? Sometimes you've got to take the long way around to get to where you need to go. That's why I'm helping you; you're my long way to what I want."

Smiling at him uncertainly, she said, "Um . . . thanks, I think." Were they both going about this all wrong? Should she just talk to Mac about her feelings? The fear of rejection was enough to make her tremble. She was taking serious chances here—doing crazy, reckless things to get his attention. Why was the risk of breaking her neck so much less scary than saying I love you?

Being a future cat lady seemed a lot simpler than what she was attempting now, that was for sure.

*   *   *

Brant and Emma were standing in the parking lot when they pulled in a few moments later. Emma looked thrilled to see her sitting on the back of a Harley with Dominic between her thighs. Brant just looked confused.

Dominic steadied her as he helped her from his bike. She was grateful for the Tylenol she had taken before leaving home, which kept her aches down to a mild throb. Emma ran over and threw her arms around Ava's neck in an unusual display of affection. "Holy hotness, I forgot what a stud Dominic is. You looked like a motorcycle queen when you rode in." Ah, now it made sense. Emma was using the hug to speak to her without the men hearing. "By the way, Brant is about to freak out over the whole thing. I give him thirty minutes before he pulls you aside and starts quoting the crash statistics of motorcycles."

As if on cue, Brant gave her a frown as Emma pulled away. Dominic said hello to the couple, looking amused at the tense expression on her brother's face. Emma, thankfully, said something about being hungry and ushered them all inside. It was so funny to Ava to see her ultraserious brother trying to control his instinctive cringe as the noise level assaulted them. She knew that he had rarely spent time in fast food restaurants before Evan and then Emma came along. That was one thing about Brant: he was always family first even if it killed him.

She studied the woman who had stolen her brother's heart for a few moments, looking for cracks in her veneer. It had been a tough few months for Emma. Her sister had drowned in a surfing accident in Florida and she knew that both she and her family were still trying to deal with the loss. That was one reason she didn't cut Emma slack at the office. When they were bickering, Emma didn't have time to be sad. She had those hours each day when she could be her normal sassy, funny self, and truthfully, it was a bright spot for Ava as well.

With Emma leading the way, they pushed through the crowded McDonald's, making their way to the play area and the rest of their family and friends. As she looked around, Ava spotted Mac sitting in a corner talking to Evan. He smiled as he saw her before frowning when he noticed Dominic behind her. Oh, shit, maybe this hadn't been the best idea. It would defeat the purpose of trying to get Mac's attention if he ended up killing Dominic and hating her in the end.

Looking for the world as if it didn't bother him at all, Dominic walked over to where Mac and Declan were now talking. With Evan back on the playground, she suspected the men were calling each other their usual unflattering nicknames. Dick-measuring contest: check.

The next people to enter the crowded room were Claire and Jason with their daughter, Chrissy, followed closely by Gray and Suzy. Suzy was sipping what looked like a frappé and wrinkling her nose in dismay. Ava walked up saying hello as Suzy said, "Come on, what's wrong with Chuckie? At least they have pizza there."

"You hated Chuck E. Cheese." Gray smiled wryly. "If I remember correctly, you told baby Henry to ask for a Hooter's party the next time."

Ava hadn't seen Nick and Beth come in, but suddenly Nick's head popped up between Suzy's and Gray's. "Henry's daddy is completely on board with that suggestion."

Beth shook her head next to her husband. "Go take Henry to play with the other kids, perv." Everyone laughed as Nick, Gray, Brant, and Jason joined the other men, leaving the women to themselves.

"Thanks for coming, everyone." Ella sighed. "I know this is the last thing you wanted to do on Sunday, but this is what Evan picked. With Julie away on her honeymoon, we've just been trying to distract him."

Ava looked across the room smiling as Evan let loose a bloodcurdling battle cry before throwing himself on Declan's back. Evan was the result of a one-night stand between Evan's mom, Julie, and Declan back when he was in the military. Declan hadn't found out until last year when he ran into Julie at Danvers. Apparently, Claire and Julie were friends. Julie had tried to track Declan down when she found out she was pregnant, but the military had a strict policy on giving out information on their servicemen. When Julie recognized Declan, she had taken the opportunity and finally told him about Evan. Even though it was a shock, Ava had been proud of the way he had stepped into the role of dad. Like Mac, Declan carried many tough memories from his time in the marines. It had taken the love of Ella and Evan to make him accept that he could have something as normal as a wife and a child. Now they were expecting their second child, which was obvious from Ella's enormous stomach. Ava had to swallow the urge to beg her to sit down as she bustled around the room and her pregnant belly jiggled alarmingly.

Claire looked to make sure that none of the men was nearby before leaning over to whisper, "So, how're things going with Mac?"

Before she could answer, Emma chimed in. "You should have seen her pulling up on the back of Dominic's bike a few minutes ago. I thought Brant would spaz out."

"Oh my God," Beth moaned, "I wish I had been here to see that."

"Me too," Suzy admitted. On cue, they all looked toward Dominic. "I know he's not the goal here, but I can't see anything bad about having that between your legs." Almost in perfect sync, they all nodded.

"True, dat," Ella said, causing everyone to laugh. "Sorry. I've been around Evan too long. That kid has his own lingo."

"He is good-looking," Ava admitted, "but he's not Mac. I will say, though, he's damn funny now that I've gotten to know him a little bit. G-lo would be crazy to let him get away." Mouths dropped as Ava told the girls why Dominic was helping her.

"Jeez, that's something right out of *Dallas*, isn't it?" Beth added. "Maybe you should just all get together and swap."

Claire raised her hand in that cute way that seemed habitual. "Question here. How far are you two willing to go to get Mac and Gwen's attention? I mean, are you also pretending to be involved now? Mac's gotta wonder if something is going on there."

Ava slumped back against the wall behind her,

frowning. "I really don't want to go that far. Mac and Dominic are friends, and I wouldn't want to change things between them. I know Mac wonders, though. He brought it up earlier . . . right before I kissed him."

"What!" Every head in the playground turned in their direction when Emma's shrill voice rang out. Emma winced, and then threw up her hand, waving everyone off. "Sorry. Just a little PMS issue. Nothing to see here." The kids looked confused at her statement, but the men immediately turned their heads away at that apparently taboo subject. "Why am I just hearing about this?" she whisper-shouted as she glared at Ava.

Ava rolled her eyes before saying, "Maybe because it just happened a few hours ago. Can you not broadcast our conversation to the whole place, please?"

"All right, girls, stop your bickering and spill the details," Suzy interjected, looking ready to smack some sense into both of them.

Looking around to make sure no one else was listening, Ava told them about initiating the kiss with Mac that morning and about his statement that she belonged to him.

"Oh my God," Ella moaned, causing her stomach to shudder. "That is so sexy. Did his voice go all deep and growly?" Fanning herself, she said, "I love it when Declan gets all dominant with me. I try to act like I don't, but I melt when he orders me around."

They all stopped to stare at the visibly flushed Ella. Looking intrigued, Suzy asked, "Did you just have an orgasm or something? Because it looked that way to me. Just sayin' . . ."

Ella flushed an even brighter shade of red before brushing her hand over her face. "Maybe a little one." Looking mortified, she added, "When I went for my checkup this week, the doctor told me to abstain from sex right now because of the Braxton Hicks contractions I've been having."

Ava looked at her brother's wife in concern. "Are you okay? Are they worried about the baby?"

Ella shook her head, not appearing worried, which helped Ava to relax slightly. "No, they say it's common. But . . ."

Beth put an arm around Ella, before finishing her friend's sentence. "You're so horny you're about to explode, huh?" Next to them, Claire nodded in understanding. Apparently, along with pregnancy came a huge rush in horniness. Ava would have thought it would be just the opposite, but maybe it was better than eating a jar of pickles every night.

Always the blunt one, Suzy deadpanned, "Well, that sucks. I mean, like, you can't do anything or just the main event?"

"I'm really not sure," Ella admitted. "I was too embarrassed to ask for specifics. It doesn't matter anyway. With the doctor saying that, Declan would cut off his hands before he would touch me down there now. He's terrified that something will happen. He won't even let me . . . help him out. I put my hand on his . . . you know last night and he jumped out of bed like I'd just violated him or something. Apparently, he thinks that if I help him come, the baby will explode out of my vagina at the same time."

Everyone started laughing at Ella's description. Only Ava shifted around uncomfortably. Hearing Ella talking about sex with Declan was a little disturbing. She liked to pretend that both Brant and Declan lived with their wives without actually doing anything sexual. It was right up there with talking about sex and your parents. Of course, Emma was constantly referring to how freaky Brant was in bed. Ava was certain that one day her eardrums would start to bleed and might never stop.

Desperately needing a change of subject, she was relieved when Ella turned to Suzy and asked, "How did the home study go last night?" Ava knew from Emma that Suzy and her husband, Gray, had suffered multiple miscarriages and were now in the process of adopting a child. She remembered everyone wishing Suzy good luck when they'd had lunch together yesterday.

Suzy groaned before putting her hands around her neck as if she were choking herself. "I think it went okay in the end, but it was a long evening." Looking across the room at Gray, she said, "I love that man, I really do, but I wanted to tape his mouth shut last night."

"Oh no," Claire whispered, "not the jokes again."

"Oh yeah. Like we hadn't discussed that very thing an hour before."

"Like dirty jokes?" Ava asked, seeming to be the only one not privy to what Suzy was talking about.

Suzy shook her head, saying, "No, not really. The thing about Gray is that when he gets nervous, he tends to start cracking stupid jokes. Apparently, it runs in the family, because his mother says Gray's father does the same thing. I mean, we're sitting at the table answering all these serious questions about our views on child-rearing and I swear out of nowhere, he looks at the woman and says, 'Knock, knock!' We both just stared at him until the woman put her pen down and asked, 'Who's there?' Then he says, 'Little Old Lady.' And then she of course stares him down some more before saying, 'Little Old Lady who?' And he says, 'Wow! I didn't know you could yodel!'" By this time, everyone was laughing, even Suzy. She gasped out, "I thought I would die, right there on the spot. The woman just looked at Gray like he had two heads, before picking her pen back up and acting like the whole thing never happened."

"Suz," Claire said, giggling, "that's completely adorable. He was probably just trying to loosen everyone up. Although it's hard to picture Gray doing that, because he's always so suave."

Ava, feeling an inexplicable need to defend the man she barely knew, spoke up. "Everyone handles stress in different ways. It sounds like he tries to inject some humor into uncomfortable situations. The jokes probably pop out before he even realizes what he's doing."

Smiling at her husband, who was now looking at Suzy with so much love in his warm gaze that Ava was envious, Suzy said softly, "I know. He's a little unpredictable, but he's mine."

Beth bumped shoulders with her sister, saying, "Well, I bet if anything his jokes show that he would be a really good parent. He should get extra points for that. God knows you need a sense of humor when you have a child."

Ella pointed to the Skylanders cake sitting on the table behind them and said, "We probably need to get started with the main event. If I don't get a huge slab of that cake within the next five minutes, I'm not responsible for my actions. At this point, it's the only thing I can have that will make my eyes roll back in my head."

Emma snickered as she helped arrange the plates on the table. "Honey, you just grab that thing again tonight and don't let go. There's no way that any man can have a woman's hand on his dick for more than five seconds without losing his mind."

"Yep," Beth agreed. "And call your doctor tomorrow to find out if you can have some fun without going all the way."

They had all been so involved in their conversation that they hadn't noticed the men moving closer. "Going all the way with what?" Declan asked as he moved up behind Ella.

"With Dominic," Ella sputtered, "Ava and Dominic."

Ava's mouth fell open in shock as Declan's smile turned to a scowl. Her eyes jerked to Mac, who appeared to have heard the whole thing if his snarl was any indication. Even the usually unflappable Dominic looked surprised. Ella turned to her, looking contrite. Great, now it appeared that Ava was going to have to be the sacrificial lamb to keep Declan from finding out that his wife was horny.

Her brothers were both looking at her as if she were the new town tramp, while Jason, Nick, and Gray seemed to be unusually interested in the playground. Ava figured they were just desperately trying to pretend that they hadn't heard anything. When Evan bounced up with Chrissy and Henry in tow begging for cake, Ava vowed to herself that he was getting the biggest gift next week that she could carry out of the damn store. He had just saved her from the awkward silence that had fallen over the entire group.

Mac stood across the table during the birthday song and the gift presentation glaring daggers at her. After a while, it started to piss her off. What right did he have to judge her? If she wanted to plan a fake sex date with her fake boyfriend, who was he to object? After all, he was probably having plenty of real sex with his real girlfriend. She hadn't even set out to make Mac jealous. That was never her goal. But damn it, how dare he stand over there looking so angry over her love life? If not for the fact that Mac and Dominic were best friends, she would walk over there right now and kiss Dominic so hard he'd never recover. Okay, maybe she wouldn't quite have the nerve to do that, but she'd do something for sure.

Emma walked up to her, forcing her from her heated eye-lock with Mac. "I think Ella rolled you under the bus there. If the big vein throbbing in Mac's cheek is any indication, though, she might have done you a favor. He looks like he's gonna combust." They both glanced back over at Mac, who refused to look away. "Well, anyway, we're gonna take off now. Brant is just itching to get over here and scold you, so I'm going to drag him out of here so he can have his tantrum in the privacy of the car. We also promised my parents we'd be back for an early dinner."

Ava turned to hug Emma, thanking her for intervening with Brant. "Please tell your parents I said hello. I'd love to see them before they go back to Florida." Emma grabbed her purse and pulled a stiff Brant out the door.

That left one brother, who took the opportunity to move to Ava's side.

"So, what's going on with you, sis?"

Trying for her best innocent expression, she said, "Just enjoying the party like everyone else."

Seeming exasperated, he said, "You know that's not what I'm talking about. What's all this with Mac and Dominic? Plus, I saw you on the back of Dom's bike. Mac's completely pissed too."

Ava had finally had enough. Did everyone give Mac a hard time when he had started dating Gwen? Were they worried about her feelings then? A little voice in her head said that she hadn't professed her love for him the whole time they were such close friends, so it was different, but she was tired of listening to that rational, reasonable voice. She felt that her own family cared more about Mac than her.

So she followed Emma's lead by grabbing her purse before turning to Declan. "You know what—how about me? Aren't you my brother? Maybe I could use a little of that support that you seem to be giving to your friend." Declan flinched at the accusation, and she felt like a complete bitch as she stalked out of McDonald's only to realize when she stood on the sidewalk that she didn't have a car. There was no way, though, that she was going to go back inside after what she knew was her childish exit. She stomped off toward the street, determined to walk home if necessary.

She had only traveled a few yards when she heard the roar of a bike and Dominic pulled up next to her. "Get on, Blondie." Not in any mood to argue and certainly having no better offers, she awkwardly climbed on the bike, wedging in behind him. For someone who'd never ridden a motorcycle, she was getting rather used to it. Regardless, it'd never be her first choice of transportation, but she didn't have many options right now. "A little heads-up about the fact that we're gonna be fucking soon would have been helpful," he threw over his shoulder before pulling away. She tried to yell a denial at him, but the bike was too noisy for a conversation, so she held it in until he pulled to a stop in her driveway.

After a particularly ugly dismount from the damn bike, she threw her hands on her hips, mad at the world. "Listen, you . . ." Ava inwardly groaned at the completely pathetic comeback. Thankfully, only a small grin pulled at his lips as he held his composure. "I did not say anything to anyone about wanting to do anything of the sort with you."

Lifting a sarcastic eyebrow, Dominic said, "Come on, babe, it's nothing to be ashamed of. Most women probably feel that way around me." Looking her up and down in a way that made her breath catch, he added, "Normally, I'd have no problem at all obliging you, but you belong to Mac. So, if you can possibly keep from mentally undressing me while we're trying to help each other out, that would be great."

Ava's mouth dropped at the sheer size of his ego. His confident pose, leaning back on his bike, was the perfect complement to his over-the-top statement. Then she snapped. She had completely had it with the men in her life, and that included the smug asshole sitting in front of her. "You fucking man—" She stood taller thinking how much an insult was with some profanity in it. "I would love nothing better than to wrap my hands around your thick neck and choke you right now!"

Dominic, appearing far from offended, said, "I think you're just looking for ways to get those hands of yours on me, aren't you, Blondie?"

She grabbed handfuls of her hair in frustration, trying to control the anger coursing through her body. "You pig! I don't want my hands anywhere on you, and for your information, I don't belong to Mac regardless of what either one of you thinks." Stabbing her chest, she added, "I belong to me, damn it, just to me!"

Dominic stepped away from his bike, walking over to her with a strange expression on his face. It looked almost like pride. Had he missed her whole rant toward him? She was so surprised when he gently took her shoulders in his hands that she stood glued in place. "It feels good, doesn't it, Blondie?"

Still puzzled, she stood staring into his handsome face before whispering, "What?"

He gave her a lazy grin in return before saying, "Being alive, being mad, and just letting the fuck loose. I'm thinking you don't do that often." The look on his face said that he didn't think she ever did it. "You're always wound so tight that you're on the verge of going over the edge. I just gave you a little push today to help you let off some steam. Feel better?"

Ava continued to gawk at him for another moment before she realized that she did feel better. Somehow the weight that usually rested on her shoulders had lessened. The persistent lump in her throat got maybe just a little smaller. She relaxed, releasing a breath. "I guess you're a shrink now too, huh?"

"Nope, but I've certainly been given enough pointers by the military to know how to deal with stress overload. Life can't always be scripted, Ava, no matter how hard we try. Only fight the big battles that matter and don't let the little things rip you to pieces."

"Wow," she murmured, "that was actually pretty profound." She looked at Dominic in new admiration. There were more layers to him than she could have imagined. He had intentionally set her off to show her the bigger picture. In that moment, she felt her eyes blur. He was so much like Mac that it was almost like sharing a moment with the man she loved so much.

He cuffed her gently on the shoulder, before throwing a leg back over his bike. "I'll text you tomorrow when Mac and I are headed back from our meeting rather than on the way there. I think it will work better. Otherwise, he's likely to lose it and blow off the whole thing, and this is a big one for us." When she nodded, he added, "You know, you can just stand up there. You don't actually have to go through with it. Mac will freak just from you being there. Another set of bruises really aren't necessary."

"I'll keep that in mind. And, Dominic . . . ?" When he turned back to look at her she said, "Thanks for today. I think I needed that." He waved a hand in her direction before taking off. With a lighter step, she walked toward her door, feeling for the first time that just maybe she could do this. She could be normal.

Chapter Nine

Mac drove through the streets of downtown Myrtle Beach listening to Dominic run through the highlights of the meeting they had just finished. Neither of them mentioned the whole scene with Ava at McDonald's the previous day. He hadn't let it go, though. He fully intended to find out just what in the hell was going on, and he doubted he could keep quiet much longer.

This morning, though, was about their company, and he had needed to keep his shit together. They were in talks with the Oceanix Resort Company to provide security for their luxury flagship hotel. A Sunday meeting had been the idea of the owner, Seth Jackson, as he was going out of town for a week beginning tomorrow morning. There had been some recent theft issues within the hotel, and Jackson suspected it was an inside job. He was extremely unhappy with the progress by his current security company and was interested in hiring East Coast Security thanks in part to a glowing recommendation from Jason Danvers. It would be a big account for them, especially with the possibility of providing security for other Oceanix properties as well.

He was completely absorbed with thoughts of expanding their business when Dominic said, "Hey, isn't that Ava?" Mac didn't have time to wonder how his friend could have recognized her from so far away. All he knew was that Dominic was pointing to the zip line ride, and as Mac squinted to look, he saw what appeared to be Ava's BMW sitting in the parking area in front of the tourist attraction. Without thinking, he did a dangerous swerve across two lanes of traffic before coming to an abrupt stop next to Ava's car.

Mac jumped out of his Tahoe, looking up the countless steep steps to the top of the zip line. Without a doubt, he recognized the blond hair gleaming in the early-afternoon sun. "Ava!" he yelled as he started climbing the wooden steps. Was it too much to ask for a damn elevator when you needed one? By the time he reached the top, he was glad that he was in good shape; otherwise, he would never have made the climb in such a short time. Ava was already in a harness with her helmet on when he stepped out on the platform. He waved off the kid trying to sell him a ticket as he stalked toward her. Another kid who didn't look old enough to shave was running through instructions when her eyes landed on him. Trying to appear halfway calm, he asked in an even voice, "What are you doing?"

She didn't seem particularly surprised to see him when she said, "Um . . . zip-lining?"

Starting forward, he said, "Yeah, not anymore. Let's get this stuff off you." When he was just a few steps from reaching her, she stunned him by sticking her tongue out . . . and letting go. He felt his heart plummet to his stomach as she went flying across the wide expanse of space toward a tower in the distance. "Fuck!" He stomped back down the steps and ran into Dominic at the bottom. When the other man opened his mouth, Mac snapped out, "Call a cab. I'm going to be busy for a while." Without waiting for a reply, he jogged across the field, making it to another set of steep steps. When he saw Ava's long, tanned legs start the descent from above, he leaned against the building, literally shaking in anger, waiting for her to reach the bottom.

"Hi." She smiled broadly as she saw him. "Did you see me up there?" Was she fucking kidding him right now? Of course he'd seen her suspended on a cable, just one false move away from snapping her slender neck.

"Let's go." Grabbing her hand, he started pulling her toward their cars in the parking area. Even as mad as he was, he was mindful of her smaller stride and adjusted his accordingly. Before she could form a protest, he had opened his passenger door and ushered her inside before walking around to the driver's side.

As they were pulling away, she finally snapped out of her daze enough to protest, "Mac, where are we going? I can't leave my car here." But he ignored her as if she hadn't spoken as he drove the familiar streets toward her apartment. The first trickle of unease prickled her skin as she wondered if she had pushed him too far this time. Maybe she should have taken Dominic's advice and not actually jumped off the zip line platform right in front of Mac. When she saw him standing there, she hadn't been planning on going through with it. She had taken herself by surprise when she jumped. It was probably the closest she had ever come to peeing her pants as she flew so high above the ground. Afterward, though, God, the rush had been so all-consuming. Her skin still tingled with adrenaline.

She wasn't sure what she had been expecting, but when Mac pulled into her parking place and came around to open her door, she was ready to make a smart remark about him having her car picked up before walking off. Instead he once again grabbed her hand and pulled her up a flight of stairs, waiting not very patiently while she opened her front door. Again, she prepared to say good-bye, but he pushed past her and she shut the door behind him, completely puzzled. Oh crap, he was glaring at her. She'd never really understood the meaning of that word before, but she did now. Raking an unsteady hand through his short hair, he said softly, "Avie, I'm so mad at you right now that I shouldn't even be here. I don't understand what's going on in your head." His eyes looked tormented as he asked, "Baby, are you trying to hurt yourself?"

Unable to bear the pain in his eyes, she rushed over to him, grabbing his hands. "No, Mac, that's not it."

Clasping their joined hands against his chest, he asked, "Then why? Why are you suddenly doing all these crazy things that are going to do nothing but get you hurt?"

Ava fought against the desire to put some space between them and steady her nerves. He was staring at her as if he was trying to see inside her head. He was in her space, and normally she wouldn't allow that to happen. This time, though, she fought herself to deepen the intimacy of the moment, knowing that she needed to start baring her soul if she were ever to have a future with him. "I need to live, Mac. I want to stop being so afraid of everything all the time."

"Is that what the kiss was about yesterday?" Mac asked softly.

Pulling one hand loose from his hold, she cupped the side of his face, stroking the stubble that was starting to break through his smooth skin. "No, that was because I wanted it." She could feel his heart gallop beneath the hand that remained against his chest. Taking a deep breath, she continued. "Mac, I want us to try . . . you know, to have a real relationship." Ava was feeling light-headed at her admission, but also proud that she had actually gotten the words out.

Mac looked stunned, opening and closing his mouth a few times before finally saying something. "Avie . . . what exactly do you mean by that?"

"You're not going to make this easy on me, are you?" She laughed nervously. Mac, on the other hand, didn't even crack a smile. "Uh . . . what I'm trying to say, apparently not very successfully, is that I'd like for us to go out, you know, like on a date. We don't have to jump right into a relationship if you don't want to, but I'd like to start somewhere—with you."

He dropped her hand and started tugging on his hair as he always did when he was agitated. She wasn't an expert on men by a long shot, but it didn't seem like a good sign to her. Maybe she had been expecting him to twirl her in his arms like some kind of romance movie plotline when instead he looked as though he was about to puke. Yeah, it was a real ego booster. With every yank of his hair, her hopes were plummeting. "Why now?" he finally asked. She quelled the urge to look at the floor to see if there was any hair lying there from his tug-of-war with his locks.

When she tried to turn away, thinking it would be easier to talk to the wall than to face him, he grabbed her arm, pulling her almost nose-to-nose, and just waited. "I don't want to lose you," she admitted.

Appearing frustrated with her answer, he asked, "Is this because of Gwen and the fact that you and I aren't spending as much time together?" He looked as if he was in physical pain when he added, "I think you just miss your buddy. I'll move things around so we can have a drink together like we used to, okay?"

She wanted to reach out and choke the man. He was talking to her as if she were a child who needed to be pacified. Either he wasn't hearing anything she was saying or he didn't want to understand. Why were all the men in her life so damn frustrating lately? "That's not what I meant, Mac! I'm not talking about our friendship or lack of it lately. I want what you've wanted from me for years, but I've been unable to give you. I want to hold your hand, kiss you, and . . . love you. Not as your friend, though. I'm ready for more."

Ava jumped when he turned away, pounding his fist in his hands. In contrast his voice was calm when he spoke. "Ava, I gave you every chance to show me that you returned my feelings. I opened my life and my heart to you, but you never gave me anything back in return other than friendship and a stiff arm if I got too close. You twisted me in knots for years. It was torture to be close to you and hell not to be. Finally, I just couldn't do it anymore. I had to move on. I *have* moved on."

He still refused to turn back around and face her, which made it easier for her to whisper, "But you love me. You always have."

Mac was quiet for so long that Ava started to wonder if he had heard her. Then he turned back to her, his eyes bleak and distant. "Sometimes it's not enough. I'm happy now. You were just discussing going all the way with Dominic yesterday, so I'm not even sure why we're having this conversation." Opening the door, he stepped outside before adding, "I'll have one of the guys drop your car off later if you'll give me the key."

Feeling a hot tear start to trickle down her cheek, she lowered her head, desperately trying to maintain a shred of her pride as she pulled the key from her pocket and handed it to him. Without another word, he closed the door behind him and Ava collapsed backward into her living room chair. One benefit of never putting herself out there was that she'd never had to feel this sting of rejection. She'd never had the man she loved tell her that he was happy with someone else . . . until now . . . and it hurt so fucking much that she just wanted to curl up into a ball and withdraw into her shell. She had never seriously considered what would happen to her if Mac wasn't willing to listen to her or if he didn't return her feelings.

Was she messing up his life—again? Should she walk away now and let him go? She would have thrown a full-blown pity party if not for one thing: he didn't seem happy. They used to laugh together. He was always smiling when they ran into each other, no matter where it was. Now he just looked so sad or—the last few days—mad whenever they were together. Wouldn't someone who was in love and happy seem, well . . . happy? Maybe it was a small hope, but it was something to cling to. If she stopped now after one rebuff, then she was right back to doing what she always had done, taking the easy way out, running away before things got tough. She had to be the one to pursue him now. If nothing else, her crazy stunts were getting to him. Maybe tomorrow she'd wear one of the new outfits she had bought at the mall and try the simple laws of attraction before deciding on her next stunt. Hopefully, she could find a new hobby to try that wasn't horribly scary. It would all be worth it in the end . . . or at least she hoped so.

He was officially in hell and had no idea what to do next. Ava's admission had him reeling, and he was pretty sure that he wasn't even fit to drive himself home at this point. He kept hearing her tell him that she wanted a relationship with him . . . wanted to start dating him. He would have given everything he had a few months ago to hear those words coming from her plump pink lips. While his head had been spinning, his cock had been rearing its eager head, raring to make his dreams a reality. He had felt physically sick when he lied to her face, telling her that he was happy now. Maybe he had been getting by and most days succeeding before she had suddenly taken a one eighty the last few days and started throwing out all kinds of mixed signals.

First she was draped all over Dominic on his bike, looking like a fallen angel, and then she was sticking that sweet little tongue of hers in his mouth and sucking his tongue hard enough to make him come in his pants. Next she was back on Dom's bike and apparently considering sleeping with him. Now suddenly today she wanted to date Mac and move forward. Shit, his mind couldn't process her behavior fast enough to figure out where she would be next.

Ava had always been a constant in his life. Even if he didn't like what she did at times, like the fucking one-night stands, she was fairly predictable. It hurt like hell, but he recovered from those because they never seemed to mean anything to her. People had needs and like her, he scratched that itch when it was necessary. Would he have rather they both scratched each other's? Hell yeah, but she'd never allowed that to happen.

One problem now was that he hadn't scratched his itch in far too long. He and Gwen had not slept together yet. They'd rounded several bases, but she had made it clear in the beginning that she wanted to start things slow and see where they went. Lately, she had seemed to be running toward third and getting close to home plate and he found himself at a crossroads he had never encountered before. Gwen wasn't the type of person to give herself physically without expecting something more in return. She was a good person, and she deserved a commitment. If he slept with her, then things would get complicated in a hurry. He had been comfortable with that fact—knowing that it was the next step to moving on—until what had happened this weekend.

Now things were more up in the air than ever before, and he felt he just needed some space to process things. Unfortunately, he was meeting Gwen for dinner tonight. She was supposed to be back in town in a few hours, and they were having an early meal before she went home. Except the last thing he wanted right now was to see either her or Ava for that matter. He was too twisted up inside.

He couldn't believe his Avie was finally on the same page that he had been on for years and he'd walked away from her. What could he do, though? His heart had been shredded by her lack of reciprocation for his feelings for so long that he had trouble believing that she meant what she was saying now. Although he didn't doubt that something had changed in her recently. There was a spark in her eyes that hadn't been there since she was a teenager . . . since that night so long ago. He felt certain that he and Ava would have been a couple; he'd probably even married her by now if not for what that bastard did to her. It had changed the sweet, funny, outgoing girl he had been patiently waiting on to grow up into a woman who wanted to close out the world.

He'd made it his job after leaving the military to spend as much time with her as possible. They'd grown as close as she would allow and sometimes he would catch her looking at him with something akin to longing in her eyes. Those times broke him apart because he felt exactly the same need for her. Then the walls would go back up and she'd bring some random man in for the night and effectively put him back in his place. Thus, the cycle continued for years with only the one kiss that he'd attempted to initiate before he'd officially decided to move on with his life.

Now he had a couple of hours to go home and relax before meeting Gwen. He felt sure the conflict that was raging inside him would be obvious to anyone who cared enough to look. He only hoped that Gwen would attribute it to something other than Ava. She had already questioned the relationship between them more than once. He knew that Gwen would be doubly suspicious after his actions in the parking garage when they'd run into Dominic and Ava as they were leaving on Dom's bike. Yeah, for someone normally so calm and cool, he seemed to be misfiring at every corner lately.

Chapter Ten

Ava fought the urge to cover her chest with her hands as she walked toward the entrance of Danvers International on Monday morning. She was wearing one of the new outfits that she had recently purchased and it was more formfitting than she was comfortable with. The Indian blue silk wrap dress molded to her slim figure as if it had been made just for her. The neckline, while still being modest enough for work, showed a hint of cleavage. Actually, it took her modest-sized girls, as Emma called them, and made them appear almost voluptuous. The hemline ended just above her knees, showing more tanned leg than she normally displayed.

She had left her long blond hair loose, and it hung down her back in waves. She had been surprised to catch more than one man staring at her as she made her way through the parking garage. When she heard a whistle from behind, she sped up, trying to reach the safety of the building. She was almost to the door when she heard male laughter then a familiar voice. "Ava Stone, what a vision you are this morning."

Whirling around, she gasped in relief when she saw

the admiring eyes of Mark DeSanto. Mark's company, the DeSanto Group, had been a partner in some projects with Brant and Ava's previous company. Through them, Mark was now working on some projects with Jason and Danvers International. One night, after one too many drinks, she had found herself back at Mark's home. Things had been fine until he had playfully held her arms above her head as he'd kissed her. Ava had completely freaked out then. She had had some small panic attacks before, but that one had been epic. Poor Mark had been on the verge of dialing 911 before finally handing her a bag to breathe in. Afterward, she had explained some of her past trauma and he had understood. Mark didn't do girlfriends, but in that moment, he had decided to make an allowance for having a woman as strictly a friend. He was a great man but seemed to have just as many issues with intimacy as she did. He didn't talk about his past, but Ava had a feeling there was a story there.

Thanks to their odd friendship of sorts, she felt herself relax. When you freak out while trying to have sex with someone, there isn't a lot left that you can do to embarrass yourself in front of him. In a weird way, it had made friendship between a man and woman almost pressure free. "Mark, I didn't know you were back in town."

Mark curled an arm around her waist before dropping a kiss on her cheek. Still holding on to her, he pulled back slightly, running his gaze along her from head to toe. "Wow, look at you, my beauty. I was sitting in my car when I saw you walk by. I was obsessed with watching your hips sway before I realized it was you."

Ava felt her cheeks color slightly at his words. She knew him well enough to know that he actually meant he was staring at her ass and thinking about picking her up before he recognized her and knew it was futile. "Er . . . thanks . . . I think. So, where have you been?" she asked as they stepped into the lobby.

With a wolfish grin, he said, "Ah, you know . . . around. Enough about me, though. Whatever has happened to my little dove? You've turned into something far more exotic since I've been away, and I'm intrigued." Before she could answer, the lobby doors opened near them, and she saw Mac striding in. She almost swallowed her tongue when his gaze immediately went to her before passing by and then coming abruptly back. If she had wanted his attention today, she had it. His mouth thinned as he took in the arm that Mark still had curved casually around her waist. She could almost see the internal debate raging within him before he walked over to them.

"Ava, DeSanto."

Without dropping his arm, Mark extended his other hand, saying, "Mac, good to see you again, buddy." Ava knew that Mark had joined her brothers and Mac for drinks on several occasions. Mark didn't seem the type to ever forget a name or a face, and he made no reaction to the frown Mac was directing his way as he returned the handshake. With a devious curl of his lips, Mark pointed to her, then back to Mac. "I was just telling Ava that she looked beautiful today. Just like a ripe, juicy peach, wouldn't you agree?"

Almost as if on cue, Ava saw the tic in Mac's jaw. She'd heard of a nervous tic, but apparently Mac had an angry one. She'd never noticed it before, but he'd also never seemed as angry around her in the past as he was now. She only hoped that was a good sign.

"She always looks beautiful," Mac said gruffly. Mark looked strangely pleased with Mac's answer for some reason that she couldn't fathom. He knew a lot of the history there, so maybe he had decided to try his hand at matchmaker as well. That probably wasn't a great idea, as she already had help from Dominic. She didn't want to go from looking desirable to other men to just downright slutty. Her mind had drifted for a moment when Mac jerked her back to the present by asking, "Can I talk to you for a minute, Avie?"

Mark took the cue, giving her arm a brief squeeze before saying, "I have an early meeting with Jason. Ava, let's have lunch one day this week, okay?" She nodded in agreement before he walked toward the elevators. The receptionist looked thrilled when he said hello as he passed. Mark was a handsome man and the expensive suit that he wore only added to his allure.

"If you're finished staring, we can grab a coffee on the way up." She turned to Mac in surprise, noting that he looked miffed. He pointed toward the cafeteria before asking, "Is he why you're dressed up today?"

She stopped in her tracks and turned to face him. "Of course not. I didn't even know he was back."

He looked doubtful for a moment before saying, "For Dominic, then?"

Now he was just starting to annoy her. So maybe her sudden association with Dominic looked a little suspicious. Did he really think that she would profess to have feelings for him yesterday while chasing after every other man in sight? Somehow she had thought that after years of friendship, his opinion of her might be a little higher than that. She stepped right up in his face, with only a few inches separating them, and said through gritted teeth, "Did you maybe think, for even a minute, that I wore this dress today for you? So maybe *you* would think I look pretty?"

Suddenly, Gage appeared over Mac's shoulder holding a steaming cup of coffee and a donut. He gave her a sexy grin before freezing in place. "Holy shit, Ava?"

Ava wanted to laugh at the look of shock on Gage's face. Then she had a sobering thought. She must look rather bad every day in her usual attire for the men around her to be so amazed by her appearance today. "Good morning, Gage."

The other man took a bite of his donut while continuing to look at her in fascination. "Honey, you look hot as the fires of—"

Before he could finish his sentence, Mac turned to glower at him. "Don't you have somewhere else to be?"

Gage wiggled his eyebrows, saying, "No, actually I don't, but you might want to consider it." At Mac's look of inquiry, Gage added, "Your girlfriend is in the cafeteria. Things look a little intense between you and your BFF here, so just a suggestion." He took the last bite of his donut and wiped his hands down his thighs before stepping forward to extend his arm to Ava. "How would you like to make my day and let me escort you to your floor?"

Ava felt a stab to the heart as Mac's mouth twisted when she reluctantly took Gage's proffered arm, but he didn't object. He stood there still as stone and let her walk away so that he could wait for Gwen. She tried to laugh at Gage's jokes, but her heart just wasn't in it. When they reached her floor, she turned to smile. "Thanks, Gage. I think I've got it from here."

Instead of letting her walk off, his words stopped her. "What're you doing, little one?"

"Er . . . going to my office?"

He gave her his usual lazy grin, but she could see a touch of seriousness that wasn't usually present. "Big picture, sweetheart. You got my boy tied up in knots again."

"I don't know what you're talking about," she protested.

"Ah, come on, Ava. I like you, I always have. You're smart, pretty as hell, and a real class act. If not for the fact that Mac would kill me, I'd have asked you out myself. But we all know how he feels about you, and none of us would ever disrespect that. Now, I don't know what's going on with Dom and you, but I damn sure know it's not sexual. Our brotherhood always comes before women."

Holding up a hand, Ava warned, "I swear if you say something like bros before hoes, I'll hurt you!"

ALWAYS LOVING YOU   115

Gage sputtered, choking on his laughter. "I'm not that crazy, honey. That's strictly a man-to-man quote there. Sounds damn funny coming from your lips, though. What I'm trying to say is whatever you've got going on, it had better be for real. Don't be trying to go after Mac just because you're jealous of Gwen."

Finding Gage's honesty oddly touching, she felt the need to be straight with him as well. "So I should just let him go with Gwen and give up. Is that what you're saying?"

Shaking his head, he said, "Well, hell no, that's not what I'm saying. If you really love Mac, then go after him. Just make sure it's for all the right reasons. No retreat, little one. Balls to the wall all the way." At her look of disgust, he added quickly, "Boobs to the wall? That work better for you?"

She put her hand over her mouth, smothering a grin, as he turned to walk off.

She was still grinning when Emma walked up, saying, "Did that hot hunk of male studliness just say 'boobs to the wall'?" At her nod, Emma moaned. "God, if your brother hadn't already completely taken care of me this morning, I'd be following that man like a dog in heat right about now."

Ava looked around quickly, relieved that no one else had witnessed either Gage's audacious comment or Emma's sexually charged response. Thankfully, the hallway was clear as she turned and walked to her office door, trailed closely by Emma. "Can you please not talk about Brant and sex? Didn't we set boundaries about that?"

"I know, I know." Emma mimicked her words. "I can mention sexual thoughts about your brother on every third Friday of the month. If Ella comes into the office, under no circumstances are we to talk about Declan or Brant naked in any way. That doesn't cover Gage, though. So, what was that man talking about?"

"You're impossible," Ava groaned as she walked through Emma's office and into her own. She took a few moments to give Emma a run-through on what had happened with Mac yesterday and then this morning.

When she was finished, the other woman looked as though she was deep in thought for a moment before asking, "So, what's next on your list? By the way, you look awesome in that dress. I bet Mac almost swallowed his tongue when he saw you."

"Um . . . thanks. I'm not sure what's next, though. I need to give it some thought."

Looking excited, Emma ran to her desk and picked up a piece of paper, waving it in the air. "I've got ya covered. I saw this on the bulletin board at the grocery store last night and thought of you."

Ava took the paper from Emma's hands. Her eyes widened as she read the large print: LEARN TO HANG GLIDE. "Are you crazy! I can't do that. People end up plastered on the sides of mountains or buildings doing that."

Emma giggled, holding up a hand and waggling a finger at her. "No, no, that's the beauty of the whole thing. You don't actually have to go through with it. You can go for the free seminar they're offering. Mac usually makes his rounds in the evening before he leaves Danvers, so I'll get Ella or one of the other girls to join me in a fake conversation about your newest hobby so that Mac can overhear. I'll make it sound really good and dangerous. That should be enough to push him off the deep end without you having to actually break your neck. Whatcha think?"

Staring at her future sister-in-law, Ava felt a grudging admiration for her deception skills. She was both impressive and scary sometimes. Poor Brant, he would never be able to sleep with both eyes closed again. "That's not bad," she admitted. "It would be nice to have one new fearless sport that I didn't really have to fear."

"Cool!" Emma enthused. "Because I already signed you up online. Your class is on Wednesday at seven. That gives me a couple of days to give Mac the four-one-one on your new death wish."

Ava grimaced but gave a resigned smile. Even if it seemed crazy, she was at her best when she had some kind of plan in place. Just as a backup, though, she vowed to hit the store at lunch and buy another armful of magazines. She had a feeling that she was going to need new ideas . . . fast.

Chapter Eleven

"I'd love to be your partner, gorgeous. It would be my pleasure to help you get into a harness." Ava cringed as the man sitting next to her in her hang gliding class continued to spray her with verbal diarrhea. From the moment she had taken her seat an hour ago, he had attached himself firmly to her side, and no matter how much she tried to deter him, nothing seemed to work. He was starting to make her uncomfortable as some of his comments veered toward being sexual and inappropriate.

Aggressive men, especially strangers, tended to throw her back to a dark place in her life, and she felt her pulse quicken as the man trailed a fingertip down her arm. She jerked away, giving him a frown and turning her body sideways to escape the unwanted attention. Just when she thought she would be forced to flee before the class ended, the instructor called an end to the evening and Ava bolted out of her seat. When the man followed her out of the room and into the parking lot, she said over her shoulder, "I've got to run, my husband is waiting on me at home." She hoped that if he thought she was married, he'd back off.

His eyes dropped to her hand. "I don't see a ring on those pretty fingers. It looks like someone likes the chase." Moving so that he was blocking her car door, he stared at her breasts, making her feel sick.

"Plea-please," she stuttered. "I've got to go." She felt herself going into full-blown panic mode. All she could remember was what had happened to her last time, so many years ago, when another man hadn't taken no for an answer. In the moment, she was reduced to a teenage girl again at the mercy of someone bigger than her. As she was backing away, a cab pulled up to the curb and without thinking, Ava turned and ran toward it. She heard someone yelling behind her, but she didn't turn.

"You call for a cab, miss?" the driver asked as she huddled in the middle of the backseat.

"Ye-yes." She gave him her address and sat trembling on the seat. When they pulled up in front of her apartment, she looked around for her purse before realizing that she must have dropped it somewhere. Oh God, she didn't have money to pay her cab fare. Digging through her pockets, she was relieved that she had stuck her keys in them instead of in her bag. "I . . . eh . . . Could you wait here while I go inside for money? I don't have my bag."

The cabdriver looked at her for a moment before giving her a kind smile. "Don't worry about it. You look like you've had a hard night. Just pay it forward sometime." Ava felt tears well in her eyes at the kindness she saw on his face. She thanked him profusely before turning across the expanse of concrete with her arms hugged tightly around her body. She was lost in her own thoughts when someone grabbed her arm and swung her around. Suddenly, the face that she had run from only moments ago was back and abject terror tore through her. Her head started spinning and it was only a moment later that darkness descended to claim and protect her.

Mac had just opened his door to find Gwen unexpectedly standing on his doorstep when his phone rang. He motioned Gwen inside uneasily, noticing that she seemed to be dressed a littler sexier than usual. "Just a second," he said while he hit the call button on his phone. "What's up, Jeff?"

"Mac, I've got a problem here, and I don't know what to do about it." Jeff worked part-time surveillance for East Coast and was filling in for one of his regular guys this week. He should be in the middle of making rounds to various locations throughout the city now.

"What's the problem?" he asked, not expecting anything major.

"It's Miss Stone. She had just arrived home when I got here to check around her place as usual, but then some guy stopped her in the parking lot, and before I could walk over to find out if she needed assistance, she just collapsed. I had the security guard at the complex detain the man until we find out what is going on."

Fear gripped Mac as he started hunting for his keys on the entryway table. All he could think about was that Ava was hurt and he needed to get to her. "Where is she now?" he growled.

"I carried her into the clubhouse here. The manager called one of the residents who's a doctor and he's checking her over. She's starting to come back around now, but she took a pretty hard lick when she hit the pavement."

"I'm on my way," Mac bit out. "Don't take your eyes off her until I get there, got it?" Without waiting for the other man's answer, Mac was racing out the door when Gwen grabbed his arm. He tried to shake her off, desperate to reach Ava, but she was stronger than she looked.

"Mac, what's going on? Has something happened to your mother?"

"No," he said, not taking any time to elaborate. He was irritated that she was slowing him down and his usual patience and good manners had deserted him. "Listen, Gwen, I've got to go. Shut the door behind you." With those words, he was gone without sparing her another thought.

He made it across town in record time, pulling in front of Ava's building in less than fifteen minutes, even with the heavy evening traffic. Scanning the area, he saw Jeff waving at him from the doorway of a small building near the swimming pool. As he drew closer, Jeff held the door for him. "She's in here. She wants to go to her apartment, and I've barely been able to keep her here. The doctor thought she should go to the hospital to be checked out from the fall and from passing out, but she refuses. Says she just wants to go home. According to the security guard, the guy who was talking to her before she passed out was from her hang gliding group.

Said she dropped her purse in the parking lot, and he was just bringing it back to her. We got his information but let him go. Seemed harmless enough."

As if sensing he was near, Ava swung her head around from where she was sitting on the couch in the corner, and Mac's heart slammed as tears welled in her big eyes. What the fuck had happened to her? She got up on shaky legs and propelled herself toward him. His arms opened automatically to embrace her as she clung to him with sobs shaking her small frame. "Oh, baby," he whispered against the top of her head, "what happened?"

Trembling, she said, "Please take me to my apartment. I want to get out of here." Without thinking, Mac swung her up in his arms and took the flight of stairs up to her place. He had to set her back on her feet so she could fish the keys from her pocket and open the door. As soon as she was across the threshold, she turned back to him. He picked her up again before settling them both on her couch.

Mac let her breathing quiet and her body relax before asking quietly, "Baby, what happened? Are you sick?" He felt her shake her head against his neck. He rubbed his hand soothingly up and down her back, letting her know that he had her.

"I got scared," she mumbled against his throat. "I . . . panicked and started to hyperventilate. It just happened so fast. I couldn't control it."

Pulling her away from him, Mac searched her eyes. She still looked so damn shaken. Every protective instinct inside him was roaring. Right now, though, she needed something to take the edge off. "I'll be right back, baby. Just sit tight for a minute." Unwinding her arms from around him, he went into her kitchen and pulled out a bottle of vodka. It would probably burn her windpipe, but it should settle her nerves. He poured a generous measure and took it back to where she was sitting. He wrapped her hands around the glass, helping her raise it to her lips. "Don't sip, Avie. Throw it back. I know it's gonna taste like fire, but drink it." She started gagging on the first sip, but he kept steady pressure on her wrist. After a few more swallows, she had downed the alcohol. He set the glass on the table and pulled her back into his arms. "Better?"

With one last full-body shudder, she nodded and seemed to finally relax against him. "I—I'm sorry. I'm so embarrassed." She sniffed against his chest.

"Honey, there's nothing to be embarrassed about. I need to know what happened, though. What scared you? Did it have something to do with the man who found your purse?" She answered him haltingly about how the man had made her uncomfortable during her meeting and then he'd followed her out into the parking area, keeping her from getting into her car. She'd been shaken enough to take a taxi home and hadn't noticed that she'd dropped her purse until she had needed to pay the driver. When she'd found the same man had followed her home, she had been so frightened. "Ah, Avie, I'm sorry. I have the guy's contact information; I can assure you that I'll be talking to him.

He's never to bother you again. According to Jeff, he was pretty shaken up over the whole thing."

"I . . . I probably overreacted. I just . . . I felt trapped."

Mac heard the slight slur to her words and knew that the vodka had hit her system. Her words were softer, almost as if she were talking to herself.

"I've never been able to let anyone touch me since that night. I tried once, but I couldn't go through with it."

Mac was completely confused by the words coming out of her mouth. Ava had had men come and go from her life for years. Hell, he'd read documentation of it in written form from his surveillance guys. Of course, they didn't go into details, but when a man came home with Ava and didn't leave until sometime in the morning, it was easy to fill in the blanks. Why was she bothering to lie about it now? It was a little late in the day to try to protect his feelings. "Avie . . . it's fine. I know you have a sex life. I understand that you don't want any attachments with the men you—see."

Her bottom lip wobbled pitifully as she turned to stare at him. "There haven't been any men, Mac. I've been too messed up for that."

Her denial was starting to upset him. It was bad enough that he'd been forced to live through it, but he damn well hated to be lied to. This whole conversation was cruel and pointless, and he was hanging on to his temper by a thread. He started shifting her aside, ready to distance himself before he snapped at her. "Whatever, let's just drop this, okay? Are you feeling better now?"

She clung to his large frame, refusing to move away from him. "Why don't you believe me? I'm trying to finally tell you how screwed up I really am and you don't believe me," she cried, obviously frustrated.

He surged up from the couch, causing her to flop backward. "Why are you doing this?" he shouted. "I know you've been involved with other men. You have one-night stands with random men. Does it make me happy? Fuck no! Does it piss me off that you'll sleep with anyone you pick up in a bar? Hell yes! Have you hurt me repeatedly by doing it, yeah, big fucking yes to that! Can we please get off this sudden Miss Innocent act? Because I'm calling bullshit on it all."

Red stained her cheeks as she gaped up at him. In their time together, he'd always treated her like spun glass. He didn't ever lose his shit around her. Both of them needed a time-out to process what had happened. He was seconds from apologizing for being an ass to her after she'd had such an upsetting evening when she spoke, sounding suddenly very sober. "I . . . I didn't mean to tell you like this. But now that I've made such a mess of it, I need to come clean with you. Would you—please sit back down for a minute?"

He opened his mouth to deny her request, wanting to go home and lick his wounds in solitude. The pleading look on her face was his undoing, though. He'd never been able to say no to her, and now was no different. Instead of taking the seat he'd recently vacated next to her, he chose the chair across the coffee table. He knew from the slight drop of her shoulders that he had somehow hurt her feelings. "All right, I'm listening."

She shifted nervously in her seat, before sighing deeply. "Please let me say everything I need to before you comment. I know you're going to be angry with me, but I need to get this out." When he nodded his agreement, she locked her eyes on his. "What I said was the truth, Mac; I haven't had sex since my attack." She held her hand up to silence him when he would have spoken up. "You promised you'd listen. Anyway, I know that you think I sleep with men on a regular basis. You believe what I've wanted you to believe. I've felt safe and secure since you started having your guys check in on me daily. I can't tell you how much that helped me and how much I appreciate you always watching over me, which makes it even harder for me to say what I'm going to say . . ." Looking guilty, she continued. "I wanted . . . to create the illusion that I'm normal. That I can have sexual relationships without having a panic attack. I didn't want you to know that I'm always alone. I can't let men close to me because then they'll see who I am no matter how much I try to hide it."

When he started to feel light-headed, Mac realized that he had been holding his breath. He was reeling from the verbal punches that she had just landed against his head and his heart. The only response he was capable of making as she sat looking terrified was "And who are you, Ava?"

She didn't waver as she answered without hesitation, "I'm a mess, Mac. When I'm in the grocery store, I get scared if a man looks at me for too long. I've left my cart in the aisle countless times when my mind convinces me that there's a threat. I don't date because the few times I tried, I had a panic attack and didn't answer the door when they came to pick me up. I don't have sex because the one time I tried, I hyperventilated until I passed out. And . . . I don't let myself get close to you because—I love you so much, and I don't want you to see how pathetic I really am."

Mac sat staring at her bent head, feeling as if she had taken a sharp knife and gutted him. If he were to believe what she was telling him, then he had suffered through the fires of hell for years while she hid who she really was away from him. He still couldn't quite believe that she had perpetrated such an elaborate cover to conceal what was going on in her life. Pinching the bridge of his nose, he closed his eyes in pain as he asked, "Who were the men who came home with you, then? Some of them were here all night. How do you explain that?"

"They were college kids that I paid to spend time with me. They did work around the house, watched movies, or played Monopoly." She gave an embarrassed laugh before catching herself and falling silent once again. When Mac looked over at her, her head was still lowered and she refused to look at him. Somehow that angered him even further. She had ripped his world apart with her words, and she couldn't do it to his face.

He jumped to his feet, feeling the anger ripple from him in waves. Without thought, he grabbed a glass vase full of flowers from the side table and hurled it against the wall. Ava was finally looking at him, her eyes wide in shock. He wasn't the type of man prone to displays of anger, but she had just taken years of his life and told him that he had needlessly suffered because of a lie, or in this case, years of lies. He felt shattered at her underlying reasons, but somehow knowing that she'd suffered through years of pain when he could have been there, helping her to heal, slew him further. Mac was a quivering, raging mass of emotion and could no longer trust himself to be near her. He'd never physically hurt her, but he couldn't guarantee that his words wouldn't wound her just as deeply. He had to get away; he needed to breathe again.

Mac heard her calling his name almost as if in a tunnel as he stalked out the door and to his car. In the back of his mind, he felt bad for leaving her to clean up the mess he had made with the vase. But he just couldn't stay there for one minute longer.

Ava stared at the door in shock, expecting Mac to come back. She waited, but it never happened. He was gone and from the look on his face, she wasn't sure if he was ever coming back to her apartment . . . or to her. She'd never seen him so out of control before. She could handle his anger, even though it was foreign to her, but the hurt. . . . God, the hurt when he looked at her was devastating. Without warning, she felt her stomach start to churn and she bolted from the couch, just making it to the bathroom before the contents of her stomach released. She slumped back to the cool tile of the bathroom floor and stared at the ceiling. Dominic had been right—Mac had lost it when he found out about her ruse. Her gentle giant had cracked before her very eyes, and it had been all her doing.

She wasn't naive; she knew Mac didn't suffer fools gladly, but somehow she always thought she would be on the other side of that. Now it seemed that he was angry with her more often than not. Of course, the anger over her new reckless hobbies was much different from his anger today. He wasn't just mad; he was a mass of seething fury. She had the shards of glass and water all over her living room to prove it.

Her anxiety levels spiked as she faced the very real possibility that she had finally driven Mac away for good. Could he ever forgive her for what she had put him through? In trying to hide her pain from him, she had caused him to suffer immeasurably. At the time, she was like a junkie trying to hide her shame from the world. She didn't want people feeling sorry for her. For months after her rape, her brothers and Mac had treated her as if she were different. She had ceased to be the kooky sister and had turned into someone whom everyone wanted to tiptoe around. Conversations stopped when she walked into a room, and concerned eyes followed her every movement. Her very identity had died that day. In their eyes, she was broken. That impression didn't change until the day that she'd decided to bury the old Ava under the persona of a new Ava. The new woman was cool, indifferent, something approaching normal. She wasn't scared of anything, including men. Or so they had all thought. Maybe after worrying about her for so long, they all saw what they wanted to see. Did that make it right? No, even though at the time she thought she was doing what was best for everyone. Now she didn't even know what choice she had other than to keep doing what she had been this past week. For, as crazy as it sounded, things had been more real with Mac than they had been in years. She only hoped he cared enough now to continue watching over her.

Chapter Twelve

Mac cursed loudly when he pulled into his driveway and saw Gwen's car still there. He'd been gone for a couple of hours, but she had stayed? He was in a foul mood and his usual diplomacy was shot to hell. He needed to get her out of there—fast. The sound of his door slamming reverberated in the darkness as he stalked toward the driver's side of her car, intending to send her on her way. He was surprised when the car appeared to be empty. Concern overrode his anger as he looked around the empty expanse of lawn, seeing no sign of movement. He walked up the steps to his deck, intending to grab a flashlight and go check the beach for her. Women liked doing crazy things like walking on the beach at midnight.

"So, you finally made it back. I was starting to think that I wasn't going to be able to stay awake long enough to satisfy my curiosity tonight." Mac's head swung to the rocker in the corner of the porch where he could just barely make out an outline.

"Gwen? What're you doing here?"

As his eyes slowly adjusted to the dark, he could see

that she was rocking lightly back and forth. "Just answering some questions that I had."

Mac was beyond frustrated with the women in his life by this point. The last thing he wanted or needed was some long, drawn-out cryptic question-and-answer session. He didn't want to take his anger at Ava out on Gwen, but damn it, he desperately needed some space. Taking a deep breath, he said, "Gwen, I'm sorry. I'm not in the best of moods right now. Let me walk you to your car and we'll talk tomorrow, yeah?"

Ignoring his attempts to get her to leave, she continued rocking. "It was Ava tonight, right? The reason you rushed out of here like the world was ending?"

"Yes," he answered warily, not sure where this was going.

"You know, the one thing that really confuses me about you, Mac, is I have no clue why you ever asked me out."

The same alarm bells that sounded in most men's heads when women said shit like what Gwen was saying were going off like high-pitched sirens. It didn't seem to matter whether he was in the mood for a talk about his feelings or not, Gwen was more than prepared to force the issue. He could hear the underlying determination in her voice. *Holy fuck.* "You're a beautiful woman, Gwen. Why wouldn't I be interested?" He cringed when he ended his comment with a question. That was a dumb move.

"Thanks, Mac," she said softly, "but I don't think that even applies here. I suspect you're looking for some meaningless sex to scratch an itch. So what I

don't understand is what's made you hold back . . .
from the sex part? I'm not the type of woman to sleep
with every guy I go out with, but I think I've shown
you after a few dates that I was interested in something
physical between us. I mean, come on, Mac. You're
sexy enough that any woman would want you. I'm just
curious to know why you always halted things before
they got that far. Your body wanted me—you can't fake
that—but your head took you out of the game every
time."

This was it, Mac thought, the official hellish ending
to a hellish evening. After having one woman tell him
that she had pretended to be screwing random men for
years, he had another asking him why he wasn't screwing her. His head was throbbing and he just wanted to
make some excuse and go inside. He couldn't do that
to Gwen, though. He owed her the truth. Walking
closer to her chair, he squatted in front of her, halting
the rocking motion of her chair. "I'm sorry if I've hurt
you, Gwen. Believe me, that was never my intention.
You're right; my attraction to you has never been the
problem. You know that Ava and I go way back. I've
had feelings for her for years that she hasn't returned.
I needed to move on with my life. It may not seem like
it, but I was slowly doing just that with you until this
last week." When she flinched, he took her hand, nest-
ling it in his larger palms. "No, I haven't slept with
Ava; I don't want you to think that. There have just
been things happening that have shaken me. I don't
know what I'm doing right now and that isn't fair to
you."

She squeezed his hand back for a moment before leaning forward to trace the curve of his face. "No, it's not. You're a good man, Mac. I could see the conflict in your eyes the last few times we've been together and I know you have been desperately trying to figure out how to make everyone happy, including me. I don't want to be your fallback plan, though and that's clearly what I am." With a soft laugh she added, "Even though I'll probably kick myself later because, God, you are a catch, I think we need to move to the friends portion of our relationship and stop trying to make pieces fit together that don't work."

Mac looked at her sad smile and felt a pang of regret. He had enjoyed his time with her, but he knew that he had hurt her. Maybe that was why he had held back on having sex. In the back of his mind, he knew he'd never be able to commit and she deserved better than someone sleeping with her and walking away. Hell, she'd deserved better than everything he'd given her during their time together. He stood, pulling her to her feet and into his arms. They hugged for a few moments before he walked her to her car. He dropped a kiss on her cheek and stood watching her taillights as she left. He felt like a bastard as he turned toward his house, because along with sadness he felt relief that he no longer had to pretend to be moving on with his life—because even now, when he was close to hating her, it was always Ava who owned his heart.

Chapter Thirteen

Ava slumped dejectedly in front of her computer. She was searching the activities calendar on the Chamber of Commerce Web site for Myrtle Beach, but her heart wasn't in it. Mac had been avoiding her for two weeks now and it was starting to really get to her. She knew from a happy Dominic that Mac and Gwen had called it quits and that Dominic was biding his time until he asked her out. She'd pointed out that he almost lost his opportunity by biding his time with her once before, but he let her know quickly that people in glass houses shouldn't throw stones. She insisted that she deserved some points for coming clean with Mac even if it hadn't done anything other than drive them farther apart.

When her cell phone rang, she grabbed it eagerly and then felt a surge of disappointment when she saw Declan's name on the caller ID. Ava tried to keep the depression from her voice when she said, "Hey, Dec."

"Hey, Av. How are you?"

"Just great," she answered, and winced at how absurdly high her voice sounded.

"Um—good. That's good. Hey, listen, I need a favor. Are you busy today?"

Something about his question made her want to laugh hysterically. Ava wanted to ask him if staring at her walls and reading more self-help magazines qualified, but Brant usually handled her sarcasm better than Declan. Brant would just start reeling off suggestions to solve her problems. Declan would throw the phone to Ella and run the other way. "Not so much," she said instead.

"Cool. Do you think you could pick Ella up today from Suzy's and stay with her until I get home from Charleston this evening? I'm meeting the rest of the guys there and dropping Ella off to spend the day. Suzy offered to let her stay at her house, but Ellie gets so tired that I know she'll be ready for bed early."

"Um . . . sure." Ava knew that Jason and Gray had recruited some of the others to take a trip to Charleston and look at some new office space there. Truthfully, she thought it was also a chance for the men to have a guys' day out, under the guise of business. Suzy had invited all the women over for a day on the beach, but Ava had declined, preferring to mope around at home. "I'll swing by there around four, and we can stop for dinner somewhere on the way home."

Declan sounded relieved as he said, "Thanks, sis. It pisses Ella off, but I don't want her being alone right now so close to her due date. She can barely reach the steering wheel in her car over her stomach, so she has no business driving."

Ava smirked as she heard Ella yelling in the background. "You better go take care of that," she teased her brother as he said a quick good-bye. She loved the man he had grown into. He still had hard edges, but his life revolved around his wife and now his family. She only hoped that someday she'd know how it felt to be a part of something like that.

She was mulling over that thought when she saw a large ad on the local Web site. CALLING ALL BEGINNERS! SET YOURSELF FREE, LEARN TO SURF TODAY! Bingo! There it was, her next hobby. Since the whole disaster with the hang gliding meeting, there was no way she could go back there again. The guy who bothered her might have just been a harmless creep, but she couldn't take any chances. The idea of setting herself free as the ad promised sounded appealing as well. Also, the training class was located just a mile from Mac's house, so there was a good likelihood she'd run into him during one of his daily runs along the beach. She quickly filled out the online registration form and clicked SEND before she chickened out. She could swim, so what was the worst thing that could happen? Her thoughts went to Emma and the death of her sister, Robyn, in a surfing accident and she froze. Oh God, there was no way she could tell Emma about this. For a moment she was prepared to abandon the idea. It said beginner, though, so surely it was perfectly safe.

It was a little after four when Ava pulled into the driveway of Gray and Suzy's large, but surprisingly homey, beach house. Mac lived only a few miles down the road, so she was very familiar with this part of town.

When she walked up the pathway and rang the doorbell, Suzy opened the door wearing tiny white shorts and a blue halter top. "She's on the couch asleep," Suzy said with a grin and gestured toward the living room.

Ava moved through the spacious entryway into a large room with vaulted ceilings and floor-to-ceiling windows. She had visited a few times for various barbecues, but she never failed to gawk at the beauty of the ocean showcased to perfection by the tall windows. "Yeah, Declan said she would want to go to bed early, but I kinda thought it would be after dinner." Looking around the empty room, she asked, "Is everyone else already gone?"

Suzy nodded. "Beth and her son Henry were the last ones other than Ella, and they left a few minutes ago. I don't know why Ella didn't just agree to stay. As you can see, she's perfectly at home here."

Ava smothered a smile as Ella snored softly, blissfully unaware of being watched. As she was wondering whether to wake her or not, Ella suddenly jerked before jumping from the couch faster than anyone with a belly her size should have been capable of. Both Ava and Suzy stared at her in surprise. Ella rubbed her back and started chanting, "No, no, no, oh God, no!"

"Els, what the hell?" Suzy asked, looking confused.

"Maybe she's talking in her sleep," Ava suggested, staring at her sister-in-law.

"Oh, Suzy, I'm so sorry," Ella moaned. "I must have peed on your couch."

At Ella's words, Suzy and Ava looked to where Ella

was pointing and a puddle of liquid was visible against the tan leather. Ava had to give Suzy points for composure as she only looked mildly green before saying, "Er—it's okay. I mean shit happens . . . or pee, I guess in this case."

Ella looked horrified and on the verge of tears before her expression froze. It was startling to see someone go blank in the blink of an eye; hell, it was rather alarming. "Ella?" Ava moved forward, putting her hand on the other woman's arm. "Is everything all right?"

Then Ella said something that put the fear of God into Ava. "I . . . I think I might be having contractions."

Suzy jumped forward as if shot from a cannon. "Oh, fuck balls! Your water broke, didn't it?"

Ella started laughing, causing both Ava and Suzy to panic. "Stop!" Suzy shouted. "My God, don't move." Pointing to Ella's belly, she added, "And try not to wiggle that thing—like at all."

"But shouldn't she sit down or lie down?" Ava asked, not knowing what to do next. Suddenly, it hit her, and she pulled her phone from her pocket. "We need to Google it. Google will tell us what to do!"

"Screw that," Suzy said. "We need nine-one-one. I don't know about you, but I've got no plans to pull a baby from Ella's vajajay today. Call for help *now*!"

"Guys, guys . . . *guys*!" Finally, Ella's yelling got through the argument that Ava and Suzy were having. "You just need to take me to the hospital. This is my first baby, so I'll be in labor for hours. Now someone please call Declan and then let's go by my house and get my suitcase."

Suzy looked at Ava, clearly perplexed. "Why is she so calm?"

"Maybe she's on something," Ava whispered back.

When Ella's stomach rippled alarmingly, they all held their breath. Ella took several deep breaths before suddenly glaring at them. "I'm not on anything, but if you two would get your fingers out of your asses, I might get to the hospital and get some drugs. Now move!"

They gaped at her, before jumping into action. With a hand on each of Ella's elbows, they helped her down the steps and to Ava's car. "Um—aren't your clothes wet?" Ava asked.

"And your point is?" Ella snapped before throwing open the door.

"Never mind," Ava squeaked out, running around the front of the car and to the driver's side. Suzy stood next to the car uncertainly. Ava jerked a thumb at the backseat. "Oh, hell no, you're not getting out of this. Get in!" Suzy bit off a curse before getting in behind Ella.

When they pulled out of the driveway, Ella started sobbing. "I'm so sorry. I can't believe I said that. I don't know what came over me. I was just so angry."

"It's fine," Ava assured her, throwing a look at Suzy in the rearview mirror.

Patting Ella's shoulder, Suzy said, "Uh-huh, no problem, Els. A little scary there for a moment, but it's all good."

When they reached Ella's house, Ava ran inside first, opening the door while Suzy helped Ella. They quickly found her some dry clothes and located the suitcase for the hospital. Ava tried to talk a very panicked Declan off the ledge. Finally, Jason took the phone and assured her that they were leaving Charleston now. Ava knew it would take them roughly two hours to make the trip home.

Ella appeared to have one more contraction in the car and they were all digging their fingernails into the leather upholstery before it was over. Ava was extremely grateful to be in the hospital surrounded by professionals who handled stuff like this every day. While she and Suzy struggled to fill out paperwork, Ella was settled into a room to impatiently await the arrival of her husband.

For some reason, Ella was determined to hold off an epidural until things were further advanced. That meant with every contraction that hit, she turned into someone with a full-blown multiple personality disorder. One moment she was her usual sweet, soft-spoken self and the next moment she was slinging insults like a pro. Suzy and Ava had been in the room with her for over an hour, and they were exhausted. When the bedside monitor showed another contraction building, they braced for the onslaught they knew was coming.

"Where in the hell is Declan?" Ella yelled through gritted teeth. "Did either of you even bother to call him?"

"Here we go again," Suzy said under her breath as she looked at a profusely sweating Ella. "Yes, dear, he's on his way, remember?"

"Don't talk to me like I'm stupid, you . . . whore bag!"

Ava couldn't help it; the look on Suzy's face was so comical that she burst into laughter. When Ella's face turned red, Ava knew she was next in line of attack and braced herself.

"What're you laughing at?" Ella snapped. "You think it's funny that your dickhead brother did this to me and then didn't have the balls to show up? I hate your whole family, you . . ."

"Wait for it . . ." Suzy muttered.

"Skinny, skanky skank!"

"Oh my God," Ava wheezed, turning away before Ella could see her laughing even harder.

"Hey," Suzy protested, "why didn't you get called a whore this time? A skank is nowhere near as bad and she even called you skinny. I hate you."

Ella, looking like a clone of Linda Blair, rose on her elbows and spat at them, "Well, you're both dirty whores! There, are you happy now!"

Suzy, finally getting wise, turned her back as well, leaving both of them staring at the wall. "Holy crap," she muttered, "exorcism stat!"

Ava bit off a laugh, saying, "Please stop before she kills us both."

"No kidding," Suzy replied. "I had no idea that she would turn into the spawn from hell during childbirth. I mean Beth had a few moments, but nothing like Sybil back there. We should be taping this. Can you imagine how many hits this would get on YouTube?"

"If you're brave enough to break out your phone, more power to you, girl, but I'll tell you right now, I'm scared of her." Ava had just finished her sentence when a Kleenex box bounced off her shoulder and hit the floor.

Suzy eyed it before taking a deep breath. "Time to get back in the trenches. Surely to God this contraction is almost over and the good Ella will return for a few minutes."

Almost as if on cue, Ella started sobbing. "I'm so sorry, you guys. I don't know what keeps happening to me. It's like these things just start pouring out of my mouth and I have no control over them. I can't believe I . . . I called you—whores."

"Ah, that's okay, honey; you're in a lot of pain," Ava said diplomatically. In truth, she was torn between laughing and running.

"Yeah, what the forgiving one said," Suzy answered, looking vastly amused. "Speaking of pain, though, I think we need to get some drugs in your system. That would mellow you right out. Just let Aunt Suzy hit that little call button on the side of your bed and you'll be flying through la-la land in no time."

As Suzy was trying to convince Ella to say yes to drugs, the door flew open and Declan ran into the room. Both Ava and Suzy sagged in relief. He gave them both a questioning look as he took in their disheveled appearance. Just then, the machine of doom, as Suzy had started calling it, began registering another contraction and they both looked at Declan in anticipation. Ella was clinging to his hand and he was looking at the machine, asking, "What does that mean?"

Ava walked up to him, patting his shoulder. "Oh, you'll find out soon enough," she said before walking toward the door.

Suzy followed closely on her heels, pausing beside Declan as well. "Welcome to the party, pal." She smirked as she walked over to join Ava.

They both shuddered with laughter when they heard sweet little Ella shout, "Where in the fuck have you been?" When he stuttered out something about being with the guys, things got worse . . . a lot worse. "Oh, really? Well, how nice for you, scumbag. I'm lying here in bed being torn in two and you're off with the guys whoring around!"

"Ba-baby. Wh-what . . . ?"

Ava and Suzy leaned against the door as it closed behind them, with tears rolling down their cheeks as they shook with laughter. "What is it with her and the whore word?" Ava mused as she tried to process all the insults that had been hurled at her in the last few hours. She might have been offended if the whole thing wasn't so funny. Having someone usually so sweet and shy yo-yo between begging for forgiveness and calling her some form of slut was actually damn hysterical. Looking at the woman she had bonded with enough today to consider a friend, she added, "Will it sound completely pathetic if I say that this is the most fun I've had in years?"

Suzy grinned. "Yeah, maybe so, but I'm right there with you. I hate to admit it, but I kinda hated to leave. Wouldn't it have been funny to listen to her rip Declan a new one? I mean, the man is probably in there on his knees sobbing. If we're her whores, what do you think she's calling him? I've got fifty bucks on bastard, whaddaya think?"

Ava considered her answer for a moment before saying, "I'm going with son of a bitch, but I'm not confident enough to bet on it. Man-whore is a possibility if she keeps with her theme of the day."

They made their way to the waiting room, stopping in surprise when they noticed it was bursting at the seams. Everyone seemed to stand at once when they walked in. Jason, Claire, Beth, Nick, Brant, Emma, and Gray stood looking at them in question. Suzy walked straight into her husband's arms. "Hey, baby," he murmured as he kissed her on the lips lightly.

Suzy reached back to hook her arm through Ava's, pulling her to stand next to them. Ava fought the urge to gawk at the handsome man rubbing his hand absently up and down his wife's back. Suzy gave Ava what could only be termed an impish grin before looking back at her husband. "So, baby, it looks like you hit the jackpot when you married me."

Gray gave her an indulgent smile while simply saying, "Indeed I did. Any particular reason why you're pointing that out right now?"

"Well," Suzy began dramatically, "it appears that you're now married to royalty. I've been named Queen of the Whores." Multiple gasps were heard, before a chain reaction of laughter rippled through the room.

Ava had to give Gray credit for looking completely unruffled by Suzy's statement. Instead he simply lifted an eyebrow and said, "That's awesome, baby. Who bestowed that title on you?"

Suzy began telling Gray about Ella's volley of insults. Ava cut in at times, sharing things that Suzy had missed.

"Oh my God." Claire gulped. "Why was she so hung up on that word? I've never even heard her use it."

Before anyone could answer, an older couple stepped into the room, and Beth whispered, "That's probably where she got it. I think that was her mother's favorite name for me not long ago." Beth turned back toward the couple, putting on a bright but strained look of welcome. "Mr. and Mrs. Webber, how great to see you again."

As everyone sat awkwardly, waiting for someone else to continue the conversation, Suzy stepped forward and threw an arm around each of Ella's parents' shoulders. "Ella is right down the hall in room 301. You should go right in and see her while you can. You'd better hurry!" Her parents turned back through the door and walked off in the direction that Suzy had indicated.

Beth howled with laughter. "You, dear sister, are bad, but I love it. I only hope Ella's got a few more choice whore words left in her. Can you imagine her mother's face if she says something like that to them? Priceless!" Ava remembered Declan telling her how Ella's parents had hated him in the beginning along with all of Ella's other friends. They had wanted their daughter to stay at home with them until they found someone for her who they felt was suitable husband material. Declan was the last man they wanted for their sweet Ella. In the end, though, Ella had shown them that she was strong enough to make her own decisions and they'd grudgingly backed off. No doubt, though, they would blame Declan if Ella said anything even close to what she had thrown at her and Suzy. Oh well, her brother was a big boy and more than capable of taking care of himself and his wife if need be.

Chapter Fourteen

Ava had no idea what she hoped to accomplish here, but she found herself rooted to Mac's doorstep at three a.m. What if he wasn't alone? For all she knew, he and Gwen had worked things out. She shuffled from one foot to the other, indecision almost choking her as she debated returning to her car and leaving. She had taken a few steps backward when the porch light suddenly lit the area and the door opened. She blinked, trying to adjust to the sudden glare. "Ava?" Mac sounded surprised, clearly not expecting to see her standing there.

"Oh . . . yeah—hi," she said lamely. She sounded like someone trying to sell Tupperware. Squeezing her eyes shut, she scrambled for something to say. Why was she here again? Oh yeah, that was right, she was now a glutton for punishment and couldn't help herself.

When she opened her eyes, Mac seemed to be looking behind her as if seeking an answer to what was going on. Her eyes dropped from his face to the naked width of his chest. Oh, holy mother, all those muscles and that smooth skin, just inches away from her . . .

When she was able to continue her downward review, she saw that he was wearing only a pair of low-slung boxers that left very little to the imagination. He had the V and the happy trail of hair that every romance novel in the world paid homage to. Ava licked her suddenly dry lips when she noticed the impressive bulge beyond the waistband of his shorts. "Ava . . . *Ava*!"

Ava's head jerked up and embarrassment flooded her at being caught ogling his assets. From the smirk on his face, he knew exactly what had been on her mind. "Mmm-hmm?"

"Why are you here? Is something wrong?" His surprise had now turned to concern as he studied her intently. He might be mad at her, but he still cared. She felt a little burst of hope. It wasn't much, but she'd take any crumbs he threw out at this point.

"Ella had her baby," she blurted out, finally remembering the reason behind her visit. Not having Mac at the hospital to share the moment had left a void inside her. Mac always came to family functions. He'd been an unofficial member of the family for so long. Brant had assured her that he'd let Mac know that Ella was in labor, but he had something come up and couldn't make it.

Mac gave her a soft smile. "Yeah, I heard. A little girl."

"Sofia Grace," Ava added. Since Ella's parents argued over which parent or grandparent the baby would be named after, Ella and Declan finally picked two completely neutral names. Her parents weren't happy about it, but the decision was now officially inked and drying on the birth certificate.

Almost as if in reflex, Mac reached out to squeeze her shoulder. "That's great. I'll have to get by to see her tomorrow."

Mac dropped his arm and they both stood staring at each other. "Mac, I'm sorry," she whispered. "I miss you . . . so much."

"Ava—don't," he said in a pained voice.

Hearing him sound so tormented was more than she could bear. Without thinking, she covered the short distance between them and wrapped her arms around his big, warm body. He stiffened against her hold, and she just knew he was going to pull away, so she clung tighter, trying to fuse her body with his. "Please, Mac, hold me. We need to get past this. I don't know how to exist without you in my life."

Just when she thought he would reject her, she felt a hand against her lower back, then another one curl around her neck. "Oh, Avie," he whispered against the top of her head as he pulled her into him. "I don't know what to do with you anymore," he admitted in a shaky voice.

Her hands moved up and down his muscular back, awed at the sheer strength under her fingertips. She trailed kisses along his chest, loving the feel of him under her tongue. "Let me stay . . . Please, Mac . . . I need you."

A growl rumbled against the back of his throat as his arms flexed around her. "Ava . . . God, don't ask me that if you don't mean it."

She moved her arms up higher, locking them around his neck. She did a quick, internal check, noting that there were no signs of panic at being this close to a man. Was it always meant to be Mac who finally helped her bury the horrors of her past? She stood on her tip-toes until she could rest her lips against his. She swiped her tongue across his full lower lip, causing him to moan in reaction. Still, he remained immobile, as if waiting to see what she would do next. His lips were parted slightly, allowing her to suck his bottom lip between her lips, nipping it lightly. "Ah . . . fucking hell," he rasped as his hands dropped to her bottom and he pulled her up against him. Going completely on instinct, she used her hands around his neck as leverage to pull her body upward, wrapping her legs around his lean waist. His hands on her ass added support as he gripped her tightly. "Avie—oh, baby . . ."

In a whirlwind of movement, she founded herself on the other side of the door and holding on tightly as Mac nearly ran through the darkened hallways of his house until he reached the door of what she knew to be his bedroom. "If you've changed your mind, you need to say it, baby. I'll stop at any time, but I'd prefer it to happen now . . . before I have you under me."

In answer, she ground her lower body against the hard length pressing against her bottom. Locking her eyes with his, she said, "I don't want to stop." Then knowing it was okay to be vulnerable with Mac, she admitted, "Just tell me if I do something wrong."

Mac dropped his forehead against hers, seeming to struggle for words. "Baby . . . there is no right or wrong. Just having your hands on me—finally—is enough to send me to heaven. We'll take it slow and if anything doesn't feel right, then we stop, okay?"

Nodding her head against his, she allowed herself the freedom to sprinkle kisses over his handsome face. Being this close to Mac was like discovering a lost Christmas present. She was both giddy with excitement and trembling with the anticipation of the unknown. "I . . . I want to touch you. Can I?"

With a grin, Mac set her gently onto her feet. "Of course, sweetheart. You never need to ask me that." He pulled her into his bedroom, stopping at the bottom of his king-size bed. Spending as much time as they had together the last few years, they'd both been in each other's home countless times. She'd been in his bedroom when he gave her the tour of his home and a few other times—well, a lot of times that he wasn't aware of. Each time she used the restroom across the hall, she crept in here and imagined what it would be like to be in a relationship with him. To sleep in Mac's arms each night without fear or hesitation. To be normal.

Now she was here, and it was finally happening. He stood still in front of her, with a hand on each side of her waist. In typical Mac style, he was waiting for her . . . always waiting for her, she thought as she reached a tentative hand to his chest, tracing the line of muscles there lightly. Only his increased breathing let her know how her touch affected him. When her exploring fingers reached the nub of his nipple, she tugged on it without thought, knowing how much pleasure she derived from doing the same thing to her own breasts. Mac moaned and his big body shifted from one foot to the other, but still he let her continue. Her hand seemed to have a mind of its own as instead of journeying upward, toward his handsome face, it skirted slowly downward, tickling through the thin trail of hair on his lower stomach. At this point, she felt that they were both holding their breaths to see what she would do next. This was uncharted territory for her, and she was fascinated. Where was her usual fear of men? She had only gotten this close with Mark, and even then, she had been a mass of nerves before he even removed his shirt. Here she was going down Mac's happy trail and getting pretty damn close to the impressive package that was tenting the front of his boxers. Did she dare go there?

Her fingernail scrapped his belly button, causing Mac to issue a muffled curse before she had the answer to her question. She was at the waistband of his boxers and this felt like some kind of sexually defining moment. As if sensing her conflict, Mac applied pressure to her hips, trying to ease her back. No, damn it, she wasn't stepping away this time. Boldly, she dropped her hand suddenly and cupped him through his boxers. He froze and she quickly loosened her grip slightly on his hard length. She had been on the verge of trying to hoist his cock in the air while yelling, "I did it, I did it!" Yeah, dismembering Mac on their first time together might ruin things a bit. She was horrified when her crazy thoughts got the best of her and she started giggling. Maybe a large part of it was just stress relief from the nerves of finally being in this moment, but the timing was certainly less than perfect. "Oh God, I'm sorry," she gasped out as her body continued to shake in laughter.

When Mac put his hand over hers, trying to pry her fingers loose, she realized that she was still gripping his cock while laughing like a loon. "Avie—baby, I'm really hoping there's no connection between my dick and your attack of the giggles."

Releasing his vulnerable flesh, she sagged against him as her laughter died off. Now mortification was starting to set in. How could she have ruined the moment like that? No man wanted to be laughed at during sex, did he? "I'm sorry," she mumbled against his naked chest. "I don't know what happened. I was just . . . so relieved that I was . . . you know . . . finally doing this, and then I pictured what would happen if I accidentally pulled your pecker off because I . . . you know . . . tried high-fiving with it . . . like a fist pump and shit. I sound like a nut job, don't I? I need to just stop talking!"

Mac's big chest rumbled under her cheek as he too finally found the humor in the situation. "Ah, baby," he said, chuckling, "while parts of that explanation have my cock wanting to hide for its own safety, I get it." Pulling back slightly, he stroked the curve of her face before wrapping his big hand around the nape of her neck. "I think this is a . . . major moment in your life. I've got you, though, Ava, and this only goes as far as you want it to. You want to hold my cock and laugh because you conquered your fears, then you fucking do it. Appreciate it if you left it intact, though."

And, just that fast, her emotions jumped to the other end of the spectrum as tears threatened to choke her. Mac . . . her Mac. The man who got her, no matter how crazy she sounded or acted. Her body should have always belonged to him—and only him. "Make love to me, Mac," she whispered.

Those words sent her gentle giant into immediate action. He undressed her, worshipping every inch of new skin he exposed with his hands and his lips. When he had her down to just her tiny black lace bra and matching bikini underwear, he stepped back. She looked in surprise at his retreating back until he clicked on one of the bedside lights. She started to protest, feeling too exposed. "I've waited my whole life to see you, Avie; I need you to come out of the shadows for me."

The new light in the room also allowed her to fully see the desire glimmering in his gaze and the unmistakable proof of his arousal straining against his shorts. Mac clearly thought she was beautiful, and in that moment, she finally saw herself through his eyes. Years of shame and revulsion started falling away as she drew strength from him. With less than steady hands, she reached for the front clasp of her bra. She needed to do this, she needed to show him that she could do anything for him . . . she could be strong for him—only him.

Her heavy breasts bounced slightly as she released them from the lace material. Mac stayed locked into place, appearing completely riveted as she dropped the scrap of fabric before lowering her hands to the waistband of her panties. This part was a little harder, but she took a calming breath before lowering her last piece of clothing to the floor and stepping out of it. *Oh God, what now?* she thought while Mac stood staring at her.

She fought the urge to cross her arms over her breasts as she continued to wait . . . and wait. Was she supposed to do something else? Had he changed his mind? Insecurity rose to choke her as her bravado began to falter. She looked at him pleadingly. The fire was still there, burning in his eyes, but his jaw had gone slack, and he was clasping and unclasping his hands in an uncharacteristically nervous gesture. Mac was one of the most confident men she had ever met, even as a teenager. If he was suddenly acting so skittish, there could only be one reason. He didn't want her after all, but he didn't want to hurt her feelings. She started backing away, not sure where she was going without her clothes, but she had to get out of this room.

Her actions seemed to break Mac out of his temporary coma, and he lurched forward. "Oh, baby, fuck—wait!"

"Mac, it's okay," she said, turning her face away. "I shouldn't have put you on the spot. I know I'm not sexy and I don't have a big—butt like Gwen." She was trying to disengage her wrist from his tight grip as she continued to inch away. "We can still be friends. I . . . I'll pretend this didn't happen . . . Just, this never happened, right?"

"The hell you will," Mac roared as he stopped her hasty exit by anchoring her body to his. "What're you doing? Baby, why would you possibly believe you aren't the sexiest woman I've ever seen, and why in the world would you mention Gwen's ass?" He seemed genuinely perplexed by his last question.

As she did so often when she was nervous, she

started stuttering. "I . . . well, I took off my clothes . . . but you . . . I mean, you didn't . . . do anything. Gwen, G-lo . . . Emma said . . . you like big butts."

"Whoa," Mac said, pulling back slightly to take her face between his hands. He kissed the tip of her nose, looking as though he was biting back a grin. "First off, I've dreamed of you naked for so damn long that the sight of you in the flesh was something I had to stop and appreciate. Not to mention, if I had touched you immediately, I'd probably have disgraced myself by blowing my load before even removing my boxers." As he pushed his hips into hers, she felt him, hard as steel, and sucked in a breath. "That's right, baby, and I'm still close to that line. As for Gwen, Emma, or whoever, the only ass I'm interested in is the one that I'm fixing to fill my hands with. "I should have told you that Gwen and I are no longer seeing each other, but you, um . . . distracted me. It's just you and me, Avie. there is no one else in this bedroom but us, baby, hear me?"

With a trembling smile, she sighed. "I hear you." After that, Mac wasted no more time with conversation. He turned her, backing her toward his bed. With a gentle push, she was sitting on the edge. He dropped to his knees, nudging between her parted thighs. He used his hands to pull her closer as he kneaded her ass. His mouth devoured hers, sipping, licking, and nipping at her lips. After an initial hesitation on her part, she shyly slipped her tongue into his willing mouth and thought that she'd never tasted anything sweeter. As he staked claim to her mouth, his hands glided up her back before slowly circling to the front. At his initial contact with her nipple, she stiffened. He used his other hand to lightly stroke her side, easing her back into a state of relaxation before he continued with her other breast. Soon, every squeeze of her sensitive peaks sent a lightning bolt of heat directly to her clit.

When he lowered his head, sucking one of her nipples into his hot mouth, she gasped in pleasure. "Oh, Mac . . . Oh . . . ah!" She continued to moan, mumbling incoherently as sensation after sensation assaulted her body. She dug her fingers into Mac's hair, pulling the short dark strands. If she was hurting him, he never let on. He eased her back on the bed, keeping her legs dangling off the end. When she would have scooted up, he held her ankles to stop her. She watched in nervous enthrallment as he shifted back before pulling one of her legs up and running his tongue down the length of it, before he repeated the process on the other leg. She looked at him uncertainly as he settled each leg over his shoulder, leaving her open and exposed, only inches from his face. Oh, dear Lord. "Mac . . . what— no! Oh!"

When she had seen his intent, she panicked, trying to wiggle away. But when he held her firm and touched his tongue to her center, she shouted in surprise and pleasure.

"Baby, you taste incredible, so sweet. I could stay between these legs forever."

At his fervent declaration, Ava felt her body start to relax. She still had to fight the urge to close herself off, but with every swipe of Mac's tongue, her inhibitions were diminishing. Within moments, all she could focus on was the throbbing in her core. She was so close to the edge she just needed something—more to push her off the edge. Mac was anchoring her hips in place and she was ready to crawl out of her skin. Hearing her moans echoing off the walls, she tried to bite down on her lip to mute the sounds. All of that went out the window, though, when Mac pushed a thick finger inside her.

A garbled scream ripped from her throat, probably waking the people a mile away as her body roared toward a toe-curling, hair-pulling, finger-clenching orgasm. *"Oh God!"*

Mac chuckled as he kissed her thigh before standing. "I'm not God, baby, but I'm flattered that you think so." With a sexy curl of his lips, he dropped his boxers and stood before her in all his glory.

Ava's eyes, which were already crossed from her epic orgasm, were about to bug out of her head as she took in all that was Mac. He made her ample-size vibrator look tiny in comparison. She felt a trickle of unease as she pondered how he could possibly fit inside her without tearing her apart. When he walked to the bedside drawer and pulled out a condom, she said, "I'm on the pill." She didn't want to put a damper on the moment and tell him that she had been since shortly after her attack. It was just another area of her life where she could ensure that she was safe. He looked surprised for a moment and then tossed the condom back in the drawer. She scooted backward on the bed as Mac started prowling toward her. He looked like a sleek jungle cat, and she felt like his trembling prey. She wanted him—so much—but now her overactive mind was worrying about the logistics of it all. "Mac," she whispered uncertainly, needing his reassurance.

As his body came down to cover hers, she felt another wave of panic. It was going to hurt, and he was going to be on top of her . . . holding her down with his weight. She grabbed his forearms, ready to fight to be free, when he suddenly shifted and in a move so fast it made her head spin, Mac was on the bottom and she was on the top. Without thought, she sat up on his stomach, feeling his hard cock pressing against her ass. Mac now had his hands firmly on her hips. "I told you, baby, you're in control here. I would never force anything to happen that you didn't want. You hold the power, you call the shots. I'm just here to give you whatever *you* want."

Ava listened to his words in surprise. How did he know? It was as if he had heard every crazy thought running through her mind. She wanted him so much, but he was right, she needed to be in control, at least this first time. All of her choices had been taken from her the last time. She had been completely helpless and at the mercy of another person. Someone bigger and stronger than she was. But now Mac was giving her back a piece of what had been so brutally ripped away from her. "Oh, Mac." She sighed as she leaned down to take his lips in hers. True to his word, his hands stayed locked on her hips as he let her take what she wanted, how she wanted. She kissed and explored every inch of his upper body that she could reach. A heady sense of power filled her as Mac shuddered at her slightest touch. He growled wildly as she licked and nipped his nipples.

She knew he could feel the dampness of her core on his stomach as she shifted restlessly, trying to ease the ache throbbing between her thighs. She wanted him inside her so badly it hurt, but in her innocence, she wasn't sure how to take him slowly from this position. "What do you need, Avie?" Mac asked as she continued to wiggle against him, biting her lips in frustration.

"I . . . just . . . need your help." She felt her face flush as she stammered her request. She was embarrassed that she had no idea what to do next. If Mac hadn't still been hard as stone against her bottom, she would be terrified that he was tired of her clumsy foreplay.

His hands shifted to her waist as he started lifting her. "I've got you, sweetheart. You're still in the driver's seat, though. You tell me when you want more, okay?" At her nod, he stopped with her suspended over his cock, before lowering her just enough to push his thick head inside. They both inhaled loudly, and the room filled with their soft pants and groans.

Mac held her weight as if she weighed no more than a feather. As she adjusted to his intrusion, she simply said, "More." He lowered her an inch at a time, always waiting for the words before he went farther. Ava's body struggled to accommodate his size, and prickles of pain warred with pleasure. She was stretched to overflowing, feeling as if his cock was sitting on her cervix when he finally stopped. His entire length was now inside her, and she was almost afraid to move. What if the pain outweighed the desire starting to burn brighter? Maybe she should start small . . . just to see. Experimentally, Ava wiggled her hips, lifting just a tiny bit before sitting back down on Mac's cock. "Ohhh myyy," she groaned, unable to comprehend the sensations brought on by that one small move. Under her, Mac had gone rigid, as if fighting for control. She lifted farther the next time, pulling up a couple of inches before slamming back down harder. Without conscious thought, her hands went to her breasts and she pinched her nipples tightly, whimpering with her need for release. "Mac, please," she begged as she ground against the base of his cock.

He thrust his hips upward, pushing his big member deeper inside her. Ava felt her vision blur as her body flew toward a bliss that she had never known before. Mac was using his big hands to lift her almost completely off his length before bringing her back down. "Lean over, baby," he demanded. She fell against his chest, feeling his cock continue to stroke in and out of her as his lips took hers in a scalding kiss. They devoured each other's mouths before he said, "Put your nipple in my mouth, Avie." She whimpered as he sucked her stiff peak. He nipped the tip, before soothing the sting with his tongue. "Baby, you feel so fucking good," he moaned as she sat back up, meeting him thrust for thrust now.

Something was happening to her, and she was almost afraid to see it through. Her entire body seemed to be tingling. She vaguely wondered if Mac was giving her a heart attack. As she tried to pull back, scared by the intensity of the feelings racing through her, Mac seated himself deeply one more time while reaching a hand to pinch her clit. Her world froze in that moment, everything seeming to happen in slow motion. Her ears roared, her breath stuttered, and then it all came back into focus in one big explosion. Her body clasped around his as an endless contraction seemed to start deep inside her. She vaguely heard him yell her name before she collapsed weightless against his heaving chest. His hands were on her back now, stroking her, as they remained joined together.

The room was still slightly out of focus when she felt Mac separate from her, despite her protests. He came back to the bed and cleaned her with a cloth before disappearing into the bathroom. She heard water running for a short time and then he was back, picking her up and sliding her under the covers and into his arms. Ava felt completely and deliciously spent as she traced lazy circles on Mac's chest. "I . . . just—wow," she said with a goofy smile. "I love your penis," she added before clapping a hand across her mouth in horror. Shit, she hadn't meant to say that aloud!

Mac's chest shook beneath her as he let out a booming laugh. "Is this the part of the night where I admit to loving your vagina as well?"

Ava buried her hot face into Mac's chest. Was she completely twisted that his praise of her vagina actually turned her on again? "Sleep, baby," he said against the top of her head. When one of his hands cupped her butt, pulling her even closer, she was amazed to find that she actually could relax enough with a man—her man—to drift away.

*   *   *

Mac lay awake long after Ava had fallen asleep. He couldn't believe the moment that he had dreamed of for most of his adult life had finally happened. Ava was tucked tightly against him after rocking him to his very foundation. He'd always expected sex with Ava would be good, but he hadn't expected it to eclipse even his wildest dreams.

He had felt her tense up while he was on top of her, and he'd known she was starting to panic. It would have killed him, but he would have stopped right then if necessary. Switching her to the power position had been his one attempt to see if she would be able to overcome her fear if she felt she was in control. He had continued to watch her for any sign that she was scared. After a few minutes, she had relaxed and taken charge. She was so incredibly sexy and responsive—he had been forced to grit his teeth and quote every useless bit of sports statistics that he could think of to keep from blowing his load early. Just the feel of her tight passage milking him as he buried himself in her inch by slow inch had damn near driven him to madness.

His cock was still hard where it nestled against her thigh. He'd love nothing better than to slip back inside her. But the last thing he wanted to do was overwhelm her after she had taken such a big step. No doubt, she was probably sore as well after their intense bout of lovemaking.

As the light of early morning started to slip into the room, he looked down at the sleeping woman in his arms. He wanted to shout his love for her at the top of his lungs, but years of loving Ava had taught him a hard and painful lesson—she would run in the blink of an eye if she felt threatened. Where his instinct was to put a ring on her finger, what he needed to do now was to take things slow. She was here, in his bed. Now he needed to give her the space to accept that they belonged together.

He'd fix Ava a nice breakfast when she woke and then take his cues from her. If she mentioned something about leaving, he would let her without making a big deal of it. He wouldn't make the first move even if it meant a constant case of blue balls. He needed to let her stay in control, because he couldn't stomach the thought of scaring her away now that things had finally progressed. "Whatever you need, baby," he whispered against the crown of her head, and he meant it. If having her meant taking a step back, he could do that. If it meant that she would be with him for good in the end, he could do whatever it took.

Chapter Fifteen

Ava had surprised Suzy by dragging her to lunch on Monday. Emma had a standing lunch date with Brant most Mondays, and Ava hadn't wanted to take her brother's fiancée away. Of course, if Emma had had any clue as to what Ava wanted to talk about, she would have kicked Brant to the curb in the blink of an eye. Truthfully, she couldn't believe that Emma hadn't picked up on what had happened to her over the weekend. She felt as if she had the words *I've had amazing sex* written across her face for all to see.

Suzy and Ava had never spent any time alone before they had been Ella's whipping board at the hospital on Saturday. After being called all sorts of creative forms of whore with her coworker, Ava felt that their relationship had moved well past acquaintance to friends. "Hey, slut." Suzy smiled, seeming genuinely happy to see her.

"Hey, tramp," Ava teased in return. Just a week ago, she couldn't have imagined calling anyone something like that so easily, but Ella had certainly changed that for them. Ava was secretly afraid that now she would start using the word "whore" as if it were a common, household word.

After studying her menu, Suzy glanced up long enough to say, "You look like you got lucky sometime recently. Care to elaborate?"

Ava's mouth dropped open as she stared at the other woman's head in shock. "Wh-what?"

Still not looking up, Suzy said, "Oh, come on, you're all loose and relaxed. No offense, but before, you were so tense and frustrated that I wanted to go into the nearest closet and masturbate for you."

Ava gawked as Suzy finally looked up at her. Eventually, she gave a resigned huff before saying, "I can see why you and Emma get along so well. Neither of you believes in holding anything back."

Suzy shrugged. "I blame it on my parents. Years of distance and many self-help books have led me to the conclusion that I had to shock them with my words to get any attention, be it good or bad. Anyway, back to you. So you obviously had sex with someone. Can I assume it was Mac?"

Ava flushed before reminding herself that she had arranged the lunch date for precisely this reason. After admitting to Suzy that she had slept with Mac, she skimmed over the details even though Suzy insisted that she elaborate on a few things. "Yes—er . . . he was very—you know—big."

Suzy banged her fist against the table, yelling, "I knew it!" loud enough to have every head in the restaurant turning toward them.

"Oh my God," Ava moaned as she slid down farther in her chair.

"Oops. Sorry about that." When one particularly nosy couple kept staring at them, Suzy stared back. "Hey, show's over, buddy. Eyes back in the front." The couple gasped before turning abruptly away. Thankfully, Suzy's voice dropped considerably when she turned back to Ava. "So, he was big and he went downtown, yay! Since you look like you're about to stroke out over there, I'll let you off the hook for now. Did you stay afterward?"

Ava propped her head in her hands, finally getting to the part that was bothering her. "Yeah, I did. It was already morning anyway. We slept late and when we got up, Mac made me breakfast. He kissed me good morning, which was good—very good. As we were eating, I felt like I should make some attempt at mentioning plans for the day so he wouldn't feel as if I was expecting him to entertain me . . . even though I wanted to stay with him. So I said that I needed to run errands and do laundry."

"And what did he say?"

"He said, 'Good deal. Call me later on if you think of it.' I sat there trying not to look disappointed that he didn't seem to care if I stayed or not. I mean . . . I thought we would, you know, do it again and spend the day together."

"Hmm," Suzy mused, "did he kiss you good-bye? I mean, not just a kiss on the cheek, but a tongue-swallowing kind of kiss."

Ava shifted around in her seat before admitting, "He

kissed me like he wanted to inhale me. He was excited, I could feel that. But then he just let me go."

"So, did you call him last night?"

Nodding, Ava said, "I called him before bed, and we talked for almost two hours. He said he missed me, but he didn't ask me to come over. I would have, you know. I'd have jumped out of bed and gone to him right then if he had given me any indication that he wanted that. So, what do you think? Am I doing something wrong?"

"Shit, I don't know." Suzy grimaced. "I mean, I'm not exactly a poster child for romance. My first steady boyfriend and fiancé cheated on me with his dentist, and Gray pursued me with the same single-minded determination that he does everything. He didn't exactly send me any mixed signals; he made sure I knew exactly what he wanted every time we were together. I never have to wonder if he wants me or if he's in the mood, because he's always in the mood—always."

Confused, Ava looked at Suzy in shock. "But . . . you give everyone advice. You're like the Danvers dating guru. Am I'm such a hopeless case that you're stumped?"

Suzy patted Ava's shoulder. "No, crap no, that's not it at all." Looking strangely uneasy, she said, "It's just that you've been through a lot, Ava, and I don't want to do anything to mess this up for you. You deserve to be happy, and you seem so close to making that happen. I'm just afraid of giving you the wrong piece of advice and screwing something up." Shredding the paper napkin she had gripped in her hands, Suzy continued. "Sometimes, when you didn't think anyone was look-ing, I saw the pain that you try so carefully to hide. I'm a people watcher, always have been. Not sure how I missed the signs that my ex was cheating on me, though. That one's still a mystery."

Ava was uncomfortable at the thought of someone studying her so closely, but also strangely touched that Suzy seemed to care about what happened to her. Squeezing the other woman's hand briefly, she swallowed the lump in her throat and attempted to lighten the mood. "Thank you . . . for caring. But if we put my past issues aside and pretend that I'm, say . . . Emma, what would you tell me to do?"

Suzy narrowed her eyes, seeming to give the question serious consideration. "Well, I guess if it ain't broke, don't fix it. In other words, all the stuff that you've been doing to get Mac's attention seems to be working like a charm. You've had sex—obviously the wonderful, dirty kind—and he's no longer with G-lo, so you hold all the cards now. Did you have something else planned to drive him crazy?"

"Well, I'm supposed to have a surf lesson today."

Suzy cringed immediately. Emma's sister's death was still fresh in all their minds. "I don't think that's the best idea. Couldn't you come up with anything else?"

"I know." Ava sighed. "But living in a beach town means most of the activities here revolve around the beach. I'm going to cancel it."

"Hey, I've got it! How about parasailing? I've done it a few times before and it's awesome. I could go with you. They'll even let us go up together. It's just down the beach from our house, so you could come over this afternoon and we'll walk there."

"And Gray doesn't freak out over you doing stuff like that?"

Suzy grinned, looking completely mischievous. "Well, of course he freaks out, but he knows he can't change me. He just makes it his mission to catch me if I fall."

"It sounds scary," Ava admitted, "but kinda fun."

"Best part, Gray has been saying for a week that he needs to get Mac to come over because he wants to upgrade our security system. I'll suggest he do that this evening while I'm out. Actually, I'll insist on it."

Feeling embarrassed, Ava asked, "You aren't going to tell Gray why, are you? I mean, I have to face him over a conference table at least once a week. I don't want him to think I'm some desperate woman trying to pick up a man. Even though I guess I am."

Shaking her head, Suzy smiled. "Nah, I won't tell him. He's a little gun-shy on the whole matchmaking thing after having his brother and my sister making out secretly in our house for weeks before we found out. I still think about them screwing on our kitchen counter when I'm in there, but what are you going to do? It happened."

Ava choked on her sip of tea at Suzy's matter-of-fact analysis of Nick and Beth's courtship. She could easily picture both Gray and Suzy avoiding their kitchen like the plague. "Oh my God, that's funny. Poor Nick and Beth."

"Poor them? Shit, poor us! I'd burn the place down if I didn't love it so much."

Their food arrived and after taking a few bites, Ava asked, "So, what time should I be at your house?"

"Can you be there around five thirty? You can wear one of my swimsuits to keep from going home first."

Ava tried not to imagine what a swimsuit of Suzy's might possibly look like. She'd have to borrow a T-shirt to put over it. "Sure, that sounds good."

"Cool, now get out your phone and text something naughty to Mac. Just to let him know where your head is."

Her sandwich dropped back onto her plate with a thump as her eyes widened. "Wh-what?"

"You did say for me to give you the same advice that I would Emma. Well, that's what I would tell her. All men love hearing that you're thinking of *THAT*. Trust me, I practice what I preach. Gray gets some interesting texts and it never fails to make for a memorable evening."

Despite herself, Ava was intrigued. She'd never done anything like that, since she'd never actually had a boyfriend. It did sound fun, though, just like something someone normal would do. "So, what would I say?"

Suzy winked at her, saying, "Well, the last one I sent Gray said something like 'thinking of you while I touch myself,' but since he knows you're at work or in this case at lunch, it might be harder to pull that one off— but not impossible, mind you. Maybe we should start off kind of mild, just so this first text doesn't send him over the edge. How about . . . 'I know you're busy today, but can you add one thing to your to-do list? Me'?"

"What?" Ava shrieked. "I can't say that!"

"Oh, come on, why not? It's perfect. It starts out as

business and ends as a party. It's just the right amount of sweet and sexy. I guarantee that he'll be busting out the zipper of his pants within sixty seconds of reading that."

Red-faced, Ava said, "Oh . . . I can't, I just—what would he think if I said something like that to him?"

"Honey, what he'd think is that you want him as much as he wants you and that you're not afraid to let him know. It'll also shock the shit out of him in an 'I'm so hard I could explode in my pants' kind of way." Eyeing Ava's clenched expression, she let out a growl. "You aren't going to do it, are you? Ugh, just go ahead and say something like 'thinking of you' or some other PG stuff."

Ava grabbed her cell phone before she could change her mind. It was just a text message. She and Mac had had sex. Honest-to-goodness, real sex. A text message was nothing. She needed to be comfortable joking around with him. This was the kind of thing that women in relationships did all the time, wasn't it? Suzy had admitted to doing it with Gray. Mac had a great sense of humor; he would love something like this. With Suzy looking on in approval, she typed out the message word for word as her friend repeated it and then hit SEND. There, it was done. No turning back now.

She really, really hoped that Mac was a lover of sexting.

Mac was in the middle of a staff meeting with Dom, Gage, and five of their employees when his phone chimed to alert him to a new text. When Gage started going through some new reporting procedures with the other men, Mac picked up his phone, surprised to see that it was from Ava. He smiled as he clicked on it, hoping that she wanted to see him tonight. He was still trying to honor his plan to let her control the pace of their relationship until she was more comfortable, but damn, he missed her already. His eyes almost bugged out of his head when he read—*I know you're busy today, but can you add one thing to your to-do list? Me.*

"Fuck me." Mac had no idea that he had uttered those words aloud until all heads at the table swiveled his way.

Gage looked at him in question before giving him a sarcastic grin. "Something you wanted to add?"

"Um—no. All good here," he grumbled in reply. Shifting uneasily in his chair, he tried to alleviate the ache in his crotch where his cock was now pushing painfully against his zipper. He didn't think he'd ever had a problem with fighting wood during a meeting with the guys before and it was damn disconcerting. Even Dom was giving him a funny look. Thank God there was no way that they could see what was happening to him under the table.

As if it hadn't done enough damage the first time, he looked at the text message again, needing to make sure that he had read it correctly. Yeah, shit, there was no mistaking what she had said. He desperately wanted to run from the room, go straight upstairs, rip her panties off, and fuck her on the top of her well-organized desk. Instead, with a none-too-steady hand, he texted back *My house tonight, eight.* His hand hovered over the SEND button before deciding on a little payback. He added two words before hitting SEND—*No panties.*

The rest of the meeting passed by in a blur. He was grateful that he had been the first to speak and had finished the items on his agenda before Ava's text. As it was, he was so scattered that both Gage and Dom had gone from looking curious to downright concerned. Wanting to avoid the questions that he knew would be coming, he'd gathered his stuff and left early for his next appointment. At moments like this he hated the fact that the men he worked with were like a bunch of nosy, gossiping women.

Chapter Sixteen

Suzy was already wearing a green string bikini when Ava arrived at her house after work. She handed Ava a black bikini that looked similar in style. "Er . . . do you have anything else—like maybe a one-piece?"

Suzy shook her head, before pushing her toward a bathroom off the hallway. "No, of course not. If I did, I wouldn't let you wear it. Mac doesn't want to see you dressed like his mother. You've got a banging body; you need to show it off."

Ava knew it was futile to argue. Instead she took the swimsuit and quickly changed. She looked at herself in the mirror and decided that even though it looked okay, she'd never felt so exposed in her whole life. Was anyone ever really comfortable in a swimsuit on the beach in front of dozens of people? Ugh! "Do you have a shirt or something I can put over this?" she yelled back through the door.

"No," Suzy yelled back. "Come on out, we've got to go. And don't put your clothes back on over that suit!"

Ava gaped at the door, wondering how the other woman had known that she was considering doing exactly that. Grumbling under her breath, she picked her clothing up and walked out the door. She came to an abrupt halt when she spotted Gray standing in the living room grabbing what looked like a handful of Suzy's butt.

Ava had started to edge backward, trying to make her escape before being spotted, when Gray's eyes landed on her. He smiled at her apologetically before swatting his wife's ass lightly and saying, "behave yourself, minx. You are embarrassing your partner in crime." Suzy spun around, narrowing her eyes as she saw Ava clutching her discarded clothing to her chest. She noticed that Gray still kept a possessive arm wrapped around Suzy's waist, seeming to want to be in constant contact with some part of her. They were the sexiest couple that Ava had ever seen.

"Ready, chica?" Suzy asked, before leaning up to kiss her husband. "We'll be back in a few hours, babe. You've got Mac coming over, right?"

Gray looked from his wife to Ava and then back again. "Mmm-hmm. Mac seemed a little surprised that I needed to meet him this evening just to discuss an upgrade. Neither he nor I could discern why it was suddenly so earth-shakingly important to my beautiful wife." When Suzy just gave him her best innocent look, he shook his head in resignation. Kissing the top of her head, he said, "Be safe, baby."

When Gray walked off into another room, Suzy wrestled the clothing from her hand and threw it into a nearby armchair. "Come on, drop the body armor. We're going out onto a beach. There are many people with swimsuits on. It doesn't matter who you are or what size you wear, just own it. Confidence is sexy." With those words, Suzy pulled her out onto the deck and then down the steps that led to the beach.

Ava felt naked with strangers around but tried to take Suzy's words to heart. Was it as simple as just seeing yourself a certain way? Even though she had been told she was attractive, a part of her had always felt ugly . . . since that night. She thought if she exposed too much skin, she was asking for bad things to happen to her. She had lived with the fear for years that she had somehow been responsible for her assault. Had she given him the wrong idea by how she dressed and the things she said? All the books said no. That there was never anything you could do to justify those acts of violence, but deep down inside, the doubts festered.

Being exposed like this now, for strangers to see, was almost paralyzing. Sure, she had worn more revealing clothes lately but always with some kind of escape plan in mind. But here and now, there was no car near, there was nothing to hide behind. If she freaked out and ran, everyone would see . . . Suzy would see.

Ava had no idea that she had stopped walking until Suzy put hand on each of her arms, shaking her lightly. "I don't think . . . ," she began to explain before letting the words trail off. Why? Why couldn't she stop being afraid?

"Hey," Suzy said quietly, "listen to me. I know you're all up in your head right now. Trust me, I recognize the signs. I'm not going to force you to see this through. But I will promise you this: I'll be with you every step of the way. I won't leave your side. We don't have to parasail today. We can just hang out. No one is going to bother you; I'll make sure of that."

Ava studied her new friend for a minute, seeing nothing but sincerity in her eyes. If there had been one ounce of pity, Ava would have collapsed, but somehow Suzy's strength fueled her own. She really looked at her surroundings for the first time, seeing other women on the beach dressed just as she was. She didn't stick out here. No one was looking at her; she was just another face in the crowd. Releasing the breath she hadn't been aware of holding, she gave a nod of agreement and a tentative smile of reassurance. "I—okay. Can we just watch other people do the parasailing before I commit, though?"

Doing a little victory dance, Suzy threw an arm around her shoulders. "Hell yeah, we can. If we're being all honest and stuff, I almost pissed my pants the first time I tried it, so I'm all for taking baby steps. Most important thing is that we're actually considering it, right? Big points for that! Hey, by the way, what was Mac's reaction to your sext today?"

Ava felt her face go up in flames as she looked around to make sure no one was listening before saying, "He said to be at his house at eight . . . with no panties."

"No, he didn't!" Suzy all but shouted. "I bet you don't make it as far as the bedroom tonight before he jumps your bones! That man probably hasn't been able to think of anything else all day. You go, girl."

Next, Ava did something she would never have

thought possible while being scantily dressed in public: she let loose a full-belly laugh and felt years of repression start to lighten from her shoulders. She'd had sex, walked on a public beach in a bikini, and done her first ever sext—all in one week—with only minor moments of panic. After so many years of almost giving up on herself, she was getting her life back, and in that moment, she felt like a carefree teenager again. Fun, fearless, and ready to take on the world.

Without stopping to overthink it, she pulled a now-worried Suzy up to the sign advertising parasailing before it hit her. "I didn't bring any money!" Maybe it was divine intervention, but she didn't want to stop now. She had been determined to see this through without letting her fears win.

Suzy looked at her disappointed expression before cursing under her breath. In a move that made the young man taking the money gawk, Suzy stuck a hand into her swimsuit top and pulled out some bills. "I know I'm going to regret this, but if you're all set to go for it, then I've got your back." The poor guy seemed to struggle not to swallow his tongue as he took the hundred-dollar bill from Suzy's outstretched hand. When he was finally able to get it together enough to return her change, he motioned for one of the thankfully older men on the beach to help them into the boat.

One man drove the boat while the other hooked them in their harnesses and then helped them onto the flight deck. The man handling the equipment explained that they would be launched and retrieved using a hydraulic winch. Ava was relieved to know that they wouldn't suddenly catapult into the water. When the winch started to launch them into the air, she felt her stomach drop to her feet. "Oh my God, why did I let you talk me into this?" she screamed over at Suzy.

"What! I was happy to stay on the ground! I told you that we'd take baby steps today. That meant walk around and think about doing this shit, but not actually do it!" Suddenly, they both looked down, realizing that the boat was now only a small speck in the distance. "Oh, holy fuck-a-moly! Remember what I said about pissing my pants? Well, it may just happen this time!"

For Ava, that was all it took. Hearing Suzy curse and toss out threats along with the adrenaline rush of doing something so completely crazy was enough to make her snap. Instead of the panic that she would normally feel, though, she started laughing. Tears rolled down her face, and she could barely breathe, but she only laughed harder. She had well and truly lost her mind this time, but in a good way. She threw her hands up into the air and started to squeal between bouts of mad laughter. "Ahhh, yayyy!" she screamed over and over. After a few minutes, she noticed someone echoing her crazy yells and turned to see Suzy doing something similar. They looked at each other, grinning like idiots.

"Girl, you are crazy!" Suzy gasped out. "Everyone within a five-mile radius can probably hear us, but who in the hell cares? This is the bomb!"

When the guy below hoisted them in, he was grinning at them, trying hard to suppress his own laughter. "Sounds like you ladies had a good time."

Instead of shying away and waiting for Suzy to answer, Ava gave him a thumbs-up. "It was off-the-charts! We'll definitely be back, right, Suzy?"

Suzy gave a small thumbs-up in return before slumping back against the boat seat. "Ur—yeah, I'm afraid we will."

After that, they took a leisurely walk on the beach, laughing over how crazy they had sounded before heading back toward Suzy's house. Ava had expected to see Mac there and was disappointed when Gray said that he had already left.

At Suzy's insistence, she left her swimsuit on but borrowed a T-shirt to throw on over it. It did seem crazy to put her work clothes back on after being on the beach. It wasn't exactly sexy lingerie, but still she hoped that Mac would like it.

Mac paced back and forth across his entryway, waiting for Ava to arrive. When he'd shown up at Gray's house earlier, the other man casually mentioned that his wife and Ava were parasailing down on the beach and would be back in a few hours. Parasailing? Holy shit! Mac's concentration had gone out the window after that. He was only half listening to Gray's questions about an alarm system upgrade as he imagined the woman he loved breaking her neck and drowning in the freaking Atlantic Ocean. It had taken everything he had not to leave Gray standing there while he marched down the beach and threw Ava over his shoulder. He thought he deserved a fucking medal for having that much self-control.

He had wanted to ask Gray how it was that he didn't

seem at all concerned about his wife's welfare but figured that being married to Suzy had probably taught the other man some patience. Mac had always heard that a smart person picked his battles, and maybe that was how Gray handled things with his wife. Mac, though, obviously wasn't that intelligent, because he was pissed and ready to start an out-and-out war with Ava the moment she arrived. That was assuming she made it there in one piece. She was supposed to arrive at eight, which was about fifteen minutes from now.

He had been in a state of near-constant arousal since her text earlier today. Couple sexual frustration with anger, and it was a volatile combination. He knew that he needed to exercise control with her, though. He couldn't risk scaring her away, after they had finally taken a step forward and made it this far. Her message had given him hope that she wanted him with the same all-consuming desire that he felt for her. He had already been hanging by a thread when he found out that she was, once again, doing something that could very well get her injured. He had hoped that after she had been so spooked by the man at the hang gliding club meeting, she would give all that up and come to her senses, but that didn't appear to be the case. These stunts just seemed to be getting worse. He wanted to kiss every inch of her delectable bottom but also itched to turn it red. The woman would be the death of him.

As he continued to seethe, he heard the unmistakable sound of a car engine followed by a slamming door. That had better be her. He truly pitied anyone else who believed this might be a good night for a visit. He looked through the side window and glimpsed her walking up the steps. He gulped as he noticed she wore nothing but a shirt that left miles of leg uncovered. *Oh, shit.* He threw the door open, noting her surprised expression as her finger hovered over the doorbell. Without a word, he took her hand and pulled her inside the darkened entry-way . . . and that was as far as they made it.

A fire ignited between them that made it impossible to think rationally. Before he could even fathom how it had happened, he had her shirt over her head and his hands on her ass, grinding her against his painfully hard erection. "Mac—yes," she moaned as he untied the strings to her skimpy swimsuit, exposing every naked inch of her to his hungry gaze.

Her small hands were on him, pushing his basketball shorts down his legs, seeming to want him just as desperately as he desired her. He hooked one hand over his back, pulling his shirt up over his head, and finally, they had what they were both hungry for—skin-on-skin contact. For Mac, self-control was gone. He was an animal in its most primitive form. "Mine," he moaned as he took one of her nipples in his mouth, sucking the rosy peak while pinching the other one between his thumb and forefinger. "I need you, baby—now," he growled, pushing the head of his thick cock against her wet entrance. His body shuddered as he waited for her permission. Even with the raging need he felt, he couldn't possess her without knowing it was what she wanted. He needed to hear the words. When she moaned against his neck, he whispered, "Say it, baby. Tell me you want me."

Wrapping a leg around his thigh, she groaned, "Yes . . . yes, Mac. God yes, I want you. Please—now, right now!" Before she finished her plea, he was pushing inside her. She was so tight that he was forced to go slow, even though he wanted nothing more than to bury himself in one stroke. He couldn't hurt her—he'd never do that, no matter how close to the edge he was. She came first; she always had. After a few shallow thrusts into her wet heat, it became apparent he wasn't the only one ready for more. With a voice full of impatience she snapped, "Harder, Mac! *Harder!*" When he felt her small teeth sink into his earlobe, he lost it.

Rearing his hips back, Mac seated himself completely inside her. She hooked both arms around his neck before wrapping her legs around his waist, pushing him impossibly deeper into her. "Ah, Avie, oh, baby, fuck yeah!" he chanted as his powerful thrusts nailed her ass against the wall. Her hips followed the movement of his, taking everything he gave her and begging for more. When the familiar tingle started at the base of his spine, he knew he was close, but damn it, he didn't want this to end. Being inside Ava transcended every other moment in his life, and he'd fucking live there if she'd let him. "I'm close, baby," he whispered against her ear, needing her to get there fast. When he would have lowered his hand to her clit, he groaned when he felt her using the base of his cock to do that very thing.

Instead of the hard thrusts that had been pushing them both to the brink of insanity, Ava was keeping him locked inside her while grinding her sensitive nub against his root. He gritted his teeth and started thinking of anything he could to delay his explosion. He was at eighty-nine bottles of beer on the wall in his head when he felt her starting to spasm around him. He was helpless to stop his own body from following hers as her contractions milked his cock dry.

When the tremors had subsided, he continued to lean against her, using the wall to support them both. His legs felt so damn weak he was afraid they'd both tumble to the floor if he moved too soon. The feel of Ava's small hand stroking against his sweaty back had his spent flesh twitching to life. Surely, there was no way he could go again so soon after releasing everything he had into her . . . could he? He had the answer to his question, as he continued to harden. Un-fucking-real. He needed somewhere soft for them to land this time, though. "Mac," Ava purred, locking her legs tighter around his waist.

"Hang on, baby," he mumbled before clutching her close and straightening to take her weight. They both moaned in pleasure as his steps toward the bedroom pushed his cock deeper. She protested as he separated from her briefly to lay her on her side on the bed. He knew that both of their bodies were tired, even if their libidos were still going strong. He curled up behind her, lifting her leg over his thigh before sliding back into her from behind.

Mac knew she approved of the new position when her head fell back against his neck on a long sigh of pleasure. "So good," she murmured as he leaned closer against her back to cup her breast. He kept up a slow and leisurely rhythm while his hand wandered over every inch of her exposed skin. He smiled at her fevered shout of approval when he slid his fingers between her legs, flicking her swollen clit. Slow sex was all but forgotten and she moved her hips impatiently, trying to quicken his pace. He tormented her for a few moments longer, actually slowing down until she raked her fingernails down his thigh. *Ouch!* It seemed as if his woman was tired of waiting.

His stroking fingers increased with the speed of his cock and he was giving her everything she wanted. They both raced toward an invisible finish line with her crossing it just as his balls started to tighten in warning. She collapsed against him so completely afterward that he moved his hand around on her chest to check her breathing. Satisfied with what he felt there, he pulled himself from her body and got out of bed to clean up. He knew that there was no way she was moving any time soon, so he returned with a washcloth, kissing her forehead and gently cleaning her as best he could before walking through the house to lock up for the evening. It was a testament to how she affected him that he hadn't even thought to lock the door before devouring her in the hallway. Yeah, both the big head and the little head only had one thought when she was around, and it damn sure wasn't safety. For someone in his line of work, that was almost a sacrilege.

When the house was secure, he settled back around her, smiling in the dark like a sap when she snuggled sleepily against him. He remembered that he had been mad as hell at her earlier with the whole parasailing stunt. Funny how that hadn't even occurred to him once his hands had touched her skin. Right now all he could feel was complete contentment that for the second time the woman he loved was sleeping next to him. Tomorrow was soon enough for him to be pissed. Tonight he just wanted to hold her and vow that she would never spend another night without him.

Chapter Seventeen

A heavy weight across her chest pulled Ava from a dreamless sleep and straight into a nightmare. Disoriented, she could only work out was that someone was holding her down. Terror raced through her body as her fight or flight instinct kicked in with a vengeance. She had to get free! Oh God, it was happening again, he was going to hurt her—he had said he would, and now he was back!

Her mind went hazy as she started to fight like a cornered animal. She wouldn't let this happen to her again. He would have to kill her this time or set her free. So she fought, she kicked and scratched every inch of skin that she could reach. She heard him howling in pain, which only fueled her need to inflict further damage. He would pay—this time she would hurt him as much as he had hurt her. This time, she would finally win.

"Ava! Ava! Goddammit, stop! Fucking hell, baby, wake up!" A familiar voice broke through the haze her bloodlust, causing her to pause. Mac? Had he come to save her this time? She turned toward his voice, wondering

why he kept telling her to wake up. Couldn't he see that she was being attacked? "Ava . . . open your eyes. Baby, look at me."

Her heart started racing as a different kind of fear set in. As her eyes fluttered open, she struggled to keep them open against the bright glare filling the room. As she blinked, slowly adjusting to the light, she looked at the man holding her pinned beneath him in dawning horror. "No, oh, please no," she whispered as she looked at the blood tricking from his nose and the corner of his mouth. Red welts dotted his cheeks and neck along his chest and arms. "Please tell me I didn't do that to you," she cried even though she knew there was no other explanation. She had been fighting what she thought was an attack against her when all the while it had been all in her head. It was Mac. The man who would never physically hurt her.

"Shhh, it's okay, baby," he whispered repeatedly as he pulled her against his battered body. She completely lost it in what she now recognized as the shelter of his arms. Her sobs filled the room along with her garbled apologies.

She couldn't understand how something like this had happened. She'd had nightmares about the night of her attack, as anyone would who had been through that sort of trauma. The dreams had almost completely stopped, though, several years ago, and she'd never once dreamed of hurting her attacker. In her dreams, she was always the victim, always. "I—I don't know what happened. I thought he . . . was back. That I was being—hurt again." When she pulled back enough to look into his face and saw the wounds she had wrought there, her stomach churned. Oh God, she was going to be sick. With no time to explain, she sprang from Mac's embrace, stumbling toward the nearest bathroom. She barely reached the toilet before her stomach upended what little it contained into the porcelain bowl.

Ava tried to protest when Mac walked up behind her, then gently pulled her hair back while she succumbed to the dry heaves racking her body. He rubbed her back, making soothing sounds until the spasms finally passed. Leading her around as if she were a child, he helped her over to the bathroom sink and brought a spare toothbrush out of the cabinet for her. He poured her a cup of water and put the toothpaste on the brush before handing it to her.

She stood before him completely naked, having slept that way. After all that had transpired between them, modesty was the furthest thing from her mind. Mac had donned a pair of boxers at some point. He reached behind her and started the shower. Without saying a word, he checked the water temperature before stepping out of his boxers and pulling her into the steamy heat with him. Then he washed her like a child, before making quick work of soaping up his own body. Even though he touched every inch of her, there was nothing sexual in his movements. They were both still traumatized by what had happened earlier.

After he had dried them both, he handed her a pair of his boxers and a clean T-shirt. The boxers hung low, but she turned the waistband down a few times and managed to keep them on. The bedside clock said seven, which meant she needed to be at the office in less than two hours. Beside her, Mac dressed in his usual business attire of a company polo shirt and cargo pants. She knew he was watching her the entire time; she could feel his eyes on her.

"Coffee?" he asked as she finally returned his stare. When she nodded, he took her hand and led her toward the kitchen. By unspoken agreement, they waited until a steaming cup sat before each of them at the bar before talking.

After taking a fortifying sip of the hot brew, she closed the distance between them. The water had washed away the blood from his face, but the heat of the shower had made the welts more prominent. She reached out to touch his face, feeling tears welling once again. "I'm so sorry, Mac."

His hands went to her waist, pulling her against him. She felt him exhale against the crown of her head. "What happened, baby? Are you having nightmares like this often?"

Sliding her hands around his waist, she let herself sink into his strength. "No, I'm not. There have been nightmares on and off but not recently. But I've never had one like this one. I was so determined to fight back. I was so angry. Even now, I can still remember all the hate coursing through me. I—I've never felt anything like it. I wanted to kill him. It wasn't him I was hurting, though." She shuddered at the recollection.

Mac was quiet for a moment, as if trying to gather his thoughts. "You said you've never . . . been with another man since that night?"

"That's right," she admitted, feeling embarrassed about the lengths she had gone to for years to convince him otherwise.

"So you haven't slept with anyone either? I mean like spent the night with someone else in your bed?"

"No," she answered, confused by his question. If she hadn't had sex, wasn't it obvious that she hadn't had a sleepover either?

He removed his arms from her, and a squeak of surprise left her lips as he lifted her up to sit on his granite countertop. He laid a hand on each of her legs, opening them enough for him to settle between them. She put her hands on his shoulders, now that they were at eye level, and waited for him to continue his earlier conversation. "I'm a light sleeper, so you woke me up moving around restlessly. You were lying half under me, with my legs across the top of yours. I think since this wasn't something—normal for you, that it might have triggered a nightmare. Feeling someone holding you down while in the midst of a dream could have changed the dynamics. Even though you were asleep, your subconscious was reacting to a threat."

Feeling a wave of alarm, she cried, "If that's true, this could happen again. Mac! I—I can't do this to you again!"

Stroking her hair, he said, "Calm down, baby. I'm just thinking aloud. I think this is probably the most rational explanation for what happened. I don't want to get into everything this morning, since we don't have much time before work. But I think we need to discuss it tonight. Have you talked to anyone about what happened to you since that night?" When she opened her mouth to answer, he held up his hand to stop her. "I mean in detail, Avie. Not just that you were . . . violated. The whole thing from start to finish and what happened afterward."

"No," she admitted, feeling almost surprised herself. Of course, people knew about her past, but she'd never really sat down and gone through everything. Even right after her attack, she had glossed over some of the details. Truthfully, she could see her grandfather's face shutting down before her eyes as she had told him what happened. After that, each time she had omitted more and more until now it was almost like a rehearsed speech. In fact, she could see that she made light of her pain. Almost as if she were talking about someone else being raped and not herself.

Mac kissed her lightly, running his hands up and down her spine. "It's going to be fine, baby. We'll figure it out." Dropping his hand to squeeze the swell of her bottom, he added, "Now move it, woman. I'll follow you to your place so you can change."

When he started to pull away, Ava gripped his hand. "What about your . . . face? You look like you've been attacked."

Raising an eyebrow, Mac said, "Rough sex?" For the first time that morning, she had a hard time smothering a grin. "What?" Mac smiled in return. "You know that's exactly what Dom and Gage will think. Might as well let 'em enjoy it."

In perfect sync, they finished their coffee before grabbing their shoes and keys. Mac followed her to her apartment and then insisted on walking her inside. He went through each room before leaving her on her doorstep, after a thorough kiss that left her feeling utterly befuddled. If he was trying to keep her mind off how she had attacked him in his own bed, he was doing a superb job. The problem was that once he and his magic mouth were gone, all Ava could think of was the long, angry scratches marring his handsome face. She felt a hum of dread. How could she be sure something like this would never happen again? She didn't want to lash out at Mac while she was asleep and dreaming of the nightmare from her past. She had a sinking feeling that the bastard who had all but ruined her life was now going to take the only man she had ever loved from her.

Mac had to give his friends credit. He'd been at work for almost an hour and neither of them had mentioned his messed-up face. He was the first to admit that men weren't the most observant of creatures, especially when it pertained to another man. A man might not notice a woman had a new hairstyle—like ever—but if the same woman got a boob job, he'd probably notice it within two minutes. The male sex just had different priorities in life. Sad maybe, definitely true. However, usually something as obvious as your friend looking as if three big-ass cats had clawed his face was at least going to get a comment if nothing else.

When they all took a seat at the conference room table for their morning roundup meeting, Gage looked first at him, then back at Dom. "Well, fuck, I'm just going to get it out there. What are you into these days, brother? I mean, we all know that the object of your affection is the demure little number a few floors above us. I don't see her ripping your ass up like that, so who have you been playing with and does she have a sister?"

Dominic hooted with laughter, causing the chair that he'd been balancing on its back legs to wobble precariously. "I like it rough sometimes myself, but I try to limit the claws to my back. You look like you had sex with the damn female equivalent of the *Lion King*."

"Funny," Mac deadpanned. "Like you two have any room to talk. I've seen you both sporting black eyes on more than one occasion."

In typical fashion, Dominic was easily distracted and turned on the man beside him. "Yeah, Gage, how about that hot little number on the second floor who kneed you in the balls last week? Might not have left a visible mark, but damn, I bet you were singing soprano all night long."

When Gage actually blushed, Mac looked at him in surprise. "Whoa, when did I miss this?" Gage kept his mouth shut and continued to look uncomfortable. Mac turned back to Dominic, saying, "I know I'm going to regret this, but explain."

Dominic smirked in obvious enjoyment. "Well, you see there's this woman in customer service who our resident Don Juan has struck out with. Not only has he *not* gotten into her panties, but she attacked the family jewels when he grabbed her in the parking garage last week. Guess she didn't hear him coming and when he put his hands on her, she thought she was being mugged or something. I saw the whole damn thing. Only wish I had gotten it on video. She was wearing some black kick-ass heels and a tight skirt. It was a fucking sexy vision when she laid our boy here out on the ground. I'm not one hundred percent certain, but I'm pretty sure I saw a tramp stamp on her lower back when she bent over to see if he was breathing afterward."

"No way." Mac laughed. It seemed as if he wasn't the only one getting his ass kicked by a woman lately. Maybe it was twisted, but it made him feel much better.

"Yeah, yeah, laugh it up, ladies. My balls might have been up around my neck for about twelve hours, but I'm still more of a man than either one of you," Gage grumbled.

Dominic snickered in reply. "That was weak, dude, but since you've been recently emasculated, I'll let it slide."

Gage whirled around in his chair, seeming to lose his usual good sense of humor. "Oh, really, Dom? Well, why don't we talk about your lack of success with the woman you've been pining over like a little bitch?"

Mac watched in interest as the smirk fell off Dominic's face to be replaced by a scowl. Shit, had he missed all the good stuff lately? Looking over at his frowning friend, he asked, "So, who are you lusting after now?" Truthfully, he was just relieved to hear that Dominic was interested in anyone else other than Ava. Unless . . . ? "Man, it had better not be my woman," he warned.

"Boy, that's hitting a little too close to home, isn't it, Dom?" Gage taunted.

"Gage," Dominic warned, "shut your damn piehole, man, before I shut it!"

Mac was starting to feel like a bobble-head as his eyes jerked from Gage to Dominic and then back again. "All right, you two are starting to piss me off." Leveling his gaze at Dominic, he added, "Ava and I are together now, so you'd better not be sniffing at her skirt or I'll kick your ass."

Gage flopped forward onto the table, seeming to find the whole thing hilarious now that he was no longer the subject of conversation. "Go back a little further, bro," Mac heard him gasp out.

"Oh, for fuck's sake," Dominic suddenly boomed as he stood up. "It's Gwen, all right? Big-mouthed Nancy over there is talking about Gwen! Now go ahead and lose your shit so we can get past this."

Floored, Mac repeated, "Gwen? You mean you like Gwen?"

Dominic looked at him warily as he said, "It's been more like I lust Gwen, but I guess like plays a part in it too."

"She does have a nice, big, juicy, round—ouch!" Gage howled as Dominic threw a pen at his head with perfect aim.

Still confused, Mac said, "So let me get this straight. You've got a thing for Gwen? How long has this been going on?" Mac knew the fact that he was more curious than upset was very telling about the level of his feelings for the woman he had just stopped seeing.

Dominic sank back into his chair, releasing a breath. "Nothing has happened between us. She doesn't even know. I mean, we live in the same apartment building, so I see her around a lot."

"So you lusted after Gwen or whatever you want to call it the whole time I was dating her?"

Dominic looked pained as he admitted, "Well, yeah, that's about right."

Mac shook his head in disgust. "Shit, Dom, why didn't you say something? I'd never have asked her out the first time if I'd known."

Dominic looked away before saying quietly, "You needed her more. Ava has kept you tied in knots for years. I figured if there was someone to get you away from all that, then what I wanted didn't really matter."

"Dom, brother," Mac began, feeling at a loss for words.

"Does anyone else feel like we're having our own *Oprah Winfrey Show*? Just sayin' . . . ," Gage said with what was almost a straight face. Luckily, his comment had effectively broken the tension that had been building in the room, and Mac was grateful.

"Um . . . yeah, let's get back on track," Mac replied. "First, though, Dom, if you like Gwen, then you have my blessing. She's a very nice woman, and you had better treat her as such. I'm just gonna assume that this sudden BFF thing that you were doing with Ava had something to do with that." Holding up his hand when Dominic would have answered, he added, "Let's just leave it at that. I may have to kill Gage if he makes another comment, and we need to finish this meeting and get back to work."

"I never get any appreciation around here," Gage grumbled as they started going through the assignments for the day.

Mac smothered a grin, thinking how odd it was that all three of them seemed to have some type of woman problems. If misery loved company, then he finally had someone around to share it with. Thing was, though, his misery seemed to be ending while theirs was just beginning. He'd try not to enjoy it too much, since his brothers had been there for him through years of bad moods and moping around. But, damn, he wanted to relish it . . . just a little.

Ava and Emma had been working steadily all morning on a presentation that Ava planned to make to a potential new customer the next day. When they stopped to have a much-needed break and a cup of coffee, Ava attempted to sound casual and said, "So, I stayed the night with Mac last night and I accidentally attacked him this morning."

Emma cursed as she took a big gulp of her hot coffee. "Ugh! Why did you do that to me? Couldn't you have given me some warning before blurting out something like that?" Wiggling her tongue around as if trying to cool it off, she set her cup down and glared at Ava. "Okay, let's try that again."

Ava couldn't control the grin that covered her face at Emma's disgruntled but still overly curious expression. "I stayed the night with Mac, but then had a nightmare this morning and . . . scratched him all up." Shaking her head, she added, "He looked terrible."

Emma's eyes were wide as she said, "Wow! Wait a minute. Am I the first person you've told about this? I'm still pissed that you told Suzy about the first time with Mac. I would have totally dumped your brother for lunch that day had you given me any indication that you had some big news to share. Speaking of . . . was it big—news?"

"Oh my God," Ava groaned, "I can't believe you asked that too! What is it with the women here and their fixation on men's penis sizes?"

"Ah, come on. Half the men here walk around so damn cocky, ha-ha, pun intended, that you want to know if there's something to back that swagger up. Suzy, Claire, Beth, and Ella all swear that their men are packing some serious digits, and it's for damn sure that your brother is . . ."

"Gross! Must all our conversations include something about sex or Brant's body parts? He might be your fiancé and apparently you two go at it like damn horny rabbits, but *he is my brother*! I really don't need to know if he's big, small, or makes your eyes roll back in your head within thirty seconds—just yuck!"

Almost as if Ava hadn't just finished a rant, Emma said, "So you're saying he's big, right?"

Ava picked a folder up from her desk and smacked it against her own forehead several times before dropping it. In a resigned voice she said, "Yes, damn you, he is."

"I knew it! Honey, those cargo pants don't hide anything. Same goes for Dominic and Gage. They might as well be holding up a sign next to their crotch that says XL," Emma joked.

Ava stared at her future sister-in-law and thought, yet again, that her brother had his work cut out for him. Of course, considering that he had always been a complete stuffed shirt, Emma was the best thing to have ever happened to him. "Does Brant know that you stare at the front of every man's pants in this building? Probably in Myrtle Beach as well? I mean, how do you do that without them noticing?"

"I could teach you," Emma offered.

Surprised, Ava asked, "Really? Like how . . . *No*! I don't want to know. Please, let's just change the subject."

Grinning at her slip, Emma said, "Okay, but if you change your mind . . . So, anyway, what happened with the whole bad dream thing this morning? I mean, do you remember what you were dreaming about when you went postal?"

Ava sat back in her chair, flipping a paper clip between her fingers. "Yeah, it was . . . about the guy who raped me. It wasn't like the first time I've dreamed about it, but this was different, more like it was happening now, and I was defending myself. It was still him, though. I was so determined that he wouldn't win this time. I was fighting him with everything I had. Mac finally woke me up by yelling at me to stop and had to keep me from ripping him apart. He . . . he had blood dripping down his face, Em. I let him keep things light afterward, but I seriously wanted to have a huge crying fit knowing that I'd done that to him. I just don't understand why it happened."

All seriousness now, Emma moved to the edge of

her seat, her eyes full of support and sympathy. "It might have scared you, and it most assuredly scared Mac, but I don't think it's that strange, considering what happened to you—"

"I get that," Ava interrupted, "but before when I dreamed about . . . him, it was just flashbacks, bits and pieces of what happened. Never once have I dreamed of fighting back. Of being pissed at what was happening to me. I was always helpless in the other dreams, but this one, I never felt that way. I felt like I could save myself . . . you know, if I just fought hard enough."

"But you've never slept with a man since that happened to you, right?"

Dropping her head to her desk, Ava shook her head. "No, I haven't. God, that was so long ago. It seems pathetic that I've kept myself in some self-imposed prison since then. I mean, I know everyone understood it for a while, but after a few years, I could see the pity in their eyes. They were starting to worry about me. Wondering if I would ever be the same. Both Brant and Declan tried to talk to me, but it was so damn awkward for all of us that eventually we avoided the subject. It's why I created this big bullshit illusion that I was normal again. I couldn't have them and Mac thinking that I was still messed up over the whole thing. I didn't want people feeling sorry for me. After I had the first fake overnighter, things were better. I made sure everyone knew it and I could almost hear their sighs of relief.

"When Mac came back from the military and opened his company, I knew that he kept an eye on me, so I continued doing it. A fake guy every now and again kept him from getting too close. I was too messed up for a real relationship, so it put him at arm's length, but I had our friendship. No pressure, nothing messy to deal with. But he was in my life in some way." Ava had told Emma in one of her weaker moments about her arrangement with the college guys who came over every few months, so the other woman knew well how far she had taken her efforts to appear normal to her friends and family.

"Ava, I believe you've pretty much answered your own question. After all this time, you suddenly have a man in your bed. You've actually let someone close to you without faking it. Your mind is probably scrambling to keep up with all these new developments. I would be more surprised if you *weren't* having some kind of issues adjusting. I mean, it's amazing that you finally realized that you needed to do something before you lost Mac, but maybe that big step has been a little harder than even you've realized." Giving Ava a beaming smile, she added, "I'm proud as hell of you, though. You went after what you wanted and you're living again. Shit, you're as different as night and day from when I first met you."

Curious, Ava asked, "I am? How do you mean?"

Rolling her eyes, Emma said, "Honey, you were always one of two ways. Either really tense or really depressed. There didn't seem to be much middle ground there. I figured that like your brother, you were probably eating antacids by the handful. Even when you were being all bitchy or condescending, I still wanted to give you a hug. Underneath the whole tough exterior, you seemed so sad. I think your brothers, bless their hearts, knew something wasn't right, but in typical male fashion, they just didn't know what to do about it. Now, even after attempting to strangle Mac this morning, you're glowing. You look *happy*."

Ava was deeply touched by Emma's words. Especially since she wasn't used to having heart-to-heart talks with anyone, and she had to admit that it felt good. Maybe if she had had a sister to turn to after her attack, it would have helped her recovery. Emma was right about one thing, though—talking about your feelings to a guy just didn't happen, or at least it hadn't happened for her with her brothers. She'd caught both Declan and Brant looking at her thoughtfully on more than one occasion through the years, but they never gave voice to their thoughts. Having their sister break down in front of them was probably right up there as one of their worst fears. She couldn't really fault them, though. She knew that they loved her and would be there in a minute if she asked. They were good boys who had grown into outstanding men. Blinking back the moisture in her eyes, she said, "Thanks, Em, for everything. For listening to me and putting up with my moods every day. No matter what I say to the contrary, I love working with you and having you in the family."

With a cocky grin, Emma said, "Yeah, I know. You Stones can't resist me. I think it has something to do with my sex appeal."

"Oh God," Ava moaned, "not again."

Chapter Eighteen

When Mac called her just as she was leaving the office, she had been both surprised and delighted by his invitation out to dinner for that evening. He had been at a client site, so their conversation had been brief. He was picking her up at seven and taking her to Ivy, one of her favorite restaurants.

As she stood in her closet, surveying the clothing hanging there, she turned her nose up in disgust until it hit her. The clothes that she had purchased with the girls at the mall were hanging in her spare bedroom. With a girlish squeal of happiness, she tore through her apartment and threw open the door to the closet. She went right to the sexy black cocktail dress that Emma had talked her into buying. It was deceptively simple in design, which only added to its appeal. The slinky material felt amazing against her skin, and the strapless bra that she was wearing pushed the creamy swells of her breasts up against the straight neckline of the dress. She loved the wraparound shoulder straps that flowed so easily into the back of the dress. The formfitting design was classy, but definitely sexy. She paired it with a pair of black Christian Louboutin peep-toe, heeled sandals that she had bought years ago in a moment of feminine weakness but had yet to wear.

When she looked at herself in the mirror, she screamed for a different reason. In her haste to find something to wear, she had completely forgotten that she had just stepped from the shower. She only had ten minutes until Mac arrived, and she knew that he wouldn't be late. She ran to the bathroom and dried her hair as quickly as possible. She had no time left to straighten it. She left it to hang down her back in a wild array of waves. Hopefully, Mac would think the carefree look was intentional. Next, she applied a light base makeup, along with blusher and eyeliner. She had just added a coat of gloss to her lips when her doorbell sounded. Yep, right on time.

She teetered for a moment as she turned quickly on her heels but was able to right herself and continue on to the door. God, she hoped she didn't land on her face tonight in the restaurant. Maybe flats would have been a better option, but these looked so good with the dress. She'd just walk slowly to compensate. Women did it all the time, right?

When she opened the door, both she and Mac gawked at each other. He stood before her looking good enough to eat in a gray suit with a purple silk tie. "Oh, wow," she gasped as her fingers itched to run across the fabric covering his broad shoulders. "You look so . . . awesome." But she swallowed hard at the sight of the scratches still marring his otherwise perfect face.

He stepped inside her entryway, still looking at her in a way that made her toes curl. "Baby, damn, look at you. You're beautiful. I'm not going to be able to think about anything but fucking you tonight." Running his finger down her cleavage, he said, "In fact, maybe we should . . ."

Grabbing his wandering hand in her own, she smirked back at him. "Oh no, Mr. Powers, you promised me dinner." Feeling her cheeks color, she added, "Then afterward, I hope you will . . . because I want you too."

With a growl, he drew her into his arms and locked his mouth on hers. When he pulled back, she had been thoroughly kissed and was completely rattled. She didn't give a damn about dinner at that point and was ready to admit it, when Mac, seeming to know exactly what she was thinking, steered her toward the door with an evil smile.

"Come on, then, let's go get you that dinner that you wanted so much. Remember?"

"Um . . . yeah." Giving him a hopeful look, she said, "We could just order a pizza, though."

He tweaked her nose, laughter rumbling from his broad chest. "I like the way you think, but there is no way I'm letting that dress go to waste. If we stay home, it'll just end up on the floor in less than five minutes. And even though that sounds like heaven, I want to look at you across the table tonight and imagine what I'm going to do to you later. There is nothing like anticipation."

Daringly, Ava ran her hand over his ass, cupping

him firmly before releasing him. "So, this is like a few hours of foreplay, right? I can't wait. Let's go!"

She grinned as she heard Mac mutter, "Fuck," under his breath before taking her hand and walking her out to his SUV.

Ava wasn't sure what had come over her, but she was determined to make Mac regret his decision to skip pizza and go somewhere public. He thought anticipation made things better. Well, she intended to give him more than he could possibly handle. She'd never been the daring type, but something about the dress, the shoes, and the man was a heady mix. Tonight, she felt powerful and sexy and she wanted to spread her wings and fly.

When they were seated in a quiet corner of the upscale restaurant, Ava waited until their server had left the table before scooting her chair closer to Mac's. She had no intention of sitting so far away from him for the next hour. He raised an eyebrow at her but didn't comment on her movement. Mac ordered a bottle of wine, and they both decided on seafood as their main course. He was just lifting his wineglass when she made her first move. She put her hand firmly on his hard thigh, only inches from his crotch. His wineglass tilted alarmingly before she quickly reached out to steady it. Leaning over, she whispered, "You better be careful. You wouldn't want to stain the tablecloth."

When she started rubbing wide circles on his leg, he quickly set his glass back down. Looking adorably rattled, he asked, "Er—baby, what're you doing?"

"Hmm? What do you mean?"

His hand dropped to cover hers, squeezing it lightly. "I mean, what's going on with this hand?"

Giving him a wicked smile, she said, "Ohhh, nothing much. You look so good tonight that I need to be touching some part of you so that I'll know that you're real."

She looked at him in fascination as he appeared to blush. Mac was a gorgeous, hot hunk of man, and she'd always assumed that he was well aware of that fact. Emma was right about one thing: the men at Danvers, Mac included, did have the cocky-walk thing going on. Was it possible that after all the years of her refusing to take their relationship past a friendship, he was insecure about her feelings toward him? Could he actually doubt that she thought he was the most beautiful man she'd ever seen? Had she ever told him that? God, she couldn't remember now. She knew he'd caught her ogling his body on more than one occasion, but she should make sure that he knew, shouldn't she?

Clearing his throat, he said, "I think that should be my line, shouldn't it?"

Taking a deep breath, she locked her eyes with his as she began, "Mac, aside from my brothers, you're the most incredible man I've ever known. I know it's not cool to say, but you're beautiful to me. Handsome just isn't a good enough word to describe you. When you walk into a room, my heart skips a beat and then speeds up to double time. Even when I was scared of my own shadow, I wanted you. You were gorgeous as a teenager, and it's only gotten better. I could sit and stare at you for hours and never grow tired of it. I've never desired anyone but you . . . always you."

She watched the emotions flicker in Mac's expressive eyes as she talked—seeing first surprise, then happiness, followed by desire. "Avie—I," he began just as their server returned with their plates. Ava wanted to turn around and roll her eyes at him for intruding on their intimate moment, but maybe it was for the best. Did she really want to have a heart-to-heart with Mac in the middle of a restaurant? They had all night for that. Right now they could return to their fun, easy flirting and enjoy their meal. This was her first real date, and she didn't want to miss a single moment of it.

Mac had ordered the lobster for himself and suggested she try the shrimp. She speared a juicy morsel on her fork and leaned over to offer it to him. With eyes smoldering, he opened his lips and allowed her to feed him. He closed his teeth on her fork, pulling it playfully before releasing it. When he offered her a bite of his lobster, she made a show of taking the morsel and then flicking her tongue against his fork before releasing it. His eyes were riveted on her mouth as she swallowed the bite. "I'm going to visit with Ella and the baby tomorrow night. Would you like to go with me?" she asked as he finally returned his attention back to his plate.

Nodding in agreement, he said, "Yeah, I'd like that. Declan says that they haven't slept in days. Maybe you and I could manage to hold the fort down while they take a nap. Do you know anything about babies?"

Alarmed, Ava shook her head frantically. "The only

thing I know is that you're supposed to give them back immediately if they start crying or smelling funny."

Mac chuckled. "Yeah, that's been my experience too. Aren't they supposed to mostly sleep at first, though?"

"I have no idea," Ava admitted. "Maybe we should Google it."

Taking a sip of his wine, Mac said, "Here's what we'll do. If the baby is asleep, and I mean really out of it, we offer to give them an hour to sleep. If she's awake or sleeping, but restless, then we keep our mouths shut. I feel bad about it, but they'd probably rather lose some sleep than have us mess the kid up."

Beaming her approval at Mac's logic, Ava agreed with him. "That's a good idea. We also need to find out how much mileage she has on the diaper she's wearing first. If the time's almost up and she's due for a change, then she might suddenly wake up freaking out."

"And the milk thing," Mac added, "don't forget that. They suddenly start raising holy hell when it's time to eat again. Shit, there's a lot to consider here, isn't there?"

"Maybe I could make a checklist before we go in?" Ava suggested. "That way we don't forget anything. We could get in there, get scared, and forget to ask some important questions."

Mac lifted a hand, clicking his finger at her. "Good idea, baby. We're likely to freeze up under pressure. Let's go through the whole list in the car right before we go in. That way we'll at least remember to cover the important points. And there's no shame in just backing down if we're not sure, agreed?"

Ava raised her glass and clicked it against his. "Absolutely. Sounds like a plan." Having finished her meal, she let her hand return to his thigh. She knew she shouldn't, as she'd never done anything like it before, but she couldn't resist. In a way, this was like a sexual milestone, and she wanted to reach it. Her hand moved upward and covered the bulge in his pants. His eyes widened and his leg jerked, causing the china on the table to shake. Oops, had she grabbed him a little too hard? Had he flinched in pain or pleasure? Biting her lip, she looked at him in concern, wondering if she had messed up her foray into public groping. Crap, according to *Cosmopolitan*, there was no such thing as a wrong touch where a man's penis was concerned. She was still a little unsure of the whole ball-tugging thing, though, and she didn't think that was possible to do while he was wearing pants anyway. She had planned to save that move for later on. "Um . . . did I hurt you?" she asked, feeling embarrassed.

Mac coughed, looking as if someone were squeezing his windpipe. "Avie . . . you know you're holding my cock, right?" he wheezed out.

She flexed her hand, marveling in the fact that he felt much bigger than he had just a minute ago. "Yes, I know. Is it okay? Am I holding Mr. Wood too tight or not tight enough?" Oh God, she was doing something wrong. His eyes looked ready to pop out of his head and his face was almost purple.

As she started to pull her hand away, he clamped down on it, holding it in place. "Mr. Wood?" he asked, sounding strained.

Ava sagged in her seat, completely disappointed. She'd done everything that the magazine suggested to seduce her man during dinner. She had flirted, touched his penis, and even given it one of the manly names that they had suggested. Nothing seemed to be working, though. Instead of looking madly aroused and ready to throw her across the table, he looked as if he was just seconds away from passing out. As tears of disappointment threatened, she whispered, "I'm a complete failure at this, aren't I? I guess you can't be taught how to be fun and sexy, because it's not working for me. I'm more like the antidote to all that. I'm sorry, Mac. I tried."

Mac looked horrified as a lone tear slid down her cheek. Reaching out to brush it away, he cupped her face in his hand. "Oh, baby, I have no idea where all this is coming from, but you just surprised me, is all. You don't have to try to be any of those things. To me you're already all of them and more." Lowering his voice, he moved the other hand that was holding hers against his cock and pushed firmly down. "I get hard just being near you. I panicked when you touched me because I knew I was dangerously close to coming in my pants for the first time in my life. You have no idea how your touch, your smell—everything about you affects me. I lose what little sophistication I've acquired through the years, and I'm back to being nothing but an out-of-control, horny teenager."

Feeling a flicker of hope, Ava asked, "Really? I do that to you—for you?"

As he grew even bigger under her hand, he lifted an

eyebrow, saying, "You don't have to take my word for it, Avie. That's all for you . . . that's what you do to me." She beamed at him, thrilled to feel the evidence of his attraction to her. Chuckling, he added, "One thing, though . . . where did you come up with the name Mr. Wood?"

Ava started giggling, now seeing the humor in her hasty attempt at seduction. Maybe she should have left that step until later as well. "Since I don't really have any experience—you know, with men—I've been reading a lot of magazines," she admitted. "That was supposed to be something like a bedroom secret that was just between us. I guess some men call their . . . penises wood, like morning wood, and since you're male, I added the Mr. part." Grimacing, she asked, "Do you hate it? We don't have to use a name if you don't want to."

"Baby, you can call my cock anything you want to as long it doesn't have the words *small*, *little*, *cute*, or *sweet* in it." He gently removed her hand from his lap and flagged down their server. Giving her a look that had her clenching her thighs together, he said, "I wanted to make this a great first date for you, but we've got to go home or we'll be doing something in here that'll probably get us locked up."

Mac grabbed the check from the server's hand and hastily threw a stack of bills on the table. They left the restaurant in what was just shy of a run. He paced as they waited for his SUV to be brought around. Ava thought they both breathed an audible sigh of relief when the doors were closed behind them and they set off toward Mac's house.

As he drove with one hand on the wheel, he used his other arm to push the material of her dress up. Soon, she felt an embarrassing flood of wetness gather between her legs. "Mac . . . ," she moaned, unable to hide the desire racing through her body.

Never taking his eyes from the road, he shifted his hand to rest against the thin silk of her panties. She knew that he could feel the moisture soaking through the material, but she was past caring. When he pushed harder, pressing against her throbbing clit, she threw her head back, needing a release from the pressure building inside her. She moved her hips restlessly, wanting more. "That's right, baby," he rasped, "ride my hand."

With those words, she lost her inhibitions. Moving her panties to the side, she pulled his hand into her damp folds and sighed in bliss when he immediately started stroking her there. "Touch me, Mac," she pleaded, needing more of what he could give her.

"I am touching you, baby," he said as he flicked her sensitive nub.

"More," she begged.

When he continued to circle her aching flesh, she planted her feet on the floor, groaning in frustration.

"Still not what you want, Avie? Tell me . . . give me the words, and I'll make it happen," he prodded, giving her nothing but maddening strokes.

Finally, she snapped, needing her release as she needed to breathe. "Put your finger inside me, Mac, now!" When he immediately thrust one of his large digits inside her wet heat, she almost wept with relief.

It felt so good. "More . . . please more." He pushed a second finger inside her, and that was it. She was free-falling, spasms racking her body as she screamed his name. She had no idea how Mac kept the car on the road as she yelled like a wild woman in the seat beside him.

She had barely come back down to earth when the car stopped, her seat belt was suddenly popping open, and she was jerked from her seat and tossed over a hard shoulder. "Can't be slow, baby," Mac grunted as he took the steps two at a time, jostling her against his back. She gripped the ass that she admired so much and held on before finding herself lying half off Mac's kitchen table with her ass in the air. Her panties were ripped from her body and in the next second all the air whooshed from her as Mac slammed home from behind. "Fucking hell!" he shouted as he pounded into her.

The feeling was building again. After her release in the car, she didn't think it was possible, but Mac was fucking her toward another orgasm, and God, she wanted it now. Pushing her hips back to meet his wild thrusts, she took him to the hilt, grinding against the root of him. "Ahhh yesss!" she screamed as her body started to spasm around his length. Only his hands on her hips kept her upright as he continued to thrust until he found his own release.

Afterward, neither of them was capable of moving for several minutes. Mac lay slumped against her back, their hearts racing in unison. "That was completely insane," he gasped against her ear. She was surprised to feel his hand tremble as he pushed her hair aside to kiss her neck. "Want a shower if I can manage to get us there?" Ava nodded her agreement, and then shrieked in surprise when he swung her up in his arms. "Just one of the amenities offered here at Casa Powers, Miss Stone."

Trailing her fingertips over his muscular chest, she asked, "And what are the other amenities?"

Giving her a wink that made her heart pound, he said, "Anything for you, baby. You name it and it's yours."

"Hmm." She pretended to mull over her request. "Do you scrub backs?"

With a wolfish grin he said, "Damn straight and I also do fronts."

Her tired body protested as her libido sprang to life at his statement. "No," she moaned. Pointing down to his semierect cock, she added, "You are officially banned from my hoo-ha for at least eight hours. Snuggling is all we have left for tonight, mister."

Mac bellowed with laughter. "Don't worry, sweetheart. I'm not going to drop you, and I promise to stay away from your whatever the hell you called it for a while. You don't mind if I think about it, though, do you?"

Waving a hand in a grand gesture, she said, "Oh no, be my guest. Thoughts are free. Now, how about that back scrub?"

True to his word, Mac pampered her by washing not only her back, but her entire body along with her hair. When they were finished, he rubbed her down with a towel before drying her hair and finding one of his T-shirts for her to wear. He then pulled on a pair of low-slung shorts for himself.

The shower had revived her somewhat and she found herself wide-awake as she lay in the bed surrounded by Mac's arms. If she was honest with herself, she would admit that she was almost afraid to go to sleep. What if she had another nightmare? She knew that to a big man like Mac, her attack on him was probably the equivalent of a bunny attacking a tiger, but still, his gorgeous face and chest were riddled with signs of her dream freak-out. Ever perceptive to her moods, he seemed to feel her tense up on him. Rubbing a hand over her stomach, he said, "It's going to be fine, Avie. Never be afraid to go to sleep in my arms. I'll always be here to catch you if you need it."

She twined her fingers with his, pulling them up to kiss his hand. "I can't stand the thought of hurting you. Maybe I should sleep in the spare room, just to see if it happens—"

Before she could finish her sentence, Mac cut her off. "No way. Not going to happen. If you're in my house, then you're in my bed. Same goes for your place. I don't care if you put me in a headlock and kick me in the balls, we sleep together. Try to keep the fighting above the belt, though, if possible."

Ava giggled, elbowing him in the ribs. No matter what, Mac found a way to inject some humor into things when she got too serious. "Maybe you should be wearing a cup or something."

"It's a thought." He chuckled. They lay there in silence for a few moments before he said, "Can I ask you something, babe?"

She was surprised and wary to hear the sudden serious tone of his voice. "Did you ever talk to anyone . . . I mean, professionally . . . after that happened to you?"

When she tried to pull away, he pulled her tight against him. "Why?" she asked.

He seemed to understand her question even though she hadn't elaborated. "If you haven't, baby, you've been carrying a lot on your shoulders for a long time. Maybe the sudden dreams are your mind's way of telling you that you need someone to listen."

"So now I'm crazy," she snapped, pissed that he was analyzing her. She knew this would happen if he knew that she wasn't normal. All those years and all those deliberate acts to deceive him into believing she was okay were wasted. Now he knew she was messed up.

Blowing out an exasperated breath, he shook her lightly. "No, damn it, that's not what I'm saying. Fuck, baby, do you have any idea how much finding you broken on my doorstep messed me up? I had dreams about it for years. I could barely function for months afterward. It tore me to pieces, Avie, and it wasn't even me that it happened to! Why do you think I packed my shit and followed your brother into the damn marines?"

Breaking his hold on her, she whirled around, trying to see his face in the darkness of the room. "What? Mac—no!"

He ran a hand through his hair, gripping the ends as if he wanted to pull it from his scalp. Ava reached over and turned on the lamp, bathing the room in a soft glow. She needed to see his face, needed to understand what he was saying. "Shit, I'm not telling you this to make you feel guilty. You were the victim, not me. I just . . . I couldn't get it out of my head. I still have a hard time dealing with it. The only reason I'm admitting this to you is to show you that there is no need to pretend with me. I understand how bad it was, maybe better than maybe anyone else. I know that trying to file something like that away without acknowledging it will eat you alive. It's a testament to how strong you are that you've not only made it but excelled despite it."

Sitting back on her heels, she whispered, "But I haven't, Mac. I've loved you for most of my life, yet I kept pushing you away and doing crazy stuff to show you that I was perfectly normal and functioning instead of admitting that I didn't know how to be what you needed. As soon as my grandfather got me home that night, he drummed into me that I needed to forget I was raped. No, actually, he never used that word at all. He called it an incident. It was as if he were talking about something as simple as a fender bender or a speeding ticket. That 'incident' he said would just embarrass me and the family and nothing would be done to the boy who did it anyway. I think he actually believed that he was doing me a favor by just making the whole thing go away. The boy who raped me got a free ride out of town with his family and that was that. You know, maybe the worst part was the aftermath. My grandfather never looked me in the eye again after that. I just tried to make myself invisible while he was around."

"Oh, baby." Mac rubbed her leg gently. "I'm so sorry he didn't stand up for you. He was always a cold man. For so long neither my parents nor I could figure out how in the hell everything had just been swept under the rug. I wanted to come to you, but you disappeared from my life. Before, I saw you almost every day, but afterward, no matter how many times I came over or hung around in your favorite spots, you were never there. You went from being the girl I had spent the last few years waiting to grow up to the haunted woman that I couldn't get out of my head or my heart. I've loved you for most of my life, and I've never known how to live without you, Avie—I never wanted to. I just didn't know how to reach you after that. When Declan decided to join the military, I figured maybe it was better for you and me both if I did something like that as well. There wasn't a day that you weren't right there with me, though.

"When I got out and we started spending time together again, I thought maybe our moment had finally arrived, but you gave no indications that you felt anything for me other than friendship. Even though you never had a regular man in your life, you seemed to be functioning okay, so I had to accept after a while that it was just me, that you didn't feel for me what I always felt for you. I tried to let you go, so many times I tried, but it always came back to you . . . always."

Ava launched herself into his arms, wrapping her legs around his waist. "I love you, Mac. You've been the only man in my life since I was old enough to have my first crush. I'm so sorry for what loving me has put you through. I . . . I was scared for so long. Even if I didn't show it, loving you was all that got me through those lonely years. I wanted to be better . . . to be normal so that I could be someone who you deserved. When you left me for Gwen, I just couldn't let you go." Grimacing, she added, "I have the scars to prove it."

"Oh, Avie." Mac put his hand on the back of her neck, keeping her eyes locked with his. "I love you too, baby. You're the only woman, well, aside from my mother, who has ever heard those words from me. I'm sorry if my decision to date Gwen hurt you. I didn't think you were ever going to return my feelings, and I know now that I was just trying to numb the pain. I hate like hell that I hurt both you and Gwen in the process. I want you to know that Gwen and I . . . we never had sex." He looked at her intently. "I haven't been a saint, baby, but I think that I knew even before I acknowledged it to myself that I couldn't have a real relationship unless it was with you."

"I love you," she whispered as she stroked his cheek. "Being here with you makes me feel safe, like no one could ever hurt me again."

"Avie, I've kept a watch on the bastard who attacked you for years, and he hasn't so much as crossed the South Carolina line. You don't have to be afraid of him anymore."

"He told me that if I ever told anyone about what happened, he would come for me. I think that was one reason why I let my grandfather make it go away. I was scared that he meant it. But after a while, I started worrying about him doing that to someone else. What if by me being a coward, I let the same thing happen again? I don't think I could ever forgive myself. Have you . . . heard anything about him?"

Ava thought it was strange that Mac suddenly seemed uncomfortable with their conversation. Maybe it bothered him to talk about what had happened to her. It had certainly been an emotional evening for both of them. So she let him pull her closer and gather her up in his arms.

She also knew that if Mac knew something he would have told her immediately. Sinking into his chest, she refused to give another moment of their time together to the monster who had ruined so much of her life. As Mac settled in bed behind her, she didn't notice that he'd never answered her question.

Chapter Nineteen

"Wow, who are all these people?" Ava asked as she looked at the cars parked in her brother's driveway.

"I recognize Jason's and Gray's cars. I believe that's Brant's. Did Emma mention coming over tonight?"

Shrugging, Ava said, "I barely saw her today. I had meetings all morning, and she was helping Brant this afternoon since his assistant quit."

Mac chuckled, shaking his head. "So another one of Brant's assistants bites the dust, huh? I thought he was a little more relaxed now that he has Emma."

"Oh, come on." Ava laughed. "How relaxed do you think it's possible for Brant to be? Of course, from the huge amount of oversharing I get from Emma on a daily basis about her and Brant, the poor thing probably walked in on them having sex on Brant's desk."

"Ain't nothing wrong with that, baby." Mac smirked, wiggling an eyebrow. "I've had a few thoughts of you on my desk as well. Like at least once an hour."

Ava stuck her bottom lip out in a pout. "Only once an hour? I must be doing something wrong."

Mac gave her a sexy smile in return, running his

hand up her leg. "Honey, you're doing everything right, but Dom and Gage might get the wrong idea if I walked around with a boner all day."

Ava felt her face flush, still not used to sexy word-play with Mac. It might embarrass her a bit, but damn, it felt so good. Just being with him made everything almost effortless. She didn't feel the need to disappear into her surroundings or walk with her head down. She wanted to embrace life, and she actually looked forward to each new day instead of dreading it. All because of the man beside her. Instead of making a teasing reply, she said simply, "I love you, Mac."

All at once, the smirk left his face, and his eyes seemed to glow. Even without his next words, she could see the love he had for her. "I love you too, baby. You don't know how long I've dreamed of that. Of hearing you say those words without prompting or hesitation."

After pressing a soft kiss on his mouth, she gently brushed the hint of lipstick that she had left behind on his soft lips. "I always thought them to myself when we were together. I'm just sorry it took me so long to say them out loud."

Mac had started to pull her across the seat and into his lap when a loud knock on the window brought their heads up. Emma stood at Mac's window with her face pressed against the glass. "All right, kids, we've been waiting on you to get out of the car for ages. Either you get out now or I'm hitting the video button on my phone and posting it on Facebook!"

"Oh my God," Ava moaned, mortified to see Brant

standing behind Emma looking decidedly uncomfortable. Beside her, Mac chuckled as if he found the whole incident highly amusing.

"Come on, baby, I don't want to star in the next viral video. We'd better go." Ava opened her door and walked around the Tahoe to take Mac's proffered hand.

One good thing about all the people gathered here was that it took the pressure off them to offer to babysit. Apparently, this time they wouldn't need to run through their checklist before offering their services. Emma walked up to her and threw an arm around her shoulders, effectively pulling her away from Mac. "So, what exactly was going on in that vehicle? I tried to get your brother to keep quiet so I could watch, but I guess the whole watching-your-sister-make-out thing is a bit weird."

"No, really?" Ava said sarcastically.

"I know, go figure." Emma laughed.

When they rang the doorbell, Suzy pulled it open, doing a little dance in place. "Hey, skinny, skanky skank!"

Emma turned to her, hands on hips, and asked, "She is talking to you, right?"

With her voice lower than Suzy's booming one, Ava replied in kind, "Hey, whore queen!"

Emma, finally realizing that they were joking about all the names that Ella had called them while she was in labor, doubled over laughing.

Mac gave her a questioning look as he came up behind her. "You women are a little rough on each other, aren't you?"

Ava knew by the pink of Ella's cheeks when she walked over to greet them that she had heard Suzy. "I can't believe I called you guys those names," she moaned, dropping her head in her hands. "I even told Declan that I was going to cut off his penis and stick it in a paper shredder. I swear he held his hand over his pecker the whole time I was in labor! Even worse, when my parents came back to see me, my mom was lecturing me about using bad language, and I told her not to let the door hit that stick in her ass on the way out!"

That was it. Everyone collapsed back against the wall laughing over what Suzy dubbed the "labor and delivery: bitch edition." As they were all trying to compose themselves, Declan walked over carrying the new Stone family addition. Little Sofia Grace seemed to be staring out at them from her daddy's arms in fascination. In truth, Ella said that she couldn't actually see much other than shapes yet. Considering their earlier conversation, Ava hoped she couldn't hear or decipher words either.

Ava was busy grinning like a besotted aunt when Declan plopped the baby in her arms and within ten seconds, both he and Ella had disappeared. "Oh crap." She looked around in alarm.

Suzy held her hands up, walking backward. "Yeah, you're on your own. Hermie has already wiped his nose on my shoulder, and Chrissy stuck her dirty little hands on my butt. I've had my quota for tonight." With those words, she took off toward Gray, walking into his arms and never looking back.

Looking helplessly at Mac, she asked, "Where did everyone go? We had a plan to cover this, but I thought we were safe with all these people here."

Rubbing her arm lightly, Mac said, "You're doing fine, Avie." Pointing to where she held a hand under the baby's bottom, he added, "If you feel any action down there, though, we need to hand off and run."

Suddenly, she could see herself in this same setting with Mac, holding a baby that they had made together. What would it be like to carry Mac's child—to have something that was a part of them both? She had never thought it would happen for her, but now she felt a small flutter of hope that she could have all that with him. From the sexy, sappy look that he was giving her, she knew she wasn't the only one thinking of their future.

When Jason and Claire walked up, Jason gave her that signature grin of his that never failed to turn her into a fumbling idiot. It wasn't that she wanted Jason; it was just that he had so much charisma and didn't seem to know it. "That looks good on you," he said, pointing at Sofia. Luckily, Mac struck up a conversation with Jason, leaving her and Claire to chat.

"Looks like things are going well between you and Mac," Claire whispered. "So, G-lo . . . crap, I mean Gwen is officially out of the picture, I hear?"

Ava couldn't suppress her giggle at Claire's slip. They would probably always know Gwen as G-lo. Maybe the other woman would even be okay with it if she knew how they all envied her booty. "Yeah, it's going well." She'd never had many personal conversations with Claire, but she found herself admitting, "We've even exchanged 'I love you.'"

Both Jason and Mac looked over at them when Claire let out a squeal before clamping a hand over her mouth. "Oops, but wow! Oh, Ava, that's wonderful. I remember the first time Jason and I said that to each other. I'm so happy for you. So, no more stunts to get his attention now?"

Ava grinned. "Oh, I don't know about that. I've found that I like experiencing new things after all this time. Mac will just have to learn to handle someone who likes to do crazy stuff sometimes."

"Good for you," Claire murmured. "I drive Jason nuts half the time. You know what a geek the man is. He likes for things to fit in neat little compartments, and he is constantly ruffled because I don't." Nudging her with her elbow, she added, "He likes to take all his frustrations out in the bedroom, though, so it works *really* well for both of us."

Ogling Mac's ass for a second longer than was acceptable in mixed company, Ava said, "I know exactly what you mean." Both she and Claire had huge smirks on their faces when the men walked back to their sides. Mac and Jason shook their heads but didn't bother to ask questions. Ava was sure that they didn't want to know.

Unbelievably, she hogged baby Sofia for the rest of the evening, even braving a diaper change, which thankfully was strictly pee. When it was time to leave, she found herself volunteering them to babysit one evening soon so Declan and Ella could have a meal out.

Mac looked at her as if she were crazy, but the baby bug had officially bitten her.

They had been back at Mac's house for a few minutes when he got a call from Gage. There had been a break-in at one of the buildings where they handled security, and even though the police had the situation under control, Mac needed to go double-check that the building was secure for the night. "I shouldn't be more than a couple of hours," he said as he grabbed his keys.

She thought about going home, but if she were going to be alone, she would rather be at Mac's house. Going back to her lonely apartment didn't hold much appeal. "Be careful," she said as she kissed Mac good-bye and said she'd see him when he returned.

An hour later, she had already showered and changed into one of Mac's T-shirts. She didn't want to go to sleep without him, so she wandered his house restlessly. When she came to his office, she decided to do what half the world did when they were bored, play Candy Crush. Mac had given her the password to his computer, so she curled up in his big leather chair and logged on. She smiled at how organized his desk was. Everything was neatly filed and labeled. You could take the boy out of the military but not the military out of the boy. Idly, she opened the desk drawers, laughing as she noted that his organizational skills extended there as well. She was just shutting the last drawer when a label on a folder caught her attention. AVA STONE. "What the hell . . . ?" she mumbled as she pulled the folder out.

As Ava thumbed through the list of reports, she wasn't really surprised. She knew that Mac had kept an eye on her for years. Maybe she thought that it was more informal than these written reports proved, but she understood where his protective instinct for her had come from. The file didn't contain a report on every man she had brought home over the years, but it was a good-sized list. The whole folder was a mirage. Now she thought of how Mac must have felt when he had these pages sitting in front of him in black-and-white. For the first time, she truthfully acknowledged to herself how much she had needed help to heal and how even though she was better, she still needed support to continue the process. She couldn't go back to the pretend life she had been living.

She was almost to the end of the folder when she found an envelope. Her name was handwritten with her address listed as in care of Brant Stone. The return address showed a location in New York. She didn't know anyone there, so she was truly puzzled as to who would be trying to contact her. Ava pulled a single sheet of paper from the envelope and felt the breath leave her body in a startled gasp as she read the first line.

Ava,

I know that I'm not supposed to have any contact with you, but I couldn't continue to live my life as though nothing ever happened. You are the only victim here, but that night and what I did to you has haunted me since I was sober enough the next day to realize what had happened. You may not believe me, but I wanted to turn myself into the police. My parents and your grandfather wouldn't hear of it, though. Your grandfather made all manner of threats to my parents if they didn't take me and leave town immediately. He said that you didn't want me to humiliate you further by contacting the police. I have no idea if that was true, but I had little choice but to do as my parents wanted.

For weeks, I had been drinking more and mixing it with any type of drugs that I could get my hands on. But that night I had too much of both. Something about the combination made me so angry and aggressive. When you said no . . . I just snapped. I had no real concept of what I was even doing. When I realized what I'd done to you, it almost destroyed me. Ava, there is no excuse that I can make, or no way to apologize enough, but I am so very sorry for what I did to you. Not a day has gone by in my life that I haven't regretted what happened that night. I'm not writing this expecting your forgiveness; I just needed you to know that as meaningless as it may be to you now, I'm sorry.

Kevin

Ava sagged in the chair, letting the letter flutter from her nerveless fingers. Turning the envelope over, she saw that it was postmarked four years earlier. "Oh my God," she whispered as her head whirled and her stomach clenched. Why had no one ever told her about this? There were at least two people who knew, Brant and Mac. She would bet that Declan did as well. Her brother had to have given the letter to Mac. Operating on pure adrenaline, she picked the letter up and ran to the door before realizing that she didn't have her car. Running back into the kitchen, she found the box near the back door and easily located the keys to Mac's truck that he rarely used. She had teased him for years about men in the South always having a truck, even if they didn't drive it often. Declan was the same way.

Accessing the garage by way of the kitchen, Ava stopped only to hit the opener mounted on the wall before climbing up into the truck. Within moments, she was speeding toward Brant's house. Her mind was buzzing with questions, and she planned to get some answers. How could they have kept something like this from her? Kevin hadn't gone into much detail about what had happened afterward, but she had a feeling that Brant knew, and she was tired of being in the dark.

It was almost eleven by the time she pulled into his driveway. She was glad to see a light glowing in the living room window. She pounded on the door several times before her disheveled brother pulled it open, blinking in surprise. "Ava . . . is something wrong?"

She pushed him aside, stalking into the entryway. A sleepy-looking Emma rounded the corner, blinking at her in shock. "Ava?"

Without answering, Ava held the envelope in Brant's face and watched him pale as he realized what she was holding. "Why am I just finding out about this?" she demanded.

Instead of answering her question, he asked one of his own. "Where did you get that?"

Ava felt as if steam were literally shooting from her ears. "That's all you've got? Where did I get the letter that you never bothered to give me? Why would Mac have this and not me?" she snapped.

Brant was nothing if not a smart man, and she could see the exact moment that he decided to try to placate her. "Av, it's not a big deal, really. I don't know why Mac would give that to you now, but it's been years since I received it."

That was so the wrong answer, and she was seconds away from blowing up when Emma stepped between them, clearly confused as to what was playing out before her. "All right, everyone in their separate corners. I have no idea what's going on here, but I think we need to talk about it somewhere else." Before Ava could reply, Emma had pulled her farther into the entryway and motioned for Brant to shut the door behind him. Apparently, Brant had been too rattled to realize that the door was still standing open. Emma ushered her into the living room and Brant followed warily behind them. "Okay, so what's in that letter you're waving around?" Emma asked while looking back and forth between Ava and Brant.

Instead of answering, Ava simply handed the envelope to Emma and watched as the other woman extracted the paper and read it. When she was finished, she handed it back to Ava, again without saying a word. Finally, Brant, never being one to enjoy strife, spoke up. "Ava, I didn't give you that letter because I didn't want you to be hurt again. You had moved on with your life and were doing so well. I was afraid it would bring back a lot of bad memories that you didn't need."

Ava stared at her normally intuitive brother, utterly amazed that he too had fallen for her smokescreen. Had he never once seen the cracks in her veneer? Dropping onto the leather chair behind her, Ava shook her head, trying to hold back tears. "But that's just it, Brant. I wasn't doing well. I haven't even been in the same zip code as what you'd consider doing well."

Brant looked alarmed by her statement, and he started to pace in his agitation. One of the things she loved about her brother was his desire to fix everything. If there was a problem, he didn't rest until he found a solution. She could see him trying to work through her statement in his head and figure out what he could do to make it all better. The problem was that he didn't fully comprehend what she was telling him. "But . . . you work, you date, you have friends. I don't understand."

Emma laid a hand on her shoulder, giving it a gentle squeeze as she said, "Tell him the truth, Ava. I think you both need it." Emma released her and then stepped over to kiss Brant on the cheek before leaving the room.

Patting the chair next to hers, Ava said, "Sit down, Brant. I think we need to talk, and I'd rather do it without you pacing."

Brant looked as though he wanted to argue but instead took the chair that she had indicated. "Tell me what I've missed with you, Ava," he said quietly.

Ava took a deep breath, knowing that this was going to be hard on both of them. She and Brant didn't really have heart-to-heart conversations about their feelings or personal life, so this was awkward, but she needed him to know. "I've had a hard time living a normal life since my . . . rape." She saw the flinch that Brant was unable to hide at her words, but he kept quiet, letting her continue. "At first, I just buried it all deep inside because that's what I was ordered to do by Granddad. I was too scared and ashamed to talk to anyone about it anyway.

"Granddad made me feel like it was all my fault and that was why we couldn't tell the police the truth. He made sure he let me know how humiliated I would be if our friends and family found out. I felt so dirty, like I was responsible for what happened to me.

"For years, I buried it away as best I could and learned to pretend that it never happened. As I started getting older, it became harder. I knew that people were beginning to wonder why I never dated or had a man in my life." When Brant shifted uncomfortably, Ava realized that Brant had had similar thoughts. "So I went to a bar in hopes of meeting a man I felt safe enough around to spend time with. Without going into many details, I met a college student instead who was sweet and felt sorry for me. He was also broke and in need of spending money, as were his friends. Before long, I had a steady line of young men who were more than willing to spend a few hours with me when I needed them. They worked around my apartment, making repairs or if nothing needed fixing, we watched a movie or played a game. It worked out perfectly. Everyone, including Mac, thought I was functioning normally, and hey, I even got my sink drains fixed anytime I needed it," Ava joked weakly.

Running a hand through his hair, Brant said, "But . . . why? Ava, I'm missing something here. I was ready to kill that little fucker Kevin for what he did to you, but Grandfather told me to leave it alone. He said that you never wanted it mentioned again and if I insisted on having Kevin thrown in jail, it would ruin your life. He insisted that I honor your wishes and leave it alone. Ava, I was so sick over the whole thing, but I finally agreed to do what you wanted even though I damn well knew it wasn't right. He said it was your idea to have Kevin and his family leave because you didn't want to face any of it."

Dropping her head into her hands, Ava simply shook her head. "It wasn't, Brant. God, I was only a scared kid. I was too traumatized to know what to do. I sure wasn't in any shape to broker a deal with Grand-dad to salvage my good name. He made me feel so guilty over being attacked that I couldn't look at you or Declan. And as for Mac, it changed everything there. I had loved him for most of my life, but after that, I never considered myself good enough for him again. As I got older, I couldn't resist the draw of being near him but only on my terms. I couldn't let him see how broken I was. I didn't want him remembering the way I looked that night when I crawled onto his porch and collapsed against his door."

"But Mac has always loved you, Av," Brant added. "There's never been anyone else for him; he's never made a secret of that."

Smiling through her tears, Ava admitted, "I know that now. I think I always knew that he loved me, but I couldn't accept it. I didn't know how to be loved by him."

"Oh, Ava," Brant sighed, looking destroyed. "I never knew what you were going through. Sometimes you would say things or just have a certain look on your face and I would think to myself that I needed to see if you were okay. But then I would see you again and you would seem perfectly normal. My mind would always go back to what Grandfather told me. That you didn't want to talk about what had happened and I had to respect your wishes. So I did . . . for years. Now I feel like an unfeeling, uncaring bastard."

"Brant, don't," she began before he held up a hand to stop her.

"It's true, Av. Maybe I just didn't want to acknowledge what was right in front of me. Let's face it, I've never been good at dealing with anyone's feelings, and I certainly had no idea how to handle something like that happening to my baby sister. It's no excuse at all, but I had no clue how to help you. I'm so sorry that I wasn't a better brother and protector to you."

Ava took her brother's hand, squeezing it tightly. "Stop, Brant. I'm not telling you this to heap guilt on your head. I became such an expert at pretending to be okay that I can't blame people for believing it. You and I both know that I'm a hell of a saleswoman, and I applied that same principle to my personal life. I sold everyone, even myself at times, on the illusion that I was fully recovered from what happened to me and that I

was living my life. The scary part is that I don't know
how long I would have continued to do that if not for
Mac shaking me up. If he hadn't decided to move on
with his life, I might never have been brave enough to
admit that I needed and loved him."

"I should have seen through it, though," Brant agonized. "You're my sister, and damn it, deep down inside, I knew you weren't okay!"

A part of her wanted to be mad at Brant for wanting
to avoid talking with her all these years about her rape,
but would it have changed anything really? Most likely
she would have brushed him off completely had he
tried or given him a bunch of false reassurances. If she
harbored ill will toward anyone, it was their grandfather. He had been her authority figure back then and
had been the one to make her feel as if she needed to
pretend that nothing had ever happened. She, Brant,
and Declan had just taken their cues from him. He
wanted it all to go away, and that was what had happened, at least on the surface. No matter how hard it
would have been for them to handle, she knew now
that if she had told either of her brothers that she was
drowning, barely keeping her head above water most
days, they would have dropped everything to help her.
But she hadn't, and they had accepted her facade as
truth.

"We did as we were told," she whispered. "I just
wish you had given me Kevin's letter years ago when
you received it."

Brant jumped to his feet, a pulse ticking visibly in his
jaw. "Why? His apology means nothing, Av. I didn't

want to upset you over something that was completely inadequate. An apology doesn't make what he did to you okay. The only reason I kept the damn thing and passed it along to Mac was that I was afraid he would try to contact you in another way when he didn't receive a reply. I asked Mac to keep track of him, so I wanted him to be aware."

Stung again by Brant's decision to keep the letter from her, Ava took a deep breath, trying to remain calm. "No, the apology from Kevin wouldn't have made what he did all right, but the rest of the letter would have helped me in a way." Looking down at her hands, she admitted, "I've always wondered if it was my fault. You know, did I lead him on or give him the impression that I wanted what happened? I've run through that night in my head over and over. When Granddad refused to let the police handle it, I felt like I was guilty. It made me feel dirty, as if I had somehow done something to make Kevin believe that we would have sex. But in the letter, he said that he had been drinking and doing drugs. He said he was so out of it that he didn't know what he was doing that night. He took the full blame for his actions instead of trying to put it back onto me."

Brant wilted back into the chair next to hers looking spent. "I just . . . I never thought that maybe you needed to hear what he had to say. In my eyes, there was never a question that any woman would be to blame for something like that happening to her. But I should have thought, with the way things were handled, that you might need any type of closure that you could get. Fuck, Av, I'm so sorry. You're right; I should never have kept that from you. At the time, I thought I was protecting you, but now I see that I was just continuing to believe everything was just perfectly fine when the proof that it wasn't was right under my nose."

Ava stood, moving to Brant's side. Then she did something that she didn't do nearly enough; she wrapped her arms around her brother and held on tight. After a brief moment of hesitation, Brant pulled her into his arms, nearly squeezing the breath out of her. He murmured his apology against the top of her head before kissing her gently on the temple. "I love you, my overbearing brother," she joked to lighten the mood.

His eyes looked suspiciously moist as he replied, "I love you too, sis." When she pulled back and returned to her own chair, he gave her a crooked grin. "So, you and Mac . . . finally?"

The usual feelings of heat raced through her body as she thought of the man she loved and how she finally had a chance of a real future with him. Alongside those feelings was also anger that he too had kept Kevin's letter from her. Even though he had to know from their recent conversations that the information it contained would have helped her to have at least a shred of resolution to the trauma. It also made her wonder if he had been keeping anything else from her for what he thought was her own good. Brant felt so guilty about the letter that he would have confessed already if he was aware of anything else concerning Kevin. She gave

Brant a rueful smile, admitting honestly, "Mac and I have some things to discuss. We do love each other, but it can only work if we're equal partners in our relationship. I can't be the woman who he's always trying to save anymore."

"Av, don't be mad at him over this. Declan and I have depended on him for far too long to watch over you, something we should have been doing ourselves. He's loved you since we were all kids, and in a way, what happened to you hit him hardest of all. I think he always felt like he let you down by not being there to prevent it."

"That's crazy." Ava sighed. "There is no way he could have known. He told me, though, how hard it was for him afterward. I never thought about what it must have done to him, to find me that way." Looking at her brother intently, she said, "So much has happened between Mac and me through the years, do you think we can ever have a normal relationship? I know he loves me, and I love him, but in the end, is it enough to overcome the baggage between us?"

Brant shifted in his chair, clearly uncomfortable. Ava hid a smile, knowing that her unflappable brother wasn't one to normally discuss romantic relationships. Just when she thought he would try to change the subject, he ran a hand through his hair, causing it to stick up in all directions. "Av . . . we both know that I suck at this sort of thing, but I will tell you this. I almost lost that woman in the other room, who probably has her ear against the wall listening to us, by trying to deny what I felt for her. The Stones seem to have problems expressing themselves and God forbid you throw in some crazy and unpredictable emotion like love. I let myself believe that I was confused over my feelings for Alexia because it gave me a reason to distance myself from Emma. I almost lost her before I finally accepted what was right in front of me. I know Declan was all over the place as well when he was falling in love with Ella. Maybe you and Mac have things that you need to settle between you, but don't lose sight of how you feel about him. That's the most important thing."

Just as Ava was opening her mouth to reply, Emma came running into the room, waving her arms. Brant jumped to his feet, reaching her in a single long stride. "What's wrong, baby?"

"I talked to Ella. Mac is freaking out because both his truck and Ava are missing. I guess you left your purse on the kitchen counter with your cell phone inside it. He called Declan and then went by your apartment. They were all beginning to panic when Brant wasn't answering his phone. I told Ella that you were here, Ava, and that Brant's phone was on the bedroom charger and we didn't hear it." Taking a breath, Emma added, "But I already knew he was looking for you, because he called right before her. He should be here any minute. Um . . . he sounded a little pissed."

Brant turned to Ava with a grimace. "I don't suppose you thought to leave him a note?"

Ava rolled her eyes. "I wasn't really thinking of anyone's feelings other than my own when I left his house. I'm sure he'll be fine now that he knows that I'm okay."

Brant gave her a skeptical look but didn't comment.

Suddenly, Mac was striding into the living room, having obviously skipped knocking at the door. Shit, apparently no one had bothered to lock it earlier. She watched him walk straight to her, drawing her into his arms and just holding her for a few moments without saying anything. When he finally pulled back, holding her at arm's length, she could see the worry and anger clouding his face. "Ava, do you have any idea how scared I've been that something happened to you?"

Trying to lighten his mood, she joked, "Ah, come on. It's not like anyone would have abducted me in your truck, right?" She knew immediately that her flippant reply was the equivalent of throwing gas on a flame.

"Are you fucking kidding me right now!" he roared as he jerked away from her. "I come home to find you gone with your purse still lying on the kitchen counter and lights on all over the house? Do you know how long it was before I realized that my truck was even gone? Even when I did, it didn't make me feel any better. After making a fool of myself ripping this town apart looking for you, you're making a joke? I thought someone took you, damn it!"

"Mac." Brant tried to intercede, stepping between them.

The anger that Ava had felt toward Mac earlier for not telling her about Kevin's letter was back in full force, fueled in part by the guilt she felt for upsetting him so much. Stalking around her brother, she picked up the letter that she had brought with her and stuck it in Mac's face. "This is why I'm here. I found it at your house tonight." He looked confused for a moment before freezing. Ava could see the exact moment that he recognized what she held in front of him. "So, excuse me if I didn't leave you a note or drop you a text before I came to see my brother. I had a little something on my mind."

"Avie . . . I," Mac began before stopping, clearly at a loss as to what to say next.

Shaking her head, Ava said, "Yeah, that seems to be everyone's reaction tonight."

Mac released a deep breath, seeming to have forgotten his earlier anger. "Let's go home, baby. We can discuss this there. It's late, and I'm sure Brant and Emma are tired."

"Oh, we're fine," Emma, blurted out before Brant could clamp his hand over her mouth.

Ava looked at her brother, seeing the tension from the evening still sitting heavily on him. Mac was right; they needed to have this discussion somewhere else. As it was, Brant would probably be popping antacids for days after this. He certainly didn't need to hear her argue with Mac. Nodding once, she said, "I'll meet you back at your house."

She had to bite her tongue to keep from snapping when Mac said, "Just leave the truck and I'll have one of the guys pick it up tomorrow. I don't want you driving this late." Ava knew it was probably petty and maybe she needed to learn to pick her battles, but if he didn't think she was capable of driving herself less than ten minutes down the street, then would he ever be able to see her as a strong, independent woman? Her personal life might have been a complete wreck for years, but professionally she was at the top of her game. Surely that counted for something. Regardless of how minor it seemed, she needed to win this small concession tonight from him.

"I'll be fine, Mac. There is no need for anyone to make a trip tomorrow to pick up the truck when I can drive it home tonight." Everyone in the room seemed to be holding their breath, including her, as Mac opened his mouth with the clear intention of arguing with her. At the last moment, he snapped it closed again and rubbed a weary hand across his eyes.

"Sure, whatever you want, Avie." They said their good-byes to Brant and Emma before walking out into the dimly lit driveway. Mac opened her door, waiting for her to get settled behind the wheel before shutting the door without another word. He then motioned for her to pull out onto the street, and he followed in his Tahoe. She was drained from her talk with Brant and wanted nothing more than to crawl into Mac's bed and go to sleep in his arms, but this conversation couldn't wait. She only hoped that afterward he didn't feel that she was more trouble than she was worth. She was counting on the fact that they were in this together for the long haul.

Chapter Twenty

Mac kept his eyes on the truck in front of him as they drove through the now-deserted streets of his neighborhood. His shoulders were tense, and his gut was still twisted. When he had walked into his house earlier, he was whistling, ready to see Ava. As he called her name and walked from room to room, he had gone from happy, to puzzled, and finally terrified. He had even resorted to looking under beds and in closets thinking that maybe something had scared her enough to hide.

Next, he had called her phone. When he got closer to the kitchen, he found it ringing faintly in her purse, sitting on the countertop. He had really lost it then. He had ripped back through the house and then taken a flashlight and walked the grounds. The garage was the last place he searched, and he had stopped in surprise when he found his truck gone. He had thought for a moment that maybe she just needed something from the store. But a quick look in her purse showed her wallet containing her money and credit cards along with her license.

Then he ran back to his Tahoe, dialing Declan as he

headed across town to her apartment. She probably needed clothes for tomorrow or some of those endless toiletries that women seemed to have by the dozens. Declan's puzzled tone when he asked if Ava was there was answer enough. He quickly ended the call, assuring a now worried Declan that he would let him know when he found her.

When he opened the door to Ava's apartment, he knew instantly she wasn't there. Everything was dark and quiet. He knew if Ava was there, her scent would still linger in the air as it did whenever she was near. He made a quick search of her home anyway but wasn't surprised to find no one there and nothing disturbed. By the time he left, he had already called Gage, asking him to check in with their sources at the local hospitals and police department. From the sound of the female voice in the background, Gage had company, but he readily agreed to make some calls ASAP and get back to him.

Mac tried Brant a few more times, still getting only his voice mail. At that moment he'd wished he had Emma's number, but there had never been a need to contact her directly before. He vowed to get the numbers of everyone that Ava knew tomorrow. Brant lived about ten minutes away, which gave him just enough time to call Gray on the outside chance that Ava had decided to do something crazy with Suzy again like night surf. He was both relieved and disappointed that Ava wasn't there, nor had they spoken with her since earlier at Declan's. However, Suzy did have Emma's number and Mac wasted little time in calling her.

He'd breathed a sigh of relief when she answered after a couple of rings. "Emma, it's Mac. Have you seen or talked to Ava since we left Declan's earlier?"

"Hey, Mac, yeah, she's here now."

Fully expecting another no, he stuttered in surprise, "Wh-what? She is?"

"Yes, she's talking to Brant in the other room. Do you need to speak to her?"

"Well, since I've been afraid she was abducted or dead in a ditch somewhere, I'd say yeah, I'd love to talk to her. No need to put her on the phone, though. I'll be there in a few minutes, thanks."

He could tell by the tone of Emma's "Mmm-kay, see you soon" that she had noticed the anger in his voice. He had been so pissed off that she was so thoughtless in not letting him know where she was that he could hardly acknowledge the relief he felt in knowing that she was okay. Why in the world would she take off to see her brother at this time of night after just seeing him earlier? Emma had sounded fine, so obviously they hadn't called her with an emergency. He'd never known the Stones to be the kind of close family who dropped in on each other on a whim.

When he stormed into the house and saw Ava looking unharmed next to Brant and Emma, he'd crossed the room to her on shaky legs, pulling her into his arms and taking a moment to absorb the feel of her soft body against his. He'd had the crazy urge to sob like a baby as he felt her heart race against his. She was okay; nothing had happened to her. He wasn't too late to save her this time. When he pulled back, to tell her how worried he had been, and she made some flippant reply, he'd lost it. She had damn near scared him into an early grave, and it was all some kind of joke to her? Did she not realize how traumatized he was still after all these years? He had told her how badly it had messed him up to find her that way, but surely, if she had really been listening, she would have understood that something like tonight was a trigger that could break him.

He had been completely floored when she held up that envelope in his face. Then he'd been just plain sick when he realized what it was. How in the hell had she gotten her hands on the letter from that bastard? Suddenly, her late-night trip to see her brother had made more sense. Fuck! He had known that it would come back to haunt him from the moment Brant placed it in his hand. He had agonized over whether to show it to Ava for years. She had seemed to have moved on, and he hated to bring it all back to her. However, since they had gotten together the last few weeks, it had been on his mind constantly. He now knew that she had been far from okay and it pained him to wonder if maybe the letter would have helped her in some small way. He'd been meaning to discuss it with Declan, who also knew, and Brant, but now it was too late. She knew, and by the expression on her face, she wasn't happy with any of them right now.

After fearing the worst earlier, he found it hard for him to let her out of his sight, but he could tell by the determined set of her small shoulders that she was digging in for a fight, and he refused to give it to her in front of Brant and Emma. So they said their good-byes and Mac clapped Brant on the back, reassuring him without words that he had himself in complete control where Ava was concerned.

When they arrived home, Ava waited for him at the door that led into the kitchen from the garage. He made quick work of the lock and followed her into his house. She stopped at the refrigerator and grabbed a bottle of water, lifting an eyebrow in question to him. He nodded and she passed him one before walking toward the living room and settling on one end of his sofa. He dropped heavily next to her but resisted the urge to pull her into his arms. He needed to see her face when they talked. He took a couple of sips of cold water, waiting for her to speak first. Truthfully, he was so happy that she was here, but beyond scared that she would leave him after this. Could she ever understand his reasoning and forgive him for keeping that damn letter from her?

She shifted in her seat, turning to face him. He felt an overwhelming urge to study his hands and avoid her stare but forced himself to make eye contact anyway. Her face was impassive, telling him nothing. Keeping him guessing, damn it. "Why didn't you tell me, Mac?"

He could delay his answer by playing dumb as to what she meant, but the time for lies and half-truths between them was over. If they were to have a future together, it needed to start tonight. "When Brant brought that letter to me years ago, the first thing I felt when I read it was anger. I wanted to rip it to pieces and then set them on fire. It brought back all the feelings of rage, sorrow, and helplessness that I'd felt when I found you. Honestly, I don't even know why I kept it. Just my anal need to always have some kind of paper trail. I tossed it into a file with your name on it and forgot it existed . . . until recently."

Ava asked with obvious curiosity, "What made you think of it again?"

"Our talk the other night. When you asked me if I'd heard anything about him. Knowing now how scared you've been all these years, I wondered if maybe Brant and I had made a mistake in not giving the letter to you. We were both just mad as hell that he'd try to contact you. You've got to know, Avie, that the men in your life would do anything to keep you from ever being hurt again."

Clasping his hand, she whispered, "I know that, Mac. And the rest of the file? Why did you keep all those reports from your men? I was surprised to find them."

Mac flinched before he could control the movement. Ava's file was full of nothing but pain for him. Would she be able to understand his reasons behind keeping something that so obviously hurt him? "I felt like the worst kind of stalker when those reports came in. Even though both you and your family were aware that you were under light surveillance from my company, it still felt strange to have that insight into your personal life. Truthfully, I'd throw a new report in your file and not read it until I needed a reminder of how you didn't want me. That folder was my reality check. Whenever I was close to coming to you and making a fool of myself, I'd flip through those pages to remind myself that you didn't feel the same way about me. You were happy and that was all that mattered."

A lone tear trickled down Ava's cheek as she put her hand on his cheek, stroking his hair tenderly with her fingers. "Oh, Mac, baby, I was never happy without you. I'm sorry I was so messed up inside that I thought I needed to prove that I wasn't. I always felt safer knowing one of your men was watching over me, but also . . . I am guilty of using that knowledge to make you see what wasn't there. I've hurt you so much you should hate me by now!"

Unable to bear her anguish, Mac pulled her small body onto his lap, wrapping his arms around her. He rested his head in the curve of her neck, inhaling her sweet scent. "It's impossible for me to do anything but love you, Avie . . . My life will be spent always loving you, baby."

For a long time, they were content to simply hold each other. Finally, Ava raised her head, kissing him lightly before speaking. "I'm not mad about the letter now; I understand what you and Brant were trying to do. From the way my grandfather handled everything, none of us ever really knew what to do or how to act going forward. I'm not saying that some embarrassing courtroom drama starring both Kevin and me would have been a miracle balm either, but it would have been some type of justice or at the very least closure. Since that never happened, we all need to make our own resolution . . . and it starts with me."

"Baby, you've done amazingly well. Look at all you have accomplished," Mac protested.

Ava smiled in answer, knowing that he would defend her until his last breath. God, she loved him so much it hurt to look at him sometimes. But she needed him to hear what she was saying. "I have done well . . . in business, but you and I both know that's not the case personally. My life and the crazy things I've done to appear normal would make a damn good TV sitcom. Going forward, though, I don't want to just try to appear normal. I want to live it." Taking a deep breath, she prepared for the hard part of their talk. Mac wasn't going to like it, but he needed to accept it for them to move forward. Actually, he was going to hate it, but if he could honor her wishes, then she thought they just might be able to turn the corner to a new chapter in their relationship. "Mac, I love you. But I need a little time to myself, a few weeks to get my bearings with everything that has changed in my life, and I no longer want any type of surveillance from you or your company."

She winced as he came off the sofa like a rocket, tumbling her backward on the couch. If he wasn't so obviously upset, she would have laughed at the absurdity of it all. How many women had this type of conversation with the man they loved?

"Ava! What in the hell . . . ?"

Ava noticed that he was again using her full name. He tended to save that for when he was upset or pissed off. She had mostly been Avie to him for her whole life. It never failed to make her feel special when he used the nickname. On the downside, she also noticed immediately when he didn't. "Mac . . . sit down and let me finish please before you go off the deep end."

He ran his hand over the back of his head, in a gesture she knew meant he was beyond frustrated. "If I sit back down, are you going to tell me that I misunderstood what you just said? Because it sounded to me like you want me gone from your life. Is that about the gist of it?"

Taking his hand, Ava pulled him back down next to her, trying to swallow the lump in her throat at the hurt in his voice. "That's not what I'm saying, Mac," she tried to reassure him gently. "Most women don't need a security detail unless they're married to the president." She knew exactly what he was going to say when he opened his mouth, so she put up a hand to stop him. "I know that Jason has someone watch his family. He's a very rich and important man, who is also a tad OCD about the safety of his wife and daughter. Claire lets him do it because she knows he needs that even if she doesn't. The difference is, Mac, that for years I was the one who needed it. When you started East Coast and added me to your rounds, I could sleep at night again. If I didn't see one of your guys passing by my window, I was tied in a knot until they did. In a way, I was almost better off before you started watching over me. With the extra security, I got along well to avoid getting the help that I needed, even though I was still torn up inside. I was just so embarrassed at my weakness and inability to get over what happened to me that I was terrified for anyone else to know the real me."

"Avie . . . ," Mac groaned, sounding completely shattered. "It wouldn't have mattered to me. Don't you see that there wasn't a side of you that I wouldn't have loved? I needed to be there for you. I still do."

"I know that and I do need you, Mac. What I'm trying to say, though, is that I need to be the person I was again before I became just a victim. I want to be the girl who had limitless dreams of the future, was never afraid of anything, and planned to marry the boy down the street who she'd loved since she was thirteen. Somewhere inside me, that girl still exists, and I want her back. In order for that to happen, I have to finally take control of my life, which includes dealing with my past and setting a course for my future. It's going to be hard for me to let my safety net go, but I want to start living my life again. I need to regain the innocence of believing that I'll never be hurt."

Mac took her hand, seeming to struggle with his words before asking, "What do you need from me, baby? What can I do to give that back to you?"

Raising his hand to her lips, she kissed it gently before saying, "You can't give it back, Mac, but you can help me find it. I know this is going to be hard for you, but I want us to step back for a couple of weeks. I'm going to get the name of Declan's therapist and make an appointment. I want to spend the nights at my apartment alone, without any of your security detail checking on me . . . and I want to go out on dates with you that end with me on my doorstep with a good night kiss that keeps me up at night—in a good way. I want us to try to start the kind of relationship that we might have had if nothing had happened to me. I need this, Mac—I want to know if I can be normal without pretending to be. If this relationship is going to work, we have to be equals. I know you're going to want to save and shield me from everything you can, and I love you for it, but I've got to save myself first."

Ava wasn't sure how long they sat there with Mac seeming to ponder her words before finally he squeezed her hand and said, "I'll try, baby. Watching over you is what I do, but I understand what you're saying and I'll do my best to give you what you need even if it fucking kills me." When she threw her arms around his neck, hugging him tightly, he whispered against her neck, "Does this mean no sex for two weeks either?" Laughter burst from her lips, until she was shaking against him. God, she loved this man. Even though she knew what she had asked was killing him inside, he managed to joke to make her feel better. He was now and would always be her gentle lion.

Chapter Twenty-one

Mac was pacing in his office restlessly when Dominic walked in. The other man had been out of town setting up security for another Oceanix location. The hotel chain was fast becoming one of their most profitable customers. It had been almost a week since he and Ava had had the talk, and they had gone on exactly two dates. The first was a late dinner, since they were swamped at work, and the second was dinner and a movie where they had made out like a couple of kids and missed most of the story. Both times, he had done as Ava requested and left her on the doorstep after a kiss that had them both panting.

He had pulled security from her apartment the next morning and had been a basket case, especially the first few nights. He'd gotten in his Tahoe more than once to go check on her himself, but her words had pulled him back. Doing as she asked had made one thing glaringly apparent—he didn't know how to cut the cord and stop worrying over her safety. It had been ingrained in him for so long that it was the first thing on his mind in the morning and the last thing in the evening. It wasn't that he didn't think she was strong enough to take care of herself. His problem came from his fear of failing her again. Her safety had been his obsession for so long that he wasn't sure how to have a normal relationship now even though he knew she needed that. She needed him to treat her as his equal and stop trying to layer her in bubble wrap every time she walked out the door. He just wasn't sure how.

Now she and most of the upper management for Danvers were in Las Vegas at a big annual trade show. It was a testament to his resolve that he was still sitting here in Myrtle Beach while she was so far away. The only thing that gave him any comfort was the fact that Brant, Emma, and Declan were there as well as Jason, Claire, Gray, Suzy, Nick, and Beth. Ella had stayed behind since she'd had a baby so recently. Apparently, her sister Crystal was going through a divorce and was staying with Ella until Declan returned. If he knew the other man though, it was probably killing him to leave his new family.

"Well, you look all kinds of pissy today," Dominic remarked as he dropped into a chair in Mac's office.

"Yeah, whatever," Mac snapped. He raised an irritated brow as Dom propped his feet on the corner of Mac's desk, seeming to settle in for the long haul. "Was there something you needed?"

"Nope." Dominic smirked. "But it looks like you need something. Who shit in your cornflakes today? I'd go with the usual guess and say Gage, but he's off somewhere crying about his unrequited love for the tramp stamp girl. So I'm gonna just take a wild guess here and go with Ava? I thought you two finally had your shit together?"

Mac gnashed his teeth, wanting to make some crude comment about Dominic's lack of success with the object of his affection, but out of respect for Gwen, he just couldn't do it. Instead he took a calming breath and completely unloaded all his problems on one of his closest friends, finishing up with "So you can see why I'm not up skipping through the office like a happy ray of fucking sunshine, yeah?"

Dominic inclined his head in a nod, saying matter-of-factly, "Sexual frustration will sure do that to you. It's even worse when you actually get it, then get it pulled right back out from under you, pun intended, of course."

"You're an asshole," Mac deadpanned, wondering what he had really expected from another guy.

Dominic laughed before scrubbing his hands over his face. "Okay, seriously, I feel you, man. And I get where Ava is coming from. No one wants to live their life being a fixer-upper project. At some point, the renovation needs to end."

"She's not my project," Mac grumbled, unsure if he was trying to convince Dominic or himself of that fact.

"But that's just it, buddy. You don't even realize it. I've known you for a long time now, and while you've had your fair share of female company, mostly all the one-night-only variety, it's always been Ava who's kept you walking the floors or pacing the fucking desert in Afghanistan. You're the most focused, intense person I've ever known. From the stories Declan has told of the two of you guys growing up, I don't think that's always been who you were." Smirking, he added, "No doubt you were born an anal perfectionist, but the rest I believe you picked up after Ava's attack." Dominic plowed on when Mac would have protested. "If you really think about it, you two never got to just be young and crazy. From the moment that happened, the course of your lives was altered. You both grew up the hard way and you've spent years being weighed down by a guilt for something none of you could have foreseen happening."

Kicking his desk in anger, Mac growled, "I should have fucking known it! If I hadn't been so busy trying to stay away from her for a few more years, until she was old enough for us to consider dating, I would have been with her that night. She was so young, though, and I wanted her to enjoy high school before over-whelming her with my feelings."

"Well, guess what, man? You're human. You can't predict the future and neither of you had a fucking clue what would happen that night. Saying it's your fault that you didn't go with her is like saying it's her fault for going without you. It's over. It was a shitty, fucked-up twist of fate that no one had any clue would happen. Now if you want a life with the woman who has kept you tied in knots for years, then it's time you trust that fate won't screw you over again and stop being her protector and start just being her man. Show her that you can check your OCD where she's concerned at the door and just be the guy she originally fell in love with all those years ago. I mean, he's there, right? Buried deep ... deep, really deep ..."

"All right! Shit, please stop." Glaring in annoyance, Mac said, "I don't think Ava's idea of a fun guy is one in prison because he strangled his smart-ass coworker. Christ, when did you and Gage become so insufferable? I hope he's not coming in next for his part of the come-to-Jesus intervention that you've got going on."

"Nope, Gage needs help almost as much as you do. I mean come on, all that whoring that he does has got to be hiding deeper problems. I'm betting that he was a bed wetter. His mama probably hung his pissed-on sheets out front for the other neighborhood kids to see. Since that early embarrassment, he's been unable to form attachments with women for fear of it happening again."

Mac threw his head back, howling with laughter. He had no idea where Dominic came up with this shit, but he was pretty sure that even Gage would be amused by the other man's assessment ... well, unless there was some truth to it. "Dr. Phil's got nothing on you, bro. I feel like I should warn Gwen or something. She might not be as amused by your deep insight as I am." At the look of dejection on Dominic's face, Mac found himself whistling. Apparently, he wasn't having any luck wooing his woman either. Getting to his feet, he clapped his friend on the shoulder. "I need you to hold down the fort for a few days. Think you can handle that?"

Dominic shrugged a shoulder, saying, "Of course. Where ya going?"

Mac grinned before throwing an imaginary three-point hoop shot. "I'm going to go be young, crazy, and reckless for once in my life. Isn't that what you just suggested?"

Cocking his finger, Dominic said, "Yep, that's about the gist of it. Wear a condom, though, son. I'm not ready to be an uncle." Mac nudged his chair in answer, laughing when Dom tumbled out on the floor shouting obscenities. God, would he and Gage never learn to keep their feet firmly planted on the floor?

Chapter Twenty-two

"Come on, Ava, we're in Vegas! We can't sit in the room eating cartons of cookie dough ice cream instead of having some fun." When Ava just opened her mouth for another heaping spoonful of the creamy goodness, Emma put her hands on her hips, releasing a long-suffering sigh. "You were more fun when you were all uptight and reserved. At least then, I had all your insults to keep me amused. Some of them were so detailed that I had to Google the meaning. Now you're just like a lovesick teenager. Binge-eating, listening to sad music, and writing Mrs. Ava Powers over and over on your notebook."

"Hey!" Ava protested around the spoon in her mouth. "I've only done that once and it wasn't on a notebook."

"Same thing," Emma grumbled. "Why don't you at least do what grown women do when they're lonely? Rent some porn and have a vibrator marathon. We're in Vegas. There's a store on the strip called Cock of the Stars. Want me to go get you an Adam Levine to test-drive? Suzy bought the Channing Tatum yesterday. She said Gray took it as a challenge and, well, long story short, she seems to have thrown her back out."

"Oh my God." Ava giggled. "Please, tell me you're kidding . . . about everything you just said. And tell me you didn't get one." Ava knew she'd made a mistake with that last sentence when Emma flashed her a wicked grin.

"Honey, I don't have anything left for a plastic friend. Brant fu—"

"Stop! I know I literally asked for that, but please don't finish your sentence. Remember, that's my brother." Ava shuddered.

"Like a champion," Emma added, laughing when Ava's spoon clattered to the floor and she ran from the room.

"So sick," Ava said under her breath as she walked into the bathroom and took a good look in the mirror. Ugh, maybe Emma was right. Her hair was sticking up in every direction and she had ice cream stains on the front of her white tank top. She had been holed up in her hotel for hours. Not seeing Mac was driving her crazy. When she imposed the two-week challenge on them, she'd completely forgotten about the trade show in Vegas. Now she was a long way from home, surrounded by mostly strangers, and damn, she missed the feeling of peace and security that came from knowing Mac was near. She was beginning to understand that it wasn't having his company keep an eye on her that made it easier for her to breathe, it was having Mac close. He was her anchor; his presence kept her grounded and all her fears at bay.

Claire had said something to her yesterday as they were walking alone to their rooms that came back to her clearly now. The other woman had been telling her how much she missed her daughter Chrissy, who was staying behind with Claire's mother and their family friend Louise. She had said that she just needed to be around Jason right now. She remembered her exact words as "I've mostly gotten used to him traveling and he has tried to scale it way back since we've been married. It's tough, though because he's my center of gravity. When he's gone, I just sort of find myself drifting." Claire had laughed sheepishly before continuing. "I don't miss a step really and life goes on until he's back, but inside, I'm just not me without him. He makes me stronger and I'm a better person all the way around. I'm the best version of myself when he's near." At the time, Ava had just smiled and returned Claire's hug before heading to her room for the night.

Now her friend's words made perfect sense to her. Instead of trying to put all these rules in place with Mac, maybe it was she that needed to accept that it wasn't wrong to rely on someone else. Was what Ava saw as weakness really just a natural part of being in love? Even Claire had admitted to being better with Jason than alone. If she really thought about it, all of her friends seemed to shine just a little brighter with the person they loved next to them. She didn't want Mac walking behind her through life, always trying to catch her before she fell. But she did want him beside her, giving her what only he could—acceptance, strength, and love.

When she heard the door shut in the other room as Emma left, she ran out of the bathroom to get her phone. She might not be able to see him, but God, she needed to hear his voice. So intent was she on her task that she didn't look up until she barreled into a hard chest. A startled squeak sounded from her throat as she jumped back. She blinked rapidly, thinking that surely her mind had conjured up the man standing in front of her grinning. "Mac! Wh-where did you come from?" As he started to answer, she jumped into his arms, wrapping her legs around his waist and her arms around his neck. "Oh, who the hell cares? You're here!" Mac emitted a startled gasp next as her mouth crashed down onto his. Her tongue immediately sought entrance into his mouth, and with a husky groan, he took charge of the kiss.

Soon Mac stumbled backward from the force of her kisses, searching until his knees made contact with the bed. Ava bounced against him as he turned, falling to his back with her on top. "I missed you so fucking much," he whispered as he plunged his tongue in her mouth while grinding his hard cock against her wet core. Even through the material of his pants and her shorts and panties, she could feel every inch of him. She broke from the kiss to grab his belt buckle, desperate to lower his pants. He reached for the hem of her shirt, pulling it over her head in one swift movement before unclipping the front clasp of her bra. She could barely concentrate on his zipper as he pinched a sensitive nipple before stroking the sting away. He lifted his hips so she could slide his pants and boxers down, and she gave a shout of victory as his huge member sprang free. Mac took over, making short work of her remaining clothing before sitting her back astride him. "Fuck me, Avie. Give us both what we need."

Rising to her knees, she hovered over his length, moaning as he started to penetrate her. She threw caution to the wind as she suddenly seated herself, taking all of him. Mac's body jerked in surprise, nearly bowing up before he moaned in desire. "I love you, I love you, I love you," she chanted as she started rising and lowering herself onto him.

"Ah, baby, I love you too. Shit, you feel so good." As shivers started to shake her body, Mac thrust his hips upward, going deeper than she believed possible. She was so close. She knew by the restless tempo of his hips that he was as well. When his fingers started circling her clit, she was gone. Her orgasm crashed into her with a suddenness that took her breath away. Her world went black and stars danced in her eyes as her body seemed to spasm forever. With a hoarse shout, she felt Mac release himself into her as he supported her now-limp body with his hands. "Fuck," he gasped out, seeming to be as overwhelmed as she was. "That was . . ."

"Yeah." She sighed as she collapsed against his chest. "It was." They lay there for long moments, simply content to just be together. Finally, Ava propped herself up on an elbow, trailing her other hand idly over his sweaty chest. Was it completely gross that she wanted to lick him? She decided to keep that question to herself, instead asking, "Not that I'm complaining, but where did you come from? I had just been discussing Adam Levine with Emma." When he raised a questioning eyebrow, she quickly added, "Don't ask. Anyway, I thought I heard her leaving and then poof, you were standing there . . . looking far too sexy."

Grinning, Mac said, "Emma let me in. I gave her the universal sign for zip your lips, and she pointed to the bathroom." As he continued to study her face, his grin slid away and he looked wary instead. "You're not mad that I came, are you? I know we had another week of the no-sex, date-only plan, but, baby, I just couldn't hold out. I was miserable without you. I deserve points for being strong enough not to stalk you or have my employees stalk you, though, right?"

He looked so hopeful that Ava was powerless to contain the soft smile on her lips. Moving a hand up to cup his face, she said, "I missed you too, and I'm so glad you're here. I was wrong to try to force rules on us now. You and I have never had a normal relationship, and maybe it's time we used that in our favor instead of against us."

Looking intense, Mac asked, "So, what are you saying exactly?"

Ava swallowed, trying to find the words to tell him how she felt, when suddenly it hit her. Emma was right, this was Vegas. Was there any better place for a grand gesture than the place where one gamble could change your entire life? So, with her heart beating wildly and the worst case of bed head in the history of bad hair, Ava slid from the bed and to her knees at the side of it. Still gripping one of Mac's hands tightly, she pulled him until he was in a sitting position, then continued to tug until he was standing in front of her.

He looked down at her in concern, probably having no clue what she was about to do—while they were both still naked. Clearing her throat, Ava took a deep breath and for the first time in her adult life, she took a leap of faith with her eyes wide-open. "Mac, I loved you even before I understood what love really was. When I was thirteen I vowed to myself that one day I'd marry you and you'd be mine forever." When she saw one tear trek down Mac's cheek, she almost lost it, but a quick squeeze from his hand to hers gave her the strength to continue. "For a long time, I was lost. I never stopped wanting that with you. I just couldn't find my way back to who we were. You're my person, Mac, my other half, and you were always meant to be a part of my journey in life. Please say that you'll marry me and—"

Ava didn't get any further, because suddenly he was on his knees in front of her, struggling to hold in his emotions as he pulled her into his arms. "Oh, Avie . . . You've always been my forever person and, baby, I can barely breathe when you aren't with me. I'm yours. I always have been." Holding her away from him, he reached a hand out to wipe away the steady flow of tears from her eyes and chuckled. "I was coming here to propose to you, but I can't tell you what it means to me that you did it. I was afraid of pushing for too much, too fast, but I don't want to be apart anymore." He turned away briefly, digging in the bag he'd dropped on the floor earlier. When he finally turned back to her, he was holding a black velvet box in his hands. Her hands flew over her mouth as she gaped at him. Looking at her with so much love and tenderness that it made her heart hurt, he said, "There is nothing in this world that I want more than to marry you." A gorgeous princess-cut diamond stole her breath away as he flipped the top of the box open. The ring was a perfect fit when Mac slid it onto her finger. When she finally lifted her gaze from it, Mac gave her a lopsided grin before asking, "I don't guess you're interested in being married by Elvis, are you?"

She amazed both herself and him when she giggled before nodding. "How about just a few velvet Elvis paintings around the wedding chapel? I would like nothing more than to leave Las Vegas as Mrs. Ava Powers." She knew she had Mac's approval when something hard poked her in the belly.

"I like the way you think," he growled as he rubbed his length against her. "Now, how about we seal the deal in a way we'll never forget?"

As Ava took his hard cock in her hand, pumping him slowly, she said, "Our deal was sealed long ago, but I definitely think we need to sign on the dotted line." Luckily for them, their clothes were still off and there was nothing left in their way . . . absolutely nothing.

Epilogue

Ava stood still in a bubble of complete bliss as a flurry of activity hummed around her. She was getting married in Vegas just two days after she and Mac had co-proposed to each other. She hadn't seen him at all today, as her friends and torturers were insistent that she not see the groom before the ceremony. That didn't mean that they hadn't texted each other like crazy for the last twenty-four hours.

She finally looked around the room where they were all busy changing clothes to see a sight that she'd never expected. She had friends, good ones who had worked tirelessly for two days to give her a dream wedding. Suzy, the party planner extraordinaire, had refused to even entertain a trip to a drive-through wedding chapel. She'd paled alarmingly when Mac had jokingly suggested it. Instead she had opened her bag of tricks and secured them a beautiful outdoor venue with a breathtaking view of Red Rock Canyon in the distance. She had handled every detail, and despite their protests, Brant had insisted on paying for the wedding, stating it was his honor as head of their family. God, she loved her uptight brother. Finally, she and her brothers felt like a family.

Truthfully, she had been more than happy to hand over all the planning to Suzy, who seemed to do it so effortlessly. Ava just wanted to get married, and a justice of the peace would have been fine to her. Now her dear friends Suzy, Emma, Claire, and Beth buzzed around her, seemingly overjoyed to be part of her special day. She missed Ella and wished that she could have been there.

A knock sounded at the door and Emma rushed to answer it. When Emma didn't return after a few moments, Ava looked over at the door to see the other woman passionately kissing Brant, and for once, Ava didn't want to shudder in horror from seeing her brother making out with his fiancée. Actually, she'd never been happier that both of her brothers had found their forever persons. Despite years of doubt, it seemed as if there was a happily-ever-after on the horizon for all the Stone siblings.

Brant's face was flushed when Emma finally pulled him into the room after ensuring that everyone was decent. He stopped in his tracks, just looking at Ava for a moment. She had chosen a simple white gown with a square neckline and delicate spaghetti straps. Tiny seed pearls were sewn on the white material, giving the dress a fairy-tale look. She had known it was her dream gown the moment she saw it. Suzy had given her an enthusiastic high five that she'd found her wedding dress within an hour.

"You look beautiful," he said as he reached her. Emma ushered everyone from the room, seeming to know that Brant wanted a moment alone with his sister. He looked at her almost shyly before pulling two boxes from his jacket pocket. "I . . . um . . . think I can help you out with two things you might need before you get married." He set one box on the table before holding a long, thin box in front of her. "You know that most of Mom's jewelry has been in a safe-deposit box since their death." When she nodded, he continued, staring at the box he held. "When you told me you were getting married, I remembered this one necklace. Mom always wore it to every party that she and Dad attended. It's the only piece of her jewelry that I can remember seeing her wear on a regular basis. I . . . well, I thought you might like to have a part of her here today. I know it's not the same, but . . ." Without finishing his sentence, he popped open the box, showing her the platinum pearl and diamond necklace nestled within. She choked on a sob as she too remembered it adorning their mother's neck on several occasions.

Brant removed it from the box, walking behind her to gently move her hair aside before fastening it around her neck. Her hand automatically flew up, feeling the cool weight against her skin. His eyes were bright as he moved back in front of her. "I, um . . . had someone send this to me for you. I thought this could be your something old."

"Oh, Brant," she cried, "I don't know what to say. I never knew how much I needed a part of them until now. Thank you for always taking care of me." When she went to hug him, he held her off, setting the empty box down before picking up the other, smaller one.

"Wait. There's another one, and I don't want you crying more than once, so try to hold it until—" As a knock sounded on the door, Brant smiled and went to open it. Ava's mouth fell open as her other brother walked in, looking equally emotional as he looked at her.

"Sorry, guys. I . . . got tied up. Oh, sis, you look beautiful." As Declan leaned over to kiss both her cheeks, he whispered in her ear, "Mac is one lucky bastard." Brushing an errant tear from her cheek, he pulled back, taking the box from Brant's hand. His eyes softened as they lit on their mother's necklace. "Looks beautiful on you, Av. I know she would have wanted you to wear it today." Clearing his throat, he held up the velvet box in his hand, saying, "Ella and I wanted to give you something new for your day." Opening the box, Declan turned it for her to see a bracelet very similar in design to the necklace that she wore. As he put it on her wrist, he continued talking. "I'm sorry if I haven't always been there when you needed me, Av, but please never doubt that I love you. There is only one man that both Brant and I would ever pass your hand along to without reservation, and you're marrying him today. He's always loved you, Ava, and I know that he always will."

After that, they all exchanged emotional embraces and just enjoyed the moment of togetherness with their feelings unguarded. As the rest of the gang filed back in, Suzy shook her head while the other women ushered the men out. "I'm not even going to bother fixing your makeup until your last visitor comes in, because I know you'll just cry again." Then in an uncharacteristic display of emotion, Suzy gave her a side hug, saying, "And you know what, you cry as much as you need to. If we can't fix it, then screw it. Mac will only see your beauty, not your makeup."

When Suzy moved back, Ella stood there holding her newborn baby, Sofia Grace, and doing a mixture of laughing and crying. They all gaped at their soft-spoken friend when she covered the baby's ears and said, "Now, would I miss the wedding of my favorite whore?" Laughter rang out in the room, and they all knew they'd never forget Ella's multiple-personality delivery and the laughs that it would bring to them for years to come. Ava smiled, thinking that now she knew how Brant had managed to get their mother's necklace here so quickly.

"Now I believe we're missing the borrowed and blue items, right?" Claire asked while holding a hand behind her back. When Ava agreed, the other woman brought her hand back around, showing Ava the pearl and diamond ring there. "My mother gave this ring to me when I got married and I thought it would go perfectly with your necklace and bracelet."

Ava wanted to protest, not sure about wearing something so special to Claire, but the other woman seemed so excited. When the ring actually fit Ava's finger, she found herself hugging Claire while trying to hold back her tears.

Next, Suzy and Beth stepped forward, holding out a long white box. Ava looked at it suspiciously, before shaking her head. "Please tell me that isn't the Channing Tatum that you bought."

Beth started laughing as Suzy winced, rubbing her lower back. "Um, no, Gray buried that at the bottom of the trash can. I think he may have stabbed it a few times for good measure."

"Then he buried something else, right?" Beth joked, holding her sides while she laughed.

Suzy, never one to be embarrassed, gave a smug grin. "Yeah, he sure did, again . . . and again. God, I love pushing that man's buttons." Beth finally had to nudge Suzy to shake her out of what appeared to be some vivid memories. "Oh, right, so, anyway, Beth and I took care of the something blue." When Ava hesitated, Beth opened the box, showing her the light blue garter belt nestled inside it. Ava sighed in relief before donning the last item.

Her friends left to join the rest of the wedding guests, while Brant and Declan returned and took their positions on each side of her. Strangely, she was barely nervous. Nothing had ever felt this right. The only thing she needed now was to be standing next to the man she loved. "Ready?" Brant asked, giving her hand a reassuring squeeze.

Before she answered, she hugged both of her brothers once again. "I'm ready," she said softly. "I'm finally ready."

All three of them knew that her words had little to do with the ceremony and everything to do with where she was in her life.

"A Thousand Years" by Christina Perri was played by a pianist and cellist as the love of his life walked down the canopy-covered aisle holding the arm of each of her brothers. Lights on the surrounding trees twinkled against the darkness, giving the whole setup a storybook feel. As Mac stood waiting for her, he truly understood that all the heartache of the past had led them to this one defining moment.

Since their group of friends and family attending the wedding was so small, they hadn't bothered with giving anyone in the wedding party formal titles. Instead everyone circled the altar, leaving just a small opening for Ava, Declan, and Brant. Mac's mom and dad, Dominic, Gage, Ella, and Sofia Grace had been able to make the last-minute ceremony thanks to the generosity of Mark DeSanto. He was a friend of the Stone family as well as a business associate to Danvers. When Brant told him about the wedding, he had insisted on helping in any way possible. His private jet had picked up their guests from Myrtle Beach earlier, and they had arrived in plenty of time for the wedding. Mac's parents were so thrilled that he and Ava were finally getting married that they wouldn't have held a grudge over missing the wedding, but he could tell they were happy to be here.

When both Declan and Brant arrived at his side, placing their sister's hand in his, they clapped him on the back, signifying without words their trust in him. He swallowed a huge lump in his throat as he nodded once to the men he thought of as brothers. Beside him, Gage whistled low under his breath as he glimpsed Ava. Dominic elbowed him in the stomach, causing the other man to let out a low groan before giving Dominic a dirty look. Mac was so grateful to have his friends there with him as he took the step he had always dreamed of with his forever girl.

He took advantage of the fact that Ava wasn't wearing a veil to lean in and give her a quick kiss on her neck. "I love you, baby," he whispered for her ears only. She mouthed the words back to him as the officiate started the ceremony. Both he and Ava had opted to have a simple service, including traditional vows. They had already said everything that was in their hearts to each other earlier in private. They answered the questions that were asked of them and repeated their promises when prompted, but their eyes never left each other. The world faded away as they were pronounced husband and wife. As Mac pressed his lips to hers, he felt the pain and sorrow of the past slip away and out of the ashes arose a beautiful commitment that staggered him with its perfection. Because he knew that, no matter what happened in the future, as long as Ava was at his side, life would be beautiful. And he intended to spend the rest of his life loving her—always loving her.

Acknowledgments

As always, a special note of thanks to my agent, Jane Dystel, and my editor at Penguin, Kerry Donovan. None of this would ever be possible without you both and I appreciate all that you do.

Also, thanks to Jenny Sims for all your help.

A huge thanks to all the readers and bloggers who continue to embrace the Danvers series. It always touches my heart at how much you love the characters that I've created. Thank you for making them as much a part of your lives as I have.

To my special friends: Amanda Lanclos and Heather Waterman from Crazy Cajun Book Addicts, Catherine Crook from A Reader Lives a Thousand Lives, Shelly Lazar from Sexy Bibliophiles, Marion Archer, Lorie Gullian, Stacia from Three Girls and a Book Obsession, Shannon with Cocktails and Books, Sarah from Smut and Bon Bons, Andrea from the Bookish Babe, Jennifer from Book Bitches Blog, Tracey Quintin, Melissa Lemons, Lisa Granger, Chantel Pentz McKinley, Nicole Tallman, Stefanie Eldrige-O'Toole, Tara Thomas, Lisa Salvary, and Jen Maxner.

About the Author

Sydney Landon is the *New York Times* and *USA Today* bestselling author of *Weekends Required*, *Not Planning on You*, *Fall for Me*, *Fighting for You*, and *Betting on You*. When she isn't writing, Sydney enjoys reading, swimming, and being a minivan-driving soccer mom. She lives in Greenville, South Carolina, with her family.

CONNECT ONLINE

sydneylandon.com
facebook.com/sydney.landonauthor
twitter.com/sydneylandon1

Read on for a special preview
of the next sexy romance
in the Danvers series,

WATCH OVER ME

Available in September wherever books
and e-books are sold.

"Well, this officially goes down as my crappiest birthday ever . . . hands down," Gwen Day moaned before looking back up into the sympathetic eyes of her friends Mia Gentry and Crystal Webber. "I'm finished with men. I mean, what do you even need them for anymore?"

Her friend Crystal, who was newly divorced, nodded her head in agreement. "You got that right girl. I have a vibrator that's always hard, doesn't talk back or leave the toilet seat up or dribble toothpaste in the bathroom sink. I've come more in the last six months with my plastic boyfriend than in the last six years combined with my ex. If I'd had one of those suckers when I was twenty, I'd have never gotten married."

Beside Crystal, Mia gave them a sheepish look. "Um . . . well . . . I like my man just fine, and trust me . . . he's always hard whenever I want it."

"You suck," Crystal grumbled. "The rest of us don't have a perfectly wonderful, hottie alpha male like Seth Jackson. You could at least share him, you know. Have you two considered broadening your horizons with a threesome because I'd totally be up for it?" Wiggling her brows, she added, "I seem to remember you mentioning a certain threesome fantasy featuring Suzy Merimon and her hubby, Gray."

The conversation between her friends distracted Gwen momentarily from her pity party before she went back to brooding. She had no interest in her vibrator, but she agreed with Crystal that men were completely overrated. She had thought all of that was changing for her when she met McKinley Powers. His company handled the security for Danvers International, where she worked. He was drop-dead handsome with his short military hair, which he still favored even after leaving the Marines, and his rock-hard body, which never failed to make her heart race and knees squeeze together. The fact that he was a genuinely nice guy was an added bonus.

When they had first started dating, Mac had been more than content with her "taking things slow" request, which maybe should have been her first red flag. After they'd been going out for a month, he still hadn't put any type of pressure on her to go beyond kissing. By the end of the next month, she was horny and frustrated. It seemed like he was the one wanting to take it slow, and by then she was ready to rip the clothes from his buff body.

They had engaged in some make-out sessions that never progressed past second base, because he always pulled back when he got too close to third base and dammit . . . crossing home plate had become just a distant dream.

Gwen knew all of the books said never let a man determine your self-worth, but she had been really struggling with that one after Mac's silent refusal to have sex with her. Until she finally put all of the pieces together and figured out that it might not be her who was the problem, but more important who she wasn't—Ava Stone.

Mac was good friends with the Stones, who also worked for Danvers. There was Declan, whom Mac had served with in the military; Brant, who was Declan's older brother; and then there was Ava. She was an attractive blonde Gwen had seen in the lobby on several different occasions. She had come to understand that there was possibly something more than friendship between Mac and Ava when she witnessed Mac completely losing it because his coworker and good friend Dominic Brady had given Ava a ride on his Harley. Mac had been so upset that warning bells had gone off in Gwen's head.

From that point on, her relationship with Mac was on borrowed time, and she knew it. He had become even more distant. He forgot to call her, didn't return her calls, and was just generally unavailable physically and emotionally.

So one evening, she had gone to his house to talk and just to spend some time with him, and he'd taken off almost immediately after receiving a call concerning Ava. Gwen had decided to wait it out and see if he came back home. When he finally did, hours later, they had ended it. There was no fight, no ugly words or insults. It was very civilized. Gwen might not be happy with Mac for dating her while he was hung up on Ava, but he had been honest with her, and she knew that it had really upset him to hurt her.

Her self-esteem had been limping along since that evening until Mia had dropped her bomb this morning. Her friend Suzy had told her that Mac and Ava had gotten married over the weekend in Las Vegas. It had been a blow that Gwen hadn't been expecting. She figured she would just be tortured for a while seeing them as a couple around the office. She had never expected Mac to break up with her and then almost immediately tie the knot. God, was she now the one whom men dated right before they found "the one"?

Gwen had been so lost in thought that she almost jumped from her seat when Mia's hand landed on her arm, shaking it excitedly. "I know, let's have a girls' night tonight! Seth's leaving this afternoon on business for a few days, so I'd love to go out. How about you, Crystal?"

Gwen was secretly hoping that the other woman would veto the whole thing because she wasn't really in the mood to socialize. She just wanted to go home, eat herself into oblivion, and watch some man-hating movies on Lifetime. Of course, she'd probably run right into Dominic in the apartment complex where they both lived. Geez, she needed to move now. Wasn't it just her luck to live doors away from Mac's friend? Dominic was already so annoying . . . okay hot—completely smoking hot—but still annoying.

It was no one's business if she peeked through her blinds every time she heard his boots in the hallway. Yes, dear Lord, she could admit to herself that she could pick out the sound of his tread from the rest of her neighbors. He just looked so good in his cargo pants and those tight

T-shirts. And some evenings she was even lucky enough to catch him in all of his masculine glory after returning from a run. Shirtless . . . and wearing low-hanging shorts. She loved the sight of him with those rippling muscles, glistening sweat, the tattoos, the . . . "Hmmm?" Gwen looked around to see both Mia and Crystal staring at her.

Crystal smirked."Honey, where was your head at? You just moaned and your eyes went crossed."

"And you have some drool on your chin," Mia pointed out helpfully.

Gwen felt her face flush as she quickly ran a hand across her mouth. Darn it, there was drool there. Freaking Dominic Brady! "I . . . er . . . was just thinking about dinner."

"Yeah, sure." Crystal grinned. "Whatever you say. So anyway, how about drinks at Hawks tonight?"

Mia rubbed her hands together. "Ohhh, going the sports bar route tonight. I like it. Seth would hate it, so it sounds perfect to me."

Gwen found herself agreeing. Surely, an evening out with her friends was better than sulking at home. After all, her ass was big enough, and adding another pint of ice cream to it wasn't going to help things any. Tonight she would have fun and forget all about Mac. How hard could that be?

Dominic Brady sprawled back on his sofa with a big sigh of contentment. Jet lag was a real kick in the ass. Maybe he was just getting old, but flying to Vegas and back in less than forty-eight hours was not something that he cared to do often. When he had been in the Marines, he and his friends had lived for quick trips like that. They'd get a few days off and make the most of it. Sin City was a frequent destination back then. Now just being home in his apartment in Myrtle Beach was much closer to heaven than the bright lights and the scantily clad women on the strip. Yeah, hell, at thirty-three he officially sounded old.

The trip this weekend had been for a good cause, though. One of his best friends had gotten married to the woman he'd loved all of his life. It had been a long, rocky, and uncertain road for them, but Mac and Ava had finally worked it out, and Dominic couldn't have been happier for them. He, Mac, and Gage owned a company called East Coast Security. They monitored and provided security for many high-end companies, including Danvers International, where their headquarters was located.

The job and the location fit Dominic perfectly. His family lived in Georgia, so he was close enough to visit when he wanted to and far enough away to keep his nosy mother and sister out of his business. He loved them dearly, but they had been trying to find him the "right woman" since he had been potty trained. If he still lived near home, they'd be herding single women past him like they were on an assembly line. The fact that his sister had married her high school sweetheart and promptly popped out two kids only put that much more pressure on him.

He had just started on his second Corona and was watching *SportsCenter* when he heard a sound at his door. It was more like someone moving against the frame than knocking. Biting off a curse, he reluctantly put his beer down on the coffee table and went to check. It was likely no one coming to visit him. His neighbor at the end of the hall liked to party, and even though he always tried to keep the noise down, occasionally there were a few lost strays in the hallway.

Dominic checked the peephole, then pulled back in surprise. This was a new one. He could make out the crown of someone's head, and that was about it. He stood there for a few moments, hoping that the person would just move on. When he heard nothing but silence, he came to the resigned conclusion that he was either going to leave the person there all night or open the door and encourage her to move on.

Swinging the door open suddenly might not have been the best idea, Dominic concluded when a soft body landed against him. He heard a feminine giggle, then a "Whoops!" He froze when hands started roaming his chest and then his torso. "Mmmm, you are sooo hard. . . . I knew you would be."

What the hell? Just as he registered that what he thought was brown hair through the peephole was actually dark red, his interloper looked up, and he gasped in shock. "Gwen?"

"Dominic," she purred back, blinking at him like an owl. Her hands continued to roam, and he didn't know whether to be thrilled or sorry that he was wearing nothing but a pair of basketball shorts. Her hands on his bare skin were having a direct effect on his cock, and the silky material wasn't doing much to contain it. On the other hand . . . it felt good. . . . No, amazing.

Maybe he was asleep, and this was a dream. There was no way Gwen, the woman he'd wanted from the first moment he'd seen her, was here now, touching him . . . damn near everywhere. "Er . . . Gwen . . . babe, did you need something?" He almost groaned aloud when her hand dropped to cover the bulge in his shorts.

"You could say that," she moaned as she pushed him back a few steps before shutting the door behind her. Just when he thought this encounter couldn't get much weirder . . . or hotter, she leaned down, grabbed the hem of the slinky black dress that she was wearing and pulled it over her head in a move that would have made a stripper proud. Then she stood before him in nothing but a black lace bra, tiny matching panties, and strappy black sandals. He was completely and totally screwed.

Still trying to be the voice of reason for some crazy reason, Dominic held out a calming hand and said, "Babe, what're we doing here? I mean . . . God, you're gorgeous!" All right, maybe that last line had slipped out, but holy hell, how was he supposed to stay calm when Gwen was standing in front of him practically naked, with a come-hither look in her eyes that was making him pant like a dog in heat?

She began to prowl forward, and he walked uncertainly backward, which he figured out was a big mistake when he tripped over his coffee table and landed in a heap on the sofa. "Oh goody." She rubbed her hands together as she stopped a few inches from where he had landed. "It looks like we're both on the same page."

Then . . . she dropped down to straddle his waist, and it was all over for him. When she grinned before pulling a strip of condoms out of her bra, he almost professed his love on the spot. Who was this woman? She looked like his beautiful neighbor, but that was where the similarities ended.

He'd caught her checking him out on more than one occasion, and yes, in his fantasies, he had wanted to believe that she desired him as he did her . . . but she'd never given him any outward reason to believe that was true. He had certainly never imagined her showing up on his doorstep like a wet dream. He forced himself to ask one last time, "Are you sure about this?" In answer, she ground herself against him before licking his neck. Well . . . that meant yes in his book.

He put his hands on what he had come to think of as the Holy Grail: her ass. It was firm and round and drove him to distraction. Dominic had never been one to desire a skinny woman. He loved soft, lush curves, and to him, Gwen had the perfect body. His only problem was deciding where he wanted to lavish his attention first.

"I need you inside of me," Gwen murmured as she bit his ear. As if to prove that point, she plastered her body against his chest, freeing his hips, before saying urgently, "Shorts off, condom on."

Dominic had always been something of an alpha male, so this role change was not only different for him, but surprisingly sexy as hell. He couldn't remember the last time he had been this uncoordinated as he did his best to push his shorts down and then fumbled to put the condom on his throbbing erection without causing it to blow early. At this point, he was hanging on to his composure by a mere thread.

After what was probably seconds but felt like hours, he was sheathed and past ready to feel her around him. "All right, baby, let me take care of you."

"Yes . . . God, yes," she breathed throatily. "I need to take my panties . . ." Refusing to let her up, he ripped one side of her flimsy excuse for panties and then the other. She lifted her hips slightly, and he pulled the fabric free, sending it sailing somewhere nearby. He ran a finger through her cleft, finding it wet and swollen. "Dom . . . I'm ready. Please now!"

Putting a supporting hand under her ass, he raised her body before bringing her down onto his waiting shaft. He held himself still as she screamed, afraid that he'd hurt her by going too fast. "Okay, baby?" he asked as he stroked her hip soothingly.

Gwen rose to her knees, sliding him almost out of her wet heat before bottoming out once again. "Move . . . harder, Dom!" Her demands broke what little control he had left. He wrapped his arms around her, pulling her close enough to devour her lips, while pumping his hips at a ruthless pace into her tight passage.

Soon they were nothing but a tangle of shifting, grinding limbs. Dominic bit, sucked, and licked every available inch of her skin, and it drove him to distraction when she did the same. He'd never really thought he would enjoy having his own nipples nipped, but damn if it wasn't off-the-charts hot. He wanted to make it last for hours, but all too soon he felt the familiar tingle at the base of his spine. When Gwen started to spasm around him, he was helpless to hold back any longer. His orgasm seemed to go on forever as black dots danced through his vision.

Dominic collapsed backward as all the blood that had been gathered down below finally redistributed throughout his body. He grazed his hand lazily up and down Gwen's spine as she nestled against him. He knew he needed to get up and dispose of the condom, but he figured he could do that when she inevitably freaked out and ran from his apartment. He was braced and waiting for that to happen. Hell he felt almost like the woman in this scenario, wanting to cuddle and talk about feelings and crap like that.

When Gwen sat up, he dropped his hand, already trying to distance himself. He was floored when she licked her lips and gave him a lopsided smile. "If you don't mind, I'm going to need to do that again. Can we? Please?"

Well, hell, it was official: He had gone and lost his heart to the girl next door . . . and his best friend's ex. In true fashion, he never took the easy route.

Also available from *New York Times*
and *USA Today* bestselling author

Sydney Landon

THE DANVERS NOVELS

Weekends Required
Claire Walters has worked for Jason Danvers as his assistant for three
years, but he never appreciated her as a woman—until the day she
jumps out of a cake at his friend's bachelor party...

Not Planning on You
Suzy Denton thought she had it all: a great job as an event planner and
a committed relationship with her high school sweetheart. But life is
never quite so simple...

Fall For Me
All her life, Beth Denton battled both her weight and her
controlling parents. And now that she's declared victory, she's looking
for one good man to share the spoils of war…

Fighting For You
Ella Webber has spent years uncomfortable around the opposite sex,
but as soon as she meets the handsome Declan Stone, she's smitten.
But can she persuade Declan that they're a perfect match?

No Denying You
Working for uptight workaholic Brant Stone is more than Emma Davis
can bear. But when the tension between them explodes, hate will turn
into lust, and then to something much more...

Available wherever books are sold or at
penguin.com

sydneylandon.com

s0436